There was a loud thump on the door.

Catherine laid down the musket and went to the window. Through it, she saw a face in the light from the torch next to it. The flame glared in a gust long enough for Catherine to identify the bad complexion and smirking lips of Frank Mapleton staring back at her. He opened his mouth in a smile of yellowed teeth. Two of his companions held a log from the woodpile ready to swing it against the thick door.

"Open the door, Edward," Catherine said.

The old man hunched his stooped shoulders even more than usual as he swung the heavy door open. A blast of cold wind rushed into the house. The two young men holding the log looked in confusion at Frank.

"Why, step back, lads," Frank said. "This is the house of a woman that we dare not trifle with. Is that not so, Mistress Williams?"

For answer, Catherine strode forward, holding the heavy barrel of the musket in front of her. Phyllis followed with the aiming stick in one hand, and the glowing brand in the other. Frank looked at the weapon but held his face in its mask of amused irony.

"Do we look like turkeys, then?" he asked, but he stepped back as Catherine approached.

"You look like what you are, a gaggle of insolent rogues," Catherine said, "who are besetting me in my house, and I mean to be rid of you by any means necessary."

Frank stepped back, holding his knife in front of him.

"Now Mistress," he said. "We wanted only to warm our bones by your fire while we waited for your savage."

"The only warmth you'll get from me," Catherine replied, "comes out of the end of this barrel."

MORE MYSTERIES FROM THE
BERKLEY PUBLISHING GROUP...

THE HERON CARVIC MISS SEETON MYSTERIES: Retired art teacher Miss Seeton steps in where Scotland Yard stumbles. "A most beguiling protagonist!"
—*New York Times*

by Heron Carvic
MISS SEETON SINGS
MISS SEETON DRAWS THE LINE
WITCH MISS SEETON
PICTURE MISS SEETON
ODDS ON MISS SEETON

by Hampton Charles
ADVANTAGE MISS SEETON
MISS SEETON AT THE HELM
MISS SEETON, BY APPOINTMENT

by Hamilton Crane
HANDS UP, MISS SEETON
MISS SEETON CRACKS THE CASE
MISS SEETON PAINTS THE TOWN
MISS SEETON BY MOONLIGHT
MISS SEETON ROCKS THE CRADLE
MISS SEETON GOES TO BAT
MISS SEETON PLANTS SUSPICION
STARRING MISS SEETON
MISS SEETON UNDERCOVER
MISS SEETON RULES
SOLD TO MISS SEETON
SWEET MISS SEETON
BONJOUR, MISS SEETON
MISS SEETON'S FINEST HOUR

KATE SHUGAK MYSTERIES: A former D.A. solves crimes in the far Alaska north...

by Dana Stabenow
A COLD DAY FOR MURDER
DEAD IN THE WATER
A FATAL THAW
BREAKUP

A COLD-BLOODED BUSINESS
PLAY WITH FIRE
BLOOD WILL TELL
KILLING GROUNDS
HUNTER'S MOON

INSPECTOR BANKS MYSTERIES: Award-winning British detective fiction at its finest... "Robinson's novels are habit-forming!"
—*West Coast Review of Books*

by Peter Robinson
THE HANGING VALLEY
WEDNESDAY'S CHILD
INNOCENT GRAVES

PAST REASON HATED
FINAL ACCOUNT
GALLOWS VIEW

CASS JAMESON MYSTERIES: Lawyer Cass Jameson seeks justice in the criminal courts of New York City in this highly acclaimed series... "A witty, gritty heroine."
—*New York Post*

by Carolyn Wheat
FRESH KILLS
MEAN STREAK
TROUBLED WATERS

DEAD MAN'S THOUGHTS
WHERE NOBODY DIES
SWORN TO DEFEND

JACK McMORROW MYSTERIES: The highly acclaimed series set in a Maine mill town and starring a newspaperman with a knack for crime solving... "Gerry Boyle is the genuine article."
—*Robert B. Parker*

by Gerry Boyle
DEADLINE
LIFELINE
BORDERLINE

BLOODLINE
POTSHOT
COVER STORY

THE BLIND
IN DARKNESS

STEPHEN LEWIS

BERKLEY PRIME CRIME, NEW YORK

THE BLIND IN DARKNESS

A Berkley Prime Crime Book / published by arrangement with the author

PRINTING HISTORY
Berkley Prime Crime edition / May 2000

The Penguin Putnam Inc. World Wide Web site address is http://www.penguinputnam.com

ISBN: 0-425-17466-2

Berkley Prime Crime Books are published by The Berkley Publishing Group, a division of Penguin Putnam Inc., 375 Hudson Street, New York, New York 10014.
The name BERKLEY PRIME CRIME and the BERKLEY PRIME CRIME design are trademarks belonging to Penguin Putnam Inc.

PRINTED IN THE UNITED STATES OF AMERICA

10 9 8 7 6 5 4 3 2 1

For Carolyn
As Always

And thou shalt grope at noonday, as the blind
gropeth in darkness, and thou shalt not prosper in
thy ways: and thou shalt be only oppressed and
spoiled evermore, and no man shall save thee.

—Deuteronomy 28:29

ONE

❧❦❧

I T WAS LATE afternoon by the time Catherine Williams turned off the main road leading north out of Newbury onto the path, usually rutted by the wooden wheels of a cart but now made smooth by six inches of freshly fallen snow. She pulled her cloak over her nose, blocking the wind she now walked against. The sky was dark with gray clouds and the temperature had been dropping all day. She looked to her left to the little house, not much more than a crude hut of wattle-and-daub construction, in which Sara Dunwood and her young husband lived. Catherine had delivered Sara of a healthy baby boy three weeks before, and now as she saw the smoke curling out of the wooden chimney, she wondered how they were doing this brutal winter in a hut ill suited to shut out the wind. However, Catherine's business this day took her past the Dunwood hovel to Sara's uncle's farm. It was the most distant from town, occupying the last area cleared before the New England forest, which surrounded Newbury on three sides with the ocean on the fourth.

Old man Powell was unusual in his willingness to confront the wilderness. The other citizens of Newbury extended themselves beyond the immediate center of the village with great caution, laying out the fields they cultivated as close to their houses as was practicable. When the topography dictated, they would plant at a distance from their homesteads, but they did so reluctantly. Isaac Powell, on the other hand, had chosen to live off by himself. He agreed to work this farm for Samuel Worthington, a wealthy Newbury merchant, in exchange for a place to live and a small percentage of the farm's meager profits. The farm was a quarter of mile past Sara, his nearest neighbor, and as though to emphasize his independence from the larger community, he planted his fields on the side of his property away from the village, felling the trees and removing the stumps where the forest met the meadow.

Catherine made her way in the semidarkness of a January afternoon beneath a sky heavy with approaching storm clouds. She had been summoned that morning by the young man who had recently come to live with Powell, and who had knocked at her door requesting that she come to do what she could to ease the old man's suffering from a wound on his hand.

She almost tripped over the dog lying motionless in the snow in front of the door. As her foot slid off the animal's back, it rose unsteadily to its feet and attempted a growl that came out more of a whine. It backed away from her and slunk off a few feet into the shadows, where it lay down and offered a feeble howl. The door opened, and standing there, shielding a candle with his hand, was the young man who had summoned her. The dog rose to its feet and took a tentative step toward the open doorway.

"Are you going to let the poor animal in?" Catherine asked.

The young man shrugged and motioned for her to enter.

"It is not for me to say," he murmured. He stood in the doorway without moving aside to let her enter, and his eyes shifted back and forth from her to the corner of the room inside where a shape sat huddled on a stool in shadow. A stub of a candle flickered on a table near the stool, and in its feeble light, Catherine could just see the head on the figure lift.

"Don't let that beast in, I say. Thomas, do you mind what I say?"

"What are you afraid of, old man?" asked Thomas.

"Ah, well you know," Isaac muttered.

The fire was low and the air in the room was chilled. Catherine looked toward the fireplace and then at the young man.

"He said I weren't to go out. I told him I need to fetch some firewood, but he would not hear anything about it. He didn't want me to open the door in case that dog was to make its way back in. So here we be, sitting in the cold. Him there afraid of an old dog like he was Jezebel her self."

"That's right," the old man said, rousing himself again. "That dog is why I sent you to seek Mistress Williams, and why she is now here."

"Is it, now?" Thomas said.

"It is."

Powell looked hard at the young man, as Catherine walked over to him, but then the old man's eyes shut. When he opened them to look up at her, he seemed unable to focus. He had a coarse blanket wrapped about him. She placed her hand on his forehead. He was warm from fever, and as if in confirmation, his shoulders convulsed with a violent shiver.

"You can go out now, and get some wood," she told Thomas.

Her voice seemed to rouse the old man.

"No, do not." He grabbed Catherine's arm. "He will run off if I am not watching him," he said.

"Do not worry about that," she said, then spoke again to the young man. "You are not planning to go anywhere, now, are you?"

Thomas's lips rose in a small smile.

"Not likely," he said in a loud, clear voice, "in a storm like this." He lowered his voice to a whisper and said words Catherine could not understand. She took a step toward him, but Powell's hand on her arm stayed her.

"Later, then," Thomas said just loudly enough to be heard.

"What does he say?" the old man asked.

"He says the fire will warm us sooner rather than later," she replied.

The young man walked over to Powell and shook his shoulder until he looked up at him.

"I am not going anywhere, what with Mistress Williams here, and the savages roaming about outside looking for an opportunity to knock me on my head. And that poor old dog is probably dead by now. I don't hear it no more."

"That is a good thing, Thomas," Powell said. "Bring in some firewood." A draft came in through the door, and the candle dimmed. He raised his left hand from beneath the blanket as though to grasp the young man's arm, but Thomas was too quick, and he stepped back with a smile that seemed more forced than genuine.

"Now, none of that," he said.

"I was only going to remind you to be careful," the old man muttered, "and I cannot see you very well. I told you to light another candle."

Thomas shrugged and took a full candle from a hook on the mantel. He lit it from the stub, and stood still for a moment, making sure that the flame caught. Catherine now got her first good look at him. She had heard of his presence, of course, newly arrived from Barbados, and his face was still tanned from the sun of that island. His features were attractive, almost delicate, with bright blue eyes and thin lips that seemed as ready to sneer as smile, but there seemed also to be a latent sensuality in his expression, perhaps in the way his nostrils flared as he breathed, or how his mouth never quite closed completely. Catherine noted that his face showed no signs of stubble, and she wondered about his age, as he was rumored to be the companion, and contemporary, of Master Worthington's son, Nathaniel, who was in his early twenties. Further, he was of a slight build, round shouldered, and not much taller than Catherine, who was herself only a little over five feet. Wisps of straggly blond hair protruded from beneath the cloak he wore over his head against the chill in the room.

"Go on about your work, then," Catherine said. "Now that you have provided us with some light, see what you can do for heat. I cannot attend to your master properly while we are both in danger of freezing."

Thomas shrugged in a gesture that seemed to make his narrow shoulders almost reach up and touch his ears, and then he turned to the door. He opened it, then stepped back as a strong gust rushed into the house. He lowered his head and walked out.

Isaac watched the door shut behind Thomas. His face wore an expression that Catherine found difficult to decipher, something between fondness and fear.

"That boy won't never make much of a farmer," he said. "You can look at his hands and see how little work he does here. Master Worthington sent him to me to teach him to farm, but he don't want to learn nothing about it." He shook his head and then nodded. "Which is not to say that he is not handy in other ways to have here." He snorted as though starting to laugh, and then clutched his arms about him and shivered.

"Let me see what is troubling you," Catherine said, "and do not waste any more of your breath on that one."

She held out her hands, but Isaac cowered in his chair. "Let me see it, then," she insisted.

He lifted his right hand, which had remained beneath the blanket. It was wrapped in a dirty cloth. Catherine took it in her own hands, as gently as she could, and yet he winced. She brought it toward the candle on the table and removed the cloth. She saw the festering wound, swollen red with a center of pus oozing out against the ingrained dirt on the back of the farmer's hand. She started to turn the hand over, but Powell winced and tucked it away beneath the blanket.

"It pains you, does it?" she asked in her gentlest voice. Powell nodded.

"Ever since that hellhound bit me. Can you help me?" he asked.

"Yes, but I'd like to see it again."

He shook his head, and she saw in his eyes the stubbornness of an old man who had lived long alone and was not used to accommodating himself to the requests of others. In any case, she concluded, she had seen enough. His hand was dripping poison that might also be in his blood and that is why he shook so violently, as though from ague. She reached into her midwife's bag and pulled out a coarse burlap pouch. She loosened the thread that pulled its top closed, and shook out a couple of roots. She put these on the table next to the candle, and then drew the thread tight and knotted it.

"Do you have a knife?" she asked.

Isaac reached his good hand beneath the blanket, and brought forth a knife with a six-inch blade.

"There's talk of them savages," he said.

"Yes," Catherine replied. "I have heard so."

"You live with one, I hear," he said, and opened his mouth in a crooked grin that revealed yellowed teeth on top and a black stump on the bottom.

"He lives on my property," she replied.

"That's not what folks say," he insisted.

"Folk say many things. When your young man comes back in, have him chop up these roots and boil them into a tea."

"What is it?" he asked.

"Ground root of the coneflower."

"A flower root," he said, shaking his head. "Maybe I better be calling in one of those the savages call powwows and he could chant some nonsense over me."

"You need not bother," Catherine said, "for it is from one of them that I learned of this remedy."

"The one what—" he began.

"No," she replied.

Powell shook his head and stared toward the door.

"It is cold," he said.

"I will see what is keeping him," she said.

"You need not."

"But I will."

Thomas was standing next to a pile of split firewood, a few steps from the door. The dog was at his feet. Snow was falling now and it clung to the boy's hair. His body convulsed with violent shivers. He opened his mouth to talk, but could not stop his teeth from chattering. Catherine took hold of his arm and tried to pull him toward the door, but he shook his head and leaned his weight back against her motion. She let go of his arm.

"Do you want to see how long it will be before you are ice?" she asked.

"I was waiting to speak with you."

He knelt down and stroked the dog.

"He's going to freeze out here, and the old man don't want him back in the house. He keeps talking about how Jezebel was eaten up by dogs."

"The dog bit him, did it not?"

Thomas shook his head.

"I would not know nothing about that. I did not see it."

She pointed to the firewood.

"You had better bring that in. Your master is half froze inside and you are mostly froze out here. Maybe we can convince him to let the animal inside again."

"There are worse things than ice," he said, and his thin lips twitched into a sneer. He swung his foot back and brought it forward in a sharp kick to the animal's rib. It howled, got up, and ran off. "I don't have no use for him, neither," he said.

"Thomas, the wood!"

Old man Powell's voice, surprisingly strong, came through the closed door.

"The fire is just about out," he called.

Thomas looked at Catherine and shrugged.

"And there is fires that burn in people as well as fireplaces," he said.

"I am too cold to deal with riddles," she said.

"Then I will be plain," Thomas replied, but before he could continue, his master was standing in the doorway. "Another time, then," the boy said.

"I will be back in a day or two to see if he is mending."

"Thomas," cried the old man.

"Then, we will speak," Thomas said, and Catherine turned her steps into the snow and the path that led to the road to Newbury. As she walked along, she saw the dog's tracks heading in the same direction. The tracks continued until the path joined the road, and then they veered off as though the animal had been frightened by something. Catherine clucked her tongue, but the dog did not reappear. She shrugged, pulled her cloak about her, and made her way onto the road home.

TWO

❧❧❧

SNOW, WET AND heavy, had been falling all night, coating the wigwam with a natural insulation so that Massaquoit could only measure the severity of the storm by the absence of the currents of cold air that usually floated into his living space through the chinks in the bark-covered walls. As he opened his eyes, the air was preternaturally still, even a little warmer than usual as the embers of his fire still glowed in the darkness, and he knew that when he pushed open the flap he would see a world turned unequivocally white.

Last night at sunset, when the storm had abated for a few hours, he had heard the tramp of a labored step through the snow, passing by his wigwam and proceeding on to Mistress Williams' house. The visitor had paused just outside of the wigwam, as he almost always did, as though continually surprised that this alien structure was still occupying space in front of the white woman's house. Massaquoit recognized the heavy breathing of the man, and knew that his coming at such an hour after so much snow had fallen could only mean that something serious had occurred.

This morning, however, he pushed the memory of that visit from his mind as he concentrated on a more immediate problem. It was Sunday, according to the English way of counting days, and he would be expected to join them in their communal house where they gathered to pray to their Father in words whose meaning he understood but whose intent baffled him still, after months of exposure to a religion he found unfathomable. He had taught himself to approach these meeting days with his mind open—not to admit the divine grace that would convert him, as the English fully expected, but to absorb as much of the foreign doctrine as he could so that he might convince the English magistrates that his conversion was possible. For as long as he was a prospective Christian and less the stubborn savage in their eyes, he was that much more secure in his private devotion to the world view in which he had been raised, a view that had comforted him at the moment he stood over the dead bodies of wife and child, and sustained him as his comrades were drowned by these same English. Perhaps the English expected the Word to irritate the lining of his soul, to engender there a pearl of Christian faith, but he knew that it only added layers to the stone of his resistance.

It almost amused him, in a bitter way, to think that the English wanted him to become as Christian as they were so they would be able to sleep more comfortably in their beds, secure in their illusion that their faith grafted onto his soul would stay his hand from violence against them. But recently, he had felt the eyes of the English bore into him with undisguised hostility. He had seen the hands of the men tighten as though in a fist or to grasp a weapon they did not then have in their hands, and he had noted how the women pulled their children behind them as they passed.

He crawled out from beneath his blanket and sat for a

moment, disconsolate before the English breeches, shirt, and jerkin he knew he had to put on, lying in a pile in the red glare cast by the embers of the fire. At least he had prevailed upon Catherine to gain him permission to wear the deerskin foot coverings he had obtained from Wequashcook instead of the insufferably clumsy leather boots, which made him feel as if he were walking through mud even when the crust of the ground was hard beneath him.

When he pushed the flap open a few minutes later, he encountered what he expected, a foot of fresh snow stretching in a rippled line, interrupted here and there by wind-driven drifts, between his wigwam and Catherine's house. Just visible, although almost covered by the snow which had resumed falling, were the tracks of last evening's visitor. He noted how the steps were close together and how the man's feet had dragged through the snow, instead of lifting from it, as he had labored to Catherine's door. He saw the smoke curling up from the chimney and his stomach encouraged him to join Catherine for breakfast, although most mornings he preferred making his own meal.

Her servant Phyllis motioned him to sit down at the table across from Catherine, and as he did she pushed a bowl of steaming samp in front of him. He waited for her to provide an implement, and she, in turn, looked to Catherine.

"Why, go ahead," Catherine said. "Give him one of the new ones."

"I suppose so," Phyllis replied, "seeing as how he has honored us with his company." She opened a drawer of the chest in the corner of the kitchen and lifted out a gleaming pewter spoon, which she placed with exaggerated care next to the wooden bowl.

"They have just arrived," Catherine said, "on the *Helmsford,* now anchored next to the governor's new wharf."

Massaquoit balanced the spoon in his hand, studying its

weight and its smooth surface. He dipped it into the samp and brought it up to his lips.

"It is good," he said.

"The spoon?" asked Phyllis.

"Both," he replied.

"I didn't cook the spoon," she said.

Catherine smiled. She enjoyed their interplay. But this morning her mood was somber as she recalled Woolsey's visit the night before. Her smile faded to a frown. Massaquoit noticed the change.

"Master Woolsey came to see you last night," he said.

Phyllis let her spoon clatter to the table.

"It is not natural," she said, "the way you see everything. If you was white, I would think you was a wizard on your way to a sabbat flying over poor Master Woolsey's head, and him still troubled as he is with the pain in his arm so he can hardly straighten it."

"Yes, he did," Catherine said, looking past Phyllis to Massaquoit.

"He brought bad news?" Massaquoit asked.

"Yes, I am afraid." She placed her own spoon down on the table, very slowly, as though the downward movement of her hand might gather the conflicting thoughts that whirled in her head. As the spoon touched the wood of the tabletop, the whirl did seem to stop and she was, for the moment, sure of the right course.

"Perhaps you should stay home today," she said.

He studied her face, looking for a clue to her intent.

"What Mistress is trying to say," Phyllis intruded, "is that because of what Master Woolsey said last night people will fear for their scalps with you sitting behind them in the meetinghouse."

"He said no such thing," Catherine corrected.

"Not in so many words, he didn't," Phyllis insisted, "but

that was what he meant to say if he was not too much of a gentleman to say it."

"Phyllis sometimes gives voice to her fancy," Catherine said in a voice that was intended to quiet her servant.

"Then how far does her fancy travel from the truth?" Massaquoit asked.

"Yesterday two men in Westwood, not fifteen miles north of here, were out gathering wood. They did not return."

"I see," Massaquoit said.

"Dead in the snow, that's how they found them," Phyllis put in. She glanced at her mistress, her mouth still open, prepared to expand upon the description, to tell what the men were wearing, and how they had been killed, and by whom, but she stopped the flow of words and contented herself with making a clucking noise.

"And because two English were killed you think I should stay home?"

"That is what Master Woolsey suggested."

"And you?" he asked.

"If you go, you will encounter hostility."

"And if I hide myself, I will feed that hostility," he said. She permitted a small smile to form on her lips.

"I thought you might think so." She pulled her cloak down from the peg next to the door.

Phyllis gathered her own cloak and threw it over her shoulders.

"Foolishness," she said, "that is what it is. Why he could stay here and help Edward mend that stool."

"Edward will do no work on the Lord's day," Catherine told her. "And Massaquoit will walk with us to meeting."

"Edward would enjoy the company, he would," Phyllis muttered, but she opened the door and waited for Catherine and Massaquoit to precede her outside. Catherine glanced up at the sky, which was dropping snow once again, and shook her head.

"I must try to make my way to Isaac Powell's house," Catherine said. "I promised I would be back to check on how his hand was mending, but the snow has been so heavy I have not done so. I will try to go today."

"If you would not mind the company," Massaquoit said, "I will walk with you."

"Do you fear for me, then?" she asked.

"Certainly not," he said.

"Then come along," she replied.

The snow was falling harder as they trudged to the meetinghouse. The wind blew the flakes against their faces so that they could barely see the snow-covered road, trodden almost flat by those who had passed before them. Catherine and Phyllis, walking in front as they always did when accompanied by Massaquoit, kept their heads bowed and saw only their feet. Massaquoit, however, held one hand over his eyes so that he could still see a few feet ahead of him. That is why he saw the movement coming from behind a tree. He seized the arm that reached for him as he passed the tree, and pulled.

He was prepared for an assault, but was not surprised when he saw instead of an English face the darker complexion of Wequashcook beneath his beaver hat. Wequashcook freed his arm from Massaquoit's grip and motioned ahead to Catherine and Phyllis, who were disappearing behind the curtain of snow.

"Did she not warn you?" he asked.

"She did," Massaquoit replied.

"And still you go to their meeting?"

"I do." He started to walk. "They will soon notice I am not with them."

"Yes, the English are marvelous for noticing, are they not?"

"What is it you want?"

"Only to add my warning to hers."

"It is pointless."

"Perhaps she does not know all of it."

"About the attack?"

"There has been another. Last night. At the English farm where that boy was sent."

Massaquoit nodded, but kept walking. Wequashcook shook his head but matched his stride to Massaquoit's.

"You have not gotten any less stubborn," he said.

"Tell me what you have heard. I have not gotten any more stupid, either."

"There is not much to tell. I was walking to meeting early this morning, as I always do, and I was behind the Thompson family. They did not notice me, because they were walking into the wind, as we are now, but the wind carried their voices back to me. That old man, Powell, he was found dead in his house. The boy has disappeared. Some say he killed his master. Others say Indians killed the old man and took the boy away."

"What do you say?"

Wequashcook shrugged.

"It could be either. The English sometimes kill each other. And sometimes Indians kill the English, as they sometimes kill us. It does not matter." He pointed ahead to Catherine and Phyllis. "You know they will never trust us. I have traded many years with Thompson. But this morning, when the wind died down for a moment, and he heard my feet crunching the snow, he turned and stared at me as though he was seeing me for the first time. That is when I decided to wait for you."

"I do not know this Thompson," Massaquoit replied. "But I know how he looked at you."

"Then you know all there is to know."

Massaquoit resumed walking, but now Wequashcook did not join him.

"I have business elsewhere," he said. "And if you were wise, you would tell your mistress that you must help me."

Massaquoit quickened his pace. When he glanced over his shoulder, Wequashcook was gone. He caught up to Catherine and took her arm.

"The man you intend to visit later is past your help," he said.

"He died? I did not think his hurt was mortal."

"That is not what killed him," Massaquoit replied.

Catherine nodded.

"I see," she said.

"See what?" Phyllis inquired.

"Old man Powell has been killed," Catherine told her.

Phyllis looked hard at Massaquoit.

"Where did you hear that? You did not know it at breakfast, and now I suppose you will say the wind told you."

"A man like the wind," Massaquoit replied, "whispered it in my ear, just now."

"Well, I saw no such man," Phyllis declared.

"Yet, he was here."

"Do you not want to turn back?" Catherine asked.

"No," Massaquoit replied. "I have done nothing wrong."

A crowd was gathered in front of the meetinghouse when they arrived. They stood before someone who seemed to be holding forth to such effect that his listeners ignored the wind-driven snow that swirled about them. They had drawn their cloaks and coats tightly around them, and these garments were now turned white so that it was impossible to distinguish the men from the women. The speaker, who was standing on the steps, looked over the crowd as Catherine, Phyllis, and Massaquoit approached. He stopped speaking, and as he did, the people turned to follow his gaze. A collective murmur arose, barely audible against the wind. But Catherine could hear its menace. She turned to Massaquoit.

"There is still time," she said. "Master Worthington is inciting their affections."

He shook his head.

"Don't be a fool," Phyllis said. "Do you not hear them?"

"I hear the wind," Massaquoit replied. "It is stronger than their voices."

"It's not the wind you have to worry about," Phyllis said. She turned to Catherine. "Mistress Williams, can you not speak sense to him?"

Catherine shook her head slowly, not so much in response to her servant's question, but in anticipation of the collision between Massaquoit's stubborn pride and the anger of the settlers.

"No," she said now to Phyllis. "Certainly not. He will do what he will do. And we will take our places at meeting." She nodded at Massaquoit as though to tell him that it was his decision to proceed, and that she would not try to dissuade him.

He watched their two figures, Catherine's short and squat, and Phyllis's a head taller but also broad-shouldered, merge with the falling snow. Then he walked toward the front of the meetinghouse, keeping his eyes on the speaker, who followed his progress. He saw the crowd divide to permit Catherine and Phyllis to pass, and then close again. He approached the knot of people, who now formed an uneven line in front of the meetinghouse. He considered walking straight into their midst to provoke the confrontation he knew they wanted, but dismissed that idea, not out of fear but because he did not want to give them the pleasure of assaulting him.

With this in mind, he quickened and lengthened his pace as though preparing to force his way through the crowd.

He sensed, rather than saw, the stiffening of those immediately in his path. When he was close enough to a man
in the middle of the line to see the fear in his eyes and to
watch his breath explode in excited bursts, he stopped and
held the man's gaze for a second or two before turning
sharply to his right. A few strides brought him to the last
citizen, an older woman who opened her mouth in a tooth-
less sneer at him, and there he turned again, not proceeding a foot farther than necessary to flank the woman. She
turned her head to follow his movement toward the door
of the meetinghouse, but neither she nor any of the others said anything, nor did they resist his progress.

Inside the building, he saw Catherine sitting on the front
bench, as befitted her position as a rich widow, and farther back, among the other servants, was Phyllis. He nodded at her as he went by to find his place on the bench at
the rear, where he was accustomed to endure the services
in the company of Wequashcook and half a dozen other
Indians, who with varying degrees of sincerity had embraced the English god. Today, however, he had the bench
to himself. He shook the snow from his head, stomped it
from his feet, rubbed his hands together, and sat down,
these gestures designed to insist that even though the
colonists had apparently decided that he was now a demon,
he was a demon whose flesh still felt the cold of the snow.

Usually, every place on the benches that crossed the
square space of the meetinghouse from the altar to the rear
wall would be filled with the settlers. Today, however, either because of the storm, or as Massaquoit surmised, because they were squeezing themselves more tightly together,
the bench immediately in front of him remained empty
until the very last moment before the service began. But
just as Minister Davis climbed up to the pulpit, a young
man in a ragged greatcoat so covered in snow that it looked
as though he must have been sleeping outside during the

storm, sat down on the very edge of that bench. He glanced at Massaquoit, and offered a crooked smile that revealed his missing front teeth. He held his gaze on Massaquoit until Minister Davis's voice rumbled through the meetinghouse and the service began. As it did, Massaquoit settled himself, with an expression of bemused attention on his face, as he did every time he was obliged to sit through a service.

Within a few moments, he heard snores rise from the young man in the greatcoat. He saw that the snow clinging to the coat had begun to melt and drip to the floor. Every few moments, a chunk of snow would be dislodged and fall with an audible splash. The young man's breath gathered as he slept and then was released through the gap in his teeth so that the snores from his nose were accompanied by a whistling through his mouth. As these sounds grew louder, those congregants nearest Massaquoit turned toward him with looks of bitter displeasure, and although he gestured in the direction of the young man, they seemed, somehow, to hold him responsible for this desecration of the service.

He realized that the only sound he had heard for the last few moments was the breathing and snoring of the young man. Minister Davis's voice, which had been floating above him in an aspirant arch toward the ceiling of the meetinghouse, on its way, no doubt, to the ear of the English god, had now ceased. He looked at the minister, standing behind the massive carved oak pulpit, so that only his upper chest and head beneath its skull cap were visible, and his glance was returned by Davis, who apparently had stopped talking so as to fix his eyes on Massaquoit. One by one, the other members of the congregation turned to stare past the snoring young man at him. He returned each gaze as it reached him as though he were parrying the thrusts of sword blades. Catherine half rose out of her seat so she could see over those sitting behind her. She held Massaquoit's eyes with hers, and then shook her head as if in sadness. With virtually everyone in the meetinghouse facing Massaquoit, Minister Davis began again to speak. As he did, the young man roused, rubbed his eyes, and looked toward the pulpit. Seeing everyone's eyes looking past him at Massaquoit, he too, turned in that direction.

"Sitting on the back bench," Minister Davis said, "is Matthew, a savage we have fondly called a 'praying Indian' because he has not only abandoned his savage name for a Christian one, but has also accepted Our Lord. But there are others of his kind who roam the woods, spilling the blood of our neighbors to remind us, surely, that our help is only in the Lord, and not in any human conviction or understanding of the reformation of a savage's natural, brutish nature, however it might appear to be informed by Grace."

Catherine now stood as if to speak, although she knew that doing so would constitute a serious breach of decorum. Minister Davis, pausing as if to underscore his point, looked at Catherine and with an almost indiscernible nod of his head conceded that he was treading on dangerous ground, that his words were like a lit match tossed into a powder keg of fear and anger. She, in turn, reading the concession in his expression, shifted her eyes back to Massaquoit and then sat back down.

Minister Davis again raised his voice.

"Yes, we see the signs of Grace turning the affections of the benighted savage toward our Lord and salvation, and we must rejoice when we see the wondrous effects wrought by the Spirit." He closed his eyes and nodded as though he were seeing this marvel with his mind's eye at that moment.

The congregation waited for him to continue, but a voice

from the back of the meetinghouse filled the silence left by the minister.

"I'm looking at this one savage right now, and all I see is a savage," the voice declared. It belonged to the sleepy young man, who had now roused himself fully and was pointing at Massaquoit, bringing his hand within six inches of Massaquoit's face. Massaquoit studied that hand, noted the encrusted dirt between the fingers and the ragged fingernails, even the dead skin from a recent case of frostbite on the tip of the index finger pointed at him, and then with a gesture slow and almost regal, he pulled that hand down. The young man tried to resist, but the strength in his arm was not nearly enough to hold against Massaquoit's force, and so he let the arm drop heavily against his side.

"You see how he attacks me!" he cried.

The congregation's disparate voices, men and women, young and old, rose to agree. Minister Davis cleared his throat loudly to signal that he would resume speaking, but the rumbling voices only grew louder, although as yet no words separated themselves from the waves of sound. When words did take shape, they were simple.

"No Christian, he," the young man said above the waves, and then the voices of the congregation agreed. "Yea, no Christian, he," they said.

"A Christian would not kill a Christian, would he?" the young man cried out above the clamor.

There was a stunned silence, and then a deep bass voice from the first row of benches, where the well-to-do sat, boomed out "No." Catherine looked at the man who had spoken, Samuel Worthington, owner of the merchant vessel that had brought Thomas and Worthington's son, Nathaniel, up from Barbados. Worthington had been embroiled in litigation with Catherine's husband, John, over some spoiled cargo, just before John died, and never encountered Catherine without betraying in his face a resid-

ual bitterness at the fact that her husband had defeated
him in court. And, in fact, he still had not paid the court-
ordered restitution to Catherine.

He was flanked by the tall, athletic figure of his son,
Nathaniel, on one side, and the shorter, more powerful figure of Lionel Osprey, a mercenary who had been with the
English settlers in Jamestown, where he had been given
the rank of lieutenant, and now worked for the merchant.
Osprey was holding his brass-buttoned greatcoat tightly
about him. Catherine noted, almost idly, that the coat was
missing a button. She tried to recall whether Osprey were
married, and then reminded herself that men who spent
their lives as soldiers, far from the company of women,
well knew how to handle a needle, although in the case of
Lionel Osprey his thick hands looked more suitable for
heavier, blunter implements. Worthington returned her
glance with a satisfied smile. "No," he repeated even louder.
"Look to Mistress Williams's savage and find blood in his
heart if not on his hands."

Catherine felt the eyes of the congregation shift from
Massaquoit to herself. In the faces of her neighbors she
read all the accusations she had heard whispered behind
her back, whispered with a deliberate loudness so that she
would hear how she had betrayed them by taking into her
house one of *them*. Their hostile glances amplified that dis-
content with Massaquoit's presence like a noxious weed
rising up from the soil fertilized by stories of Indian atroc-
ities.

Catherine felt all this palpably, as though their accusatory
looks had hardened into sounds, and the sounds into words.
In her heart, she knew that some of what her neighbors
thought was in fact true. Massaquoit did not, and would
not any time soon, embrace the English god. But he would
not, for that reason, spill the blood of those who did.

Minister Davis tried clearing his throat loudly, but that

gesture, which ordinarily would have produced immediate silence, was ineffectual. The unkempt young man and Worthington tossed remarks back and forth over the heads of the congregation, and each statement elicited a response of increasing intensity and anger. Massaquoit stood up and stared stonily ahead as though he could silence the babble by meeting it with his own steadfast silence.

The minister slammed the covers of his huge Bible together as loudly as he could. Worthington turned back to face the minister and his face blanched. Davis was holding the tome over his head as though he meant to throw it out among the congregants. Those nearest the front recoiled and quieted, and the quiet rolled back through the congregation until only the young man remained standing. He muttered a steady stream of insults. Minister Davis let the Bible down, gently, onto the lectern. His face was red and glowing with sweat.

"Remember whose house we are in," he said, and his voice filled the meetinghouse. The people, now docile before the authority of their shepherd, settled back in their places, ready to be instructed. Davis looked at Catherine.

"It would be well," he said, "if you took Matthew home now. The Lord will understand." The minister nodded at her with an expression he reserved for those occasions when he had opened a difficult passage of Scripture. She also recognized that both his words and expression were intended much more for the congregation than for her. Introducing the Lord into this situation was intended only to invoke a presence that might erect a temporary screen behind which she would be able to escort Massaquoit home.

For his part, Massaquoit's face revealed no response to either the minister's words or the threats of the congregation, while in his mind he wondered what the English god could possibly think of his people's mindless rage and their unprovoked attack on an innocent man. He knew well

enough that his people would avenge the murder of one
of their own, but they would be very careful, as the English were not, to make sure that they identified the murderer by something more specific than the color of skin.
When English blood was spilled, all Indians became the
enemy.

He took a step toward the aisle. He would show them
neither fear nor an answering hostility. The young man in
the row in front of him mirrored his movements so that
when Massaquoit reached the end of his row he stood in
his path.

"You should listen to your minister," Massaquoit said.
"He does not think your god wants me in this house today."
He took a step toward him.

"Or any day, for that matter," the ragged fellow sneered.

The murmuring in the meetinghouse had stopped with
Massaquoit's movements. Catherine edged her way into the
aisle, casting a glance at Worthington. Osprey took a half
step forward toward the aisle, but the merchant, his eyes
holding Catherine's, grabbed his arm and muttered something in his ear. Nathaniel leaned forward to hear what his
father was saying.

"But Thomas . . ." Nathaniel said. "He is Thomasine's
brother."

"Well I know it—Thomas," replied Worthington. Then
he nodded at Catherine as though the remark indicated to
her that their differences, dating back to her husband, and
now amplified by his son's relationship to the missing
Thomas, would have to be confronted.

Catherine shook her head slowly from side to side in a
gesture she would employ with a recalcitrant child. Then
she beckoned for Massaquoit to come toward her.

"Stand by," she called out to the young man blocking
his way.

Massaquoit stared hard at the insolent fellow, and then

with deliberation took a step directly forward. He paused
and watched the arrogance fade from the young man's face,
replaced for a moment with a petulant stubbornness. Still,
he presented his body as an impediment. Massaquoit put
a hand on each of the fellow's shoulders and pressed until
his knees buckled. Then he spun him around with a push
that sent him staggering into the row between the benches.
He steadied himself and again stepped in front of Massaquoit.

"You do not think to stop me, do you?" Massaquoit said.

The fellow glanced about him, but those closest by
shifted their bodies away from a confrontation they wanted
no part of. He shrugged.

"I see how it is," he said.

Massaquoit paced straight ahead so that he was now
chest to chest with the young man. He could smell his beer-
rich breath. The young man stepped aside and bowed as
Massaquoit passed him by.

Everyone's eyes were on Massaquoit as he made his
slow progress up the aisle. Nobody said a word, and no
one offered resistance, but there was a stir as he came
abreast the row where the servants sat. He sensed the movement of a body forcing its way through irresolute resistance, and he smiled inwardly as Phyllis fell in behind him.
As he walked by each row now, there was an audible release of breath, as though those sitting there had been unable to exhale until he passed. Catherine waited until he
was a few feet from her, and then she moved to join him.

Worthington looked up to Minister Davis.

"Do you not think it meet to question the savage?" the
merchant demanded. "He will surely flee into the woods."

"This is God's house," Minister Davis replied.

Catherine broke from Massaquoit's side and strode to
Worthington, a tall, portly man who towered over her.

"Anyone who wants to talk to Matthew knows where

to find him. But as for Isaac Powell, I was the one who traveled to his farm to tend to his hurt hand. Matthew was nowhere near that old man's house."

"So say you," Worthington retorted, his lips curled back.

"That I do," Catherine replied. She rejoined Massaquoit and Phyllis. Worthington now placed himself in their path, and the ragged young man walked up the aisle to form a hostile bookend. Massaquoit looked at Catherine and then at Worthington, but she shook her head.

"That would not be wise," she said. She looked beyond Worthington to the tall figure of Governor Peters, who was now rising from his seat. In one long stride, the governor was at Worthington's side. He leaned down and whispered something in his ear. Worthington shook his head, but when Peters seemed to repeat his point, this time with more emphasis so that the words "not now" floated into the otherwise tense silence, the merchant nodded, and stepped aside.

"Thank you for your timely aid," Catherine said as they walked by. She did not think he noticed the irony in her tone.

As they reached the front door, the congregation regained its collective voice, and there were various cries hurled in their direction. One or two voices above the others said, "Vengeance. We want vengeance." And a third, a high-pitched soprano, belonging perhaps to a young woman, screamed, "Stop him!"

And then the rich baritone of the minister filled the meetinghouse like a wave overrunning the confused swirl of the surf.

"Vengeance, indeed," the minister declared. "Yea, vengeance saith the Lord is mine."

Catherine paused to see if the minister's voice had its usual calming effect, and when she saw that it did she led her companions through the door.

Once outside, Catherine took Massaquoit's arm.

"That young man who was stirring things up, I think I remember seeing him."

"Do you not know him, then?" Phyllis asked.

"I cannot place him."

"Well, it takes one to know one, I suppose. To the rest, some are invisible."

"Make yourself clear," Catherine said.

"Servants, I am talking about," Phyllis replied. "There are those that do not even see us, even when we be standing right in front of them. That lad came up from Barbados with the one what was living with Isaac Powell when he got himself killed. He was taken in by Master Worthington until he run away, which was some little time ago. I heard that the boy was slinking about the door of the house looking to see if Master Worthington would have him back."

"I guess he did," Catherine said, "and has him plying a new trade."

"What might that be, then?" Phyllis asked.

"I would say a rabble rouser," Catherine replied.

THREE

THEY STARTED DOWN the road leading away from Newbury Center toward Catherine's house, making slow
progress as the wind was now blowing horizontal waves
of snow into their faces. Phyllis walked ahead so that her
broad-shouldered body could shield her mistress, and Massaquoit fell in behind. They had taken only a few difficult
steps when Phyllis stopped and extended her arm toward
a large house on their left. Squinting to see through the
curtain of snowflakes, Catherine looked in that direction.

"I see him," she said. "You go on ahead."

"Do you not want us to wait for you?" Phyllis asked.

Catherine shook her head.

"You know how Master Woolsey is. He will want to
speak to me alone. You two go on ahead."

Massaquoit lowered his head so that his voice could be
heard above the rush of the wind.

"I will walk with Phyllis to your house. And then I think
I will make my way to that farm."

"I am not sure that is wise."

"But everybody is now here, are they not?" he said, and
pointed to the meetinghouse.

"Yes," Catherine conceded.

"Then this is the best time for me to go."

As was his custom when he made up his mind, Massaquoit did not wait for an answer, but beckoned Phyllis to follow him. She glanced at her mistress, shrugged, and then walked after him.

Joseph Woolsey stood in the doorway of his house, a heavy, fringed wool shawl drawn tight about his shoulders. Every moment or two, he took his right hand from beneath the shawl to wipe away the snow that plastered his cheeks or flew into his eyes. He looked decidedly uncomfortable, but Catherine knew that her old friend, the magistrate, was perfectly capable of ignoring physical discomfort, and the pained expression on his face probably had a good deal more to do with Isaac Powell and the suspicions now centering on Massaquoit than it did with the flakes that seemed ready to turn him into a living snowman.

"Get on inside with you," she said, as soon as she was near enough for her voice to carry above the wind.

"I must speak with you," he called out. "I did not feel strong enough to attend meeting, but I fear I should have. Seeing you and him leave early gives me some comfort that my worst fears have not been realized, but also confirms that I was justified in having such fears."

"Right you are, as usual, Joseph," she said as she reached his side and placed her hand on his arm to guide him back into the house. "Your fears were well grounded, and we took the opportunity to leave before something worse happened."

He let himself be led back into his own house, where a servant girl, her expression showing no apparent interest in either her master or his guest, waited just inside the door. The door opened into a narrow hallway, an unusual architectural feature found only in the largest Newbury houses owned by the most affluent citizens, one of whom was

Master Joseph Woolsey, whose wealth and service to the community ranked him with Governor Peters and Minister Davis in the social hierarchy of the community. To the right of the hallway was a spacious front room, and to the left a much smaller study, dominated by an elaborately carved oaken desk. The servant girl took a step toward the large, front room.

"No, Dorothy," Master Woolsey said, "the wind blows through that room as though we were standing outside." He pointed to the study. "In there. Build the fire, if you please."

Dorothy, a thin girl of sixteen, with a pointed chin and long nose that detracted from her otherwise pretty face, said nothing, but preceded them into the study and applied a pair of bellows to the smoldering fire. Woolsey sat behind his desk and motioned for Catherine to take the one other chair, which had a cane back and seat. It was decorated with interlocking wooden loops on the top of the back and between the front legs.

"Sit," Woolsey said, as Catherine hesitated.

"Will it hold my weight? Or my dignity?" she asked.

"I have just had it from Cartwright in London. It arrived on the *Helmsford*."

Catherine sat down gingerly.

"You did not call me here to show off your new chair, I warrant."

"Certainly not. I am only sorry that my ague kept me abed this morning. I strove mightily to overcome it. Is that not so, Dorothy?"

The girl, her face reddened and perspired from building the fire, turned and nodded, a barely perceptible motion that gave her the appearance of a bird pecking at a minute morsel.

"What's that, child?" Woolsey demanded.

Dorothy rose to her feet. Her eyes were suddenly bright and her features animated as though waking from a trance.

"It is as he says, Mistress. It was a great struggle I had, to tell him not to go out, for he would surely take badly ill and then what would I do, just come to this colony and my master in the grave?"

Catherine found herself smiling at this unexpected linguistic assault, so contrary to the girl's reserved manner and frail body.

"You did right, child," Catherine said. "But you need not worry about your place. Good Master Woolsey I have known since I was a girl, and he will live a while longer, without doubt, and should you need to you can always come stay with me. My own servant Phyllis has a tongue that oftentimes outpaces her brain, and I see you would be a fine match for her."

"I thank you, Mistress, but as you say and can see for yourself, I am very happy here with Master Woolsey, as long as he will be sensible about his health." She knelt by the fire, her face again blank, and applied the poker with a disinterested persistence that soon brought the fire to a blaze.

Catherine regained her focus.

"Samuel Worthington," she said, "is not a man to forget an imagined grievance, even when the object of his concern is long in the ground."

"Your John and he had their differences," Woolsey said. "But I think I can shed further light on his present anger. His son, Nathaniel, is betrothed to the sister of that very lad who was living with Isaac Powell, and he told me himself how ill his son has taken the lad's disappearance. Nathaniel's betrothed is coming on the next ship up from the islands."

"That might explain his displeasure, but it does not excuse how at meeting today he was inciting the people against Massaquoit."

Woolsey let out an audible sigh.

"I feared something of the sort, but I did not know it would be him."

"It was."

"It is time you took my advice and sent Matthew to Niantic."

"He has no interest in joining what he calls 'white Indians.' "

"White Indians, indeed," Woolsey said with a violent explosion of breath that left a trail of spittle running down his chin. He swiped at it, and shook his head. "They at Niantic have accepted Our Lord, they pray to Him, and some even are learning to read His word."

"He will not go. And if he would, I fear it is too late. His presence would only bring the wrath of those incited by Worthington."

"Such insufferable pride."

"Who?"

Woolsey started.

"Why, your man, of course."

"That is precisely the point. He is not my man, nor yours, but his own. As he should be, as we should want him to be."

"Well may that be, but what are we to do? In the current circumstance, he represents a danger, not only to himself, but to you, as his, if you will pardon the term, mistress."

"I pardon it. As to what we are to do, I hope that you begin by talking to Master Worthington, as he is not likely to listen to anything I might have to say."

"And what would you have me say to him?"

"Why, that he is doing nobody a favor by inciting to riot in the Lord's house."

"I should think Minister Davis could make that point."

"He did, but to little effect. And, further, you can instruct him to leash his dog."

"His dog?"

"The young man he has recently taken back into his household, and who was most responsible for this morning's difficulty."

"That would be Frank Mapleton."

The voice came from the side of the fireplace, where Dorothy had been sitting, as though in a trance, throughout Woolsey and Catherine's conversation.

"Know you him, then?" Woolsey asked.

"No. But I have heard of him."

"What do you hear, child?" Catherine asked.

"That he will do what a man pays him to do, and that his master has plenty of coin to have him do his bidding." She stood up. "But it is Nathaniel you must look to."

"How is that?" Catherine asked.

"People say he was very attached to this boy Thomas. In truth, that is what I have heard, and I have no reason not to believe it." She sat back down and stared at the fire.

"Wondrous strange," Catherine muttered.

Woolsey shrugged.

"That she is, but she tends the fire well, as she does her other household chores."

"And you need not fear her chattering."

Woolsey permitted himself a small smile.

"No," he said, "I do not."

Massaquoit squatted in the snow fifty yards from Isaac Powell's house. It was late afternoon, the snow had stopped an hour before, and the sun had already slid to an acute angle as it lowered toward the horizon. It shone like a bright yellow ball, yet distant and feeble, so that the heat its glow promised was illusory, and the air remained frigid.

Massaquoit, though, welcomed the cold. He felt as though he would like to strip to his naked flesh and roll in the snow until its icy white crystals covered every inch of his body. Then, perhaps, the hot rage that had been welling in him since they left the meetinghouse might be cooled.

Vengeance they want, he thought, but what do they know? Their wise man says that vengeance belongs to their god. Just like the English, to thrust off their responsibilities on their god. *Vengeance is mine,* he said to himself, *and I have not taken it, not for my wife, or my child, or my comrades tossed into the ocean by these English, jabbering about their god.*

He grabbed a handful of snow and felt its coldness numb his fingers. When it had melted, he ran the cold water over his face, and then he took another handful, and this time he drank the water.

He looked toward the house. Inside was a white man he had never seen, lying dead. Massaquoit was not anxious to view that body. He stood up, as though with great effort, and looked at the yellow stain at his feet. He had squatted on this spot half an hour before to examine this trace of some animal, possibly a dog. And he had seen the faint imprint of the paws heading off into the woods on the right. For some reason, he knew that he must follow those tracks, but first he steeled himself to confront Isaac Powell for the first and last time.

The door was ajar, but a low mound of wind-driven snow had piled up against it. He yanked the door hard, and when it would not move, he peered in through the crack. He saw the shape of the body, lying on the floor only a few feet inside the door, but there was not enough light for him to see clearly. He hesitated, aware that the English would probably explain the half-open door as presenting some message from their god; he had heard enough of their sermons to realize how fond they were of so explaining such simple facts of the natural world as a drift of snow against a door. He thought for a moment longer, but could not come up with an interpretation such as the English favored, and so he knelt and began scooping the ice-encrusted snow from the door. It was slow going, and his fingers ached after a few moments, but he persisted until he had cleared the snow level with the bottom of the door. He stood up and pulled it open a few more inches.

The rays of the setting sun shone over his shoulder and fell on the body, giving it a preternatural aura, with what appeared to be a reddish corona about the dead man's head. Massaquoit pulled hard on the door, forcing it through the ice-encrusted snow that he had not succeeded in scraping away. Now the sun more fully illuminated the body, and he could see that the red about the man's head was not from the sun's rays. It was his blood.

Powell was lying on his back with his arms stretched over his head, and his legs splayed. Two pools of dried blood gathered where his hands should have been. Massaquoit felt a chill wind that seemed to come from within the house, and he knew that the dead man's spirit was pushing him back. He steeled himself against the spirit, for he had to examine the body more closely. He lowered his shoulder as though forcing his body through a gale, and pushed himself into the house.

He stepped to the side of the body where the cold wind seemed a little weaker, and he dropped to one knee. The reports he had heard this morning from Wequashcook and from the English, whose snippets of conversation had drifted to him as he sat in the meetinghouse waiting for the service to begin, all agreed that the man lying before him had been killed with an ax or hatchet that had split his head. And he saw the dull glint of a hatchet blade several feet to the side of the corpse, as though it had been tossed there after its work had been completed. The man's head was a mass of torn flesh and dried blood.

Massaquoit took a deep breath and leaned over to look more closely, being careful not to touch the body. Something brushed the back of his neck, and he shivered against the shock of that contact. He turned around, but saw nothing, and heard only the wind howling outside the house. Yet he knew the man's spirit was very angry with him, and it was only because his own manitou was stronger that he was not at that moment blown back out of the house to die under a mound of suffocating snow. His spirit's strength would not be able to contest that of the dead man for very long.

He studied the head wound. It seemed to start on the forehead and then rip up into the old man's white hair, and this area was solid with clots of blood. Massaquoit then saw that in the center of the wound was a round hole entering the skull. The light seemed to dim, as though the sun were now behind a cloud, and he strained to examine the wound against the background of shadows that had crept into the house. Suddenly, he heard the roar of the wind outside increase, and then there was a loud thud as the door closed behind him and he was plunged into darkness.

He felt himself being drawn down toward the body, and with all his strength he pushed against that force and staggered to his feet. He reached in the darkness for the door, found it, and hurled his body against it. It opened, and he tumbled into the snow. For a moment, he thought his vision of suffocation beneath a mound of snow was about to be realized, but then he understood that he had only fallen, and he could get up again if he so chose.

He rose and shook off the snow that clung to him. Turning, he looked at the door with a shudder, and vowed that he would not trouble the dead again. He set his step away from the house and toward the spot where he had seen the animal tracks. The clouds obscuring the sun had been swept away by the constant wind, and he knew he had about half an hour of daylight left to see where those tracks led.

He found the spot where he had been kneeling in the snow, and there were the tracks heading off into the woods. Judging by the distance between the paw prints, the animal that made those tracks was walking rather than running, and not walking very fast at that, as the prints were close together, and the impressions fairly deep to indicate the animal was not lifting its leg very much as it moved along. He followed the tracks for another ten feet or so, and then he noticed a peculiarity: between the paw prints another, dull line appeared as though the animal were dragging something. That, he figured, would account for the slowness of its movements. It had found, or killed, something that it was dragging into the secrecy of the woods.

He did not have to proceed too much farther to uncover this mystery. Just as he reached the first row of pines at the edge of the cleared space surrounding the house, he saw something lying motionless in the snow. Having no weapon with him, Massaquoit stood absolutely still until his muscles ached. The animal neither lifted its head or made any movement at all. He took another step and waited. Again, the animal remained stock-still. Massaquoit knelt down and picked up a small ball of snow. He tossed it beyond the animal so that if it started, it might run toward him rather than away, but it did not move at all. Massaquoit walked briskly to it and looked down at the frozen shape of a black dog, lying on its side, its ribs clearly visible beneath its flanks. Next to its muzzle lay a human hand, and nearby another that still retained the bandage in which Catherine had wrapped it.

The dog's fur was coated with ice. Its legs were bent as though it had been trying to gather itself to rise from the snow when its strength had failed, and it had collapsed. Its eyes were wide, staring at the hand it had hoped to consume. Its mouth hung open, its tongue jutting out, frozen at an unnatural angle. It was the mouth that drew Massaquoit's attention, and he knelt down to examine it. He needed to get a better look, and he touched the stiff hairs protruding from its lower jaw. Nothing happened, and so he concluded that no spirit was hovering nearby to protect the dog as it had the man in the house. He lifted the head to peer into the mouth. He saw worn-down molars, but where the fangs should have been were only the broken stumps of ruined teeth. The animal would have had a difficult time tearing a piece of flesh off that hand, and maybe it had died trying.

Massaquoit stood up. There was perhaps a quarter hour of light remaining, and he wanted to make the best use of it. He had no enthusiasm for returning to this place. He left the dog and the hands to feed whatever animal might wander by, and trotted back toward the house, but giving it a wide berth, circling so that he could approach its back. As he expected, having seen the logs piled up at the front, there was no rear door where wood chopping might otherwise have been done. He stepped carefully toward the corner of the house, looking at the snow both on the side and to the rear. He saw nothing until he changed his direction to go more directly to the back. There, coming from around the house on the other side and moving past the house and into the woods beyond, were tracks. Massaquoit walked toward the house, keeping his eyes on the tracks until he came to a place where the snow had been packed down beneath a jumble of impressions. He studied the area until his eye rested on a shiny object just poking through the crusted snow. He knelt down and put it in a pouch he wore around his waist.

He looked again at the line of tracks as they headed

away from the house and toward the woods. They seemed to have been made by boots, and there were two sets emerging from the trampled area. Judging by the distance between the steps of the smaller prints, that person had been running. The larger tracks were close together, as though the owner of those feet had been more slowly pursuing the smaller individual. Massaquoit followed the tracks into the woods for a few feet, then lost them in the enveloping shadows as once again a cloud blocked the sun.

He turned his steps back toward Newbury.

He was weary and shaken by his encounter with the dead man, and puzzled by the dead dog and the tracks leading off into the woods. He made his way slowly, without his usual attention to his environment, which was now in darkness, as he sought to recover his mental and emotional equilibrium. That is why he was taken unawares by the glare of torches that started out of the blackness surrounding Catherine's house.

Still fifty yards from the house, he was sure that none of the people gathered there would be able to see him. Nevertheless, he stopped in his tracks, and then moved with deliberate slowness into the line of trees that edged the path he had been walking. He worked his way ten feet into the shelter of the forest, then proceeded toward the house. As he got closer, he could count the torches to the number of six, formed in a ragged line between his wigwam and the front of Catherine's house. A few more steps, and he could begin to hear a chanting rising above the steady roar of the wind, which had not abated as night fell. They were chanting the same words they had used in the meetinghouse earlier in the day.

"No Christian, he," they said, again and again, louder and louder, their angry voices contesting with the wind.

He edged closer, keeping the trees between him and the

torches. He stopped behind a thick-trunked oak that had been standing in that spot long before the English had come. It was surrounded by a deep drift, so that he was standing in snow that reached well above his knees, and he could soon feel the chill working its way through his breeches. The chanting had stopped and for a moment he thought somebody must have seen him. He stood motionless, and his legs began to feel numb. He peered around the trunk of the tree just enough to get a clear view. Somebody had come out of the house and that was why the chanting had stopped. The person was short and round and she was carrying a candle. Behind her stood a bulkier figure.

"Get on home, now," Catherine said, and she waved the lit candle in a sweeping gesture toward the road that led back to Newbury. She shivered as the wind rose, causing the torches to flicker. The flames dipped before the breeze and then flared back to life when it died down. Her eyes watered against the cold and in response to the changing light, almost dark and then unevenly bright again as the fires danced. She pulled her cloak about her and then turned to Phyllis.

"You must go to Master Woolsey. Wake him if you must."

"I cannot leave you," she said.

"It is not me they want."

"Well I know that. But they will tire of waiting for him, and then they will find you a target for their anger at him."

"I do not think it. But that is why I send you to Master Woolsey. In the event I am wrong. Go. There is no time now for your stubborn disobedience."

"Hmph!" Phyllis said, the sound an explosion of breath in the frigid air. But she began to walk toward the torches. Catherine tugged on her arm.

"It would be well to go into the house and then leave again."

"Well it might be. But I will walk straight ahead. I do not think they will stop me." Phyllis took another step, and the line of torches formed a tight arc that threatened to enclose her.

"Where might you be going?" said a voice from the center of the line.

Catherine strained to see the face belonging to the voice, and recognized the ragged young man from the meeting, only now he was wearing a substantial greatcoat with bright brass buttons that reflected the glare of the torches.

"Is it you, then," she asked, "doing Master Worthington's bidding and disrupting the peace of my household?"

"No, Mistress," Frank Mapleton replied. His face was clean now, but the smirk from the morning remained. "It is the Lord's business I do, I warrant."

"I do not think so," Catherine said.

"Step aside," Phyllis demanded, but instead the torchbearers on the end of the line closed in toward her, like the pincers of a scorpion, leaving Frank as its venomous tail.

"I cannot," Frank said. "I have business with the savage you keep tethered hereabout."

Phyllis lowered her shoulder as though to force her way through. Frank tilted his torch until it was directly in front of her face. She stopped and stared hard at him, the torch's red glare matching the red anger in her face. The flames flickered no more than an inch or two from her. Catherine grabbed Phyllis's arm and pulled her back. She herself stepped forward to confront the torch. She waited, and Frank lifted the torch away from her.

"We want your savage, Mistress," he said.

"That you cannot have," she replied.

"My mate was living with that old farmer," Frank said. "Maybe your savage can tell me where he was taken."

"We want your savage," the other torchbearers said, and then repeated the cry from the morning: "No Christian, he."

"Nor you," Catherine shouted over their voices, but she knew that these young men, for that is what she now saw they were, all under the spell of Frank Mapleton, would not be deterred by her words. And as her shout blended with the wind, they all took a step forward. Catherine turned to Phyllis.

"Let us go back into the house. You do remember how much my John liked to hunt, do you not?"

Phyllis looked at her blankly.

"I will explain," Catherine said. "In the house."

From his vantage point, Massaquoit watched the torches advance on Catherine. He fought the urge to run forward, and he breathed a small sigh when he saw Catherine and Phyllis walk unmolested into the house. He waited to see if the little mob would follow, but the torches remained in the curved line that had moments before threatened to close in on the two women. He debated the question for only a moment, and the answer came swiftly. He could not place himself between the mob and the women. He was only one, and even if he succeeded, he would reveal himself and invite being hunted down. Further, he did not know whether the women would decide to cooperate with the English boys now surrounding the house. He could not be sure they would protect him. He had no choice, and so he trotted off through the woods in a direction that would bring him to the frozen swamp.

After feeling his way slowly for a quarter of a mile through the dark shadows of the woods he reached a clearing, piled deep in virgin snow. The moon had risen while he was in the shelter of the trees, and it now cast its soft yellow light on the white of the rolling drifts. He did not think anyone would follow him here, but remembering the vicious glint in the eye of the ragged young man and the chant expressing the English hatred for him, Massaquoit chose to take no chances.

He stepped into the snow and made deliberate tracks through it to a path on the southeast corner of the square-edged clearing. His tracks led to a path he would not take. Instead, he retraced his steps, this time keeping on his toes so as not to mar the formed outlines of his feet pointing in the direction he wanted any pursuer to think he had taken. When he reached the side of the clearing where he had begun, he stepped back into the woods and worked his way around to the southwest corner, where another, barely visible path led off to the swamp.

Even though the path was buried a foot deep in snow as it wound its way through the trees, around boulders, and down declivities caused by the rills of melting spring snow, Massaquoit's feet remembered it from the last time he had traveled here, now over a year and a half ago. Then, he had been with his comrades, all of whom were now dead, as they raced ahead of the pursuing English to lead them into the swamp, where they hoped to lose them in the mud and maze of fallen tree trunks covered with twisting vines, thick with mosquitoes and flies. If their pursuers insisted on following them, they would make them pay for their stubbornness.

The women and children, those few who had survived the massacre at the fort, were huddled in hastily constructed wigwams, eating only a little of the remaining food stores. Their sacrifice enabled the men to refresh themselves before confronting the English. The cornmeal bread restored their strength but the English were too many, too persistent, too filled with determination to eradicate an enemy they had decided they could no longer live next to as neighbors. Massaquoit and his few companions fought, and ran, hoping to tire and confuse the enemy, but after three days with their scant food supplies almost gone, their bodies exhausted, and their stoic women no longer able to quiet the starving children, they had surrendered on a promise of their lives, a promise the English violated as soon as they had their prisoners under control. The women and children were distributed as war booty, sent into slavery, and the sachems were taken on board a ship and fed to the waters, all but Massaquoit, saved, against his will, by Catherine Williams.

All this he remembered as his feet took him without conscious direction back into that swamp, now covered in snow and devoid of all human life, where among those sad memories he would wait and think what to do now that his seemingly implacable enemies had once again manifested their hatred for him. He pushed his way through the desiccated and frozen brambles and vines, which caught at his feet. The path narrowed until it was almost impassable, and then it forked both east and west. East led only deeper into the swamp, he knew, but westward, after twenty or thirty more yards, would take him to another clearing and a surviving wigwam where he might hope to find a store of cornmeal. He now began to snap off low-hanging branches, so that when he arrived at the clearing he had the makings of a fire.

Edward was lurking behind the door when Catherine and Phyllis re-entered the house. The elderly servant peered around them, and then withdrew, shaking his head, and muttering.

"Get a brand from the fire," Catherine said to him.

He looked at her without comprehension.

"A brand," she repeated, "one that has a bit of fire on

its end." She took his arm, and gave him a gentle push toward the fireplace. She followed, and as he knelt to see if he could find the cold end of a burning stick, she lifted the old matchlock musket from the pegs that secured it to the wall. She shifted the weight of the heavy weapon in her arms and sat down on the bench next to the plank table on which meals were served. She laid the gun in front of her.

"Find some powder and shot," she said to Phyllis, "and the aiming stick that should be in there." She pointed to a corner cupboard, against which a notched pole rested. "The powder and shot are on the top shelf."

"I do work in this house," Phyllis said. "And just what do you think you are going to do with a fowling piece? I do not recall that your husband ever brought home much game with it. He always said it did not sight properly."

"It was John that did not see clearly," Catherine replied. "And what we are going to do is take this musket outside and see what those young men are made of."

Edward snapped a twig off the end of a log that had not yet ignited, and held it at the edge of the flame until it caught.

"That will do nicely," Catherine said. She bent over the musket.

"I think I will stay inside," Edward said. "Those boys out there are of flesh and blood. I know that well enough."

Catherine looked up from the matchlock and nodded.

"Just keep that brand burning until we need it, then," she said. She adjusted the length of the match cord in the serpentine clamp, and then she squeezed the leverlike trigger. The end of the match cord did not quite reach the pan, so she loosened the clamp, pulled another quarter of an inch of cord through the clamp, and tried again. This time the end of the cord butted against the closed pan.

Phyllis was standing behind her, holding three pouches.

"Do you remember which goes where?" she asked.

"The coarse powder down the muzzle, then the ball wrapped in a piece of rag. Then the fine powder here in the pan." She uncovered the lid of the pan. Edward blew on the end of the brand until it glowed red, and then he knocked the ash off.

"Then," he said to Phyllis, "you just light the cord while Mistress Williams aims."

"Why then, you should come and show me how," Phyllis replied.

There was a loud thump on the door. Catherine laid down the musket and went to the window next to the door. Through it, she saw a face brightening and darkening as the light from the torch next to it waxed and waned in the wind. The flame glared in a gust long enough for Catherine to identify the bad complexion and smirking lips of Frank Mapleton staring back at her. He opened his mouth in a smile of yellowed teeth. Two of his companions held a log from the woodpile ready to swing against the thick door. Frank hunched his shoulders and shivered.

"Mistress," he called out, "it is frightful cold out here. And we see the smoke from your chimney."

Catherine went back to the table and set the musket on its stock. Phyllis opened up one pouch, put it aside, and then tried the other. She held it over the muzzle and let the coarse powder slide in. Catherine watched, and then held up her hand.

"Enough," she said. "Now the ball."

Phyllis held a lead ball over the muzzle.

"You need a bit of rag," Edward said. He pulled out his knife and slit a piece of cloth from his shirt, then took the ball from Phyllis and wrapped the cloth about it. He put it in the muzzle and rammed it home. Catherine righted the musket and opened the pan. Phyllis poured in the finer-grained powder.

"Take the aiming stick, Phyllis, and Edward, open the door."

"Mistress," came the cry again from outside, and the log thudded against the door. "Mistress, we are cold."

"Open the door, Edward," Catherine said again.

The old man hunched his stooped shoulders even more than usual in an apparent attempt to render himself invisible as he swung the heavy door open. A blast of cold air rushed into the house. The two young men holding the log looked in confusion at Frank.

"Why, step back, lads," Frank said. "This is the house of a woman that we dare not trifle with. Is that not so, Mistress Williams?"

For answer, Catherine strode forward, holding the heavy barrel of the musket in front of her. Phyllis followed with the aiming stick in one hand and the glowing brand in the other. Frank looked at the weapon but kept his face masked in amused irony.

"Do we look like turkeys, then?" he asked, but he stepped back as Catherine approached.

"You look like what you are, a gaggle of insolent rogues," Catherine said, "who are besetting me in my house, and I mean to be rid of you, by any means necessary."

She walked into the snow outside her door and motioned Phyllis forward.

"Right there," she said, pointing to a spot in the snow immediately in front of her. "Put it there."

Edward's hand emerged from the shadows inside the house, grabbed the door, and pulled it closed.

"Your man seems to be feeling a bit of a chill," Frank remarked.

Phyllis planted the aiming stick, and Catherine let the muzzle down into its notch. She swung the musket in an arc, sighting at each of the half-dozen young men in turn, then pointed it at Frank. He flapped his arm in imitation of a startled game bird.

"I don't believe that old matchlock will fire," he said. He pulled a six-inch knife from his belt. Its blade glinted in the glare of the torchlight.

"The cord," Catherine demanded of Phyllis.

Phyllis blew on the end of the brand until it glowed red, and held it to the short end of the match cord, exposed at the end of the serpentine.

"Light it," Catherine said.

Phyllis brought the brand to the end of the match cord, and held it until the cord sputtered and ignited. Frank stepped back, holding his knife in front of him.

"As you know how this weapon works," Catherine said, "you understand that if I do not pull the trigger before the cord burns down, I will have to adjust the cord, pull out another length, light it again. And it is so cold, as you have said." She pulled open the firing pan lid. "Perhaps I should just see if this old fowling piece still fires."

Frank retreated another step, still waving the knife in front of him.

"Now, Mistress," he said. "We wanted only to warm our bones by your fire while we waited for your savage."

"The only warmth you get from me," Catherine retorted, "comes out from the end of this barrel."

They stood in silence for a few moments, their breath coming out in frozen puffs. Then, the quiet was interrupted by the crunch of feet breaking through the crusted snow. Master Worthington, accompanied as he had been in the morning by Nathaniel and Osprey, approached at a trot. Worthington and his son, both tall, pulled thick woolen cloaks over their faces against the wind; the shorter Osprey strode ahead of them, holding a wheel lock pistol in one hand while he pulled his greatcoat tightly around him with the other. The snow had started again, coating his exposed face and beard. By the time he arrived a few feet in front of Catherine, he and his weapon were white. Phyllis, noting the new snow, was leaning over the smoldering match cord, shielding it from the heavy wet flakes that were rapidly covering everyone and everything.

Worthington caught up to Osprey and put his gloved hand on the pistol, but he did not yet push it down.

"How now, Mistress Williams," he said, "what have we here?"

"That is for you to tell me," Catherine replied.

"I am sure I do not know."

"Do these men not have your coin in their pocket?" she asked, swiveling the musket from one to the other.

"Certainly not," Worthington said.

Catherine leveled the piece at Frank.

"And not this one?"

"He is my servant," Worthington replied, "but I believe that what he is doing here, he can best explain."

A flicker of a frown shadowed Frank's face, and then he smiled.

"As you can see, sir, it is a bitter night, and my mates and me was just looking for a little warmth as we passed by."

Phyllis kept her hands cupped over the match cord, but turned to offer a look heavy with contempt at the young man. Then she glanced down at the match cord.

"I think you need pull that trigger now, Mistress," she said.

Frank stepped back, and Osprey forward, placing his bulk between the boy and Catherine's musket. He pointed the pistol at Catherine. Worthington again put his hand on the pistol, and this time pushed it down.

"Not so," he said. "Mistress, I mean you no harm, but I do seek your savage."

"You must find him yourself, then," Catherine replied.

"And if you seek him, you will need more than this lot," she said.

"He need ask only me," Osprey muttered.

"I have the governor's commission to raise a force to pursue those who killed Isaac Powell, and that means I will be seeking your savage as well, so that he might point the way."

"And I will be leading that force," Nathaniel said. His father turned toward him.

"That is not yet approved."

"And yet I will."

Worthington shivered in a blast of snow-laden air, and then he turned. The others, without a word, followed. When they were some hundred yards away and disappearing into the white blanket of falling snow, Catherine lifted the heavy weapon from the aiming stick, pointed it at the heavens, and pulled the leverlike trigger. The cord came down and ignited the powder in the pan into a flash, followed by a loud explosion that echoed against the howling of the wind.

Whether Worthington or his men heard the shot, she did not know, but as she turned back to the house Catherine felt the better for its sound giving voice to the violent anger she felt at the indignity of having her peace and her house so assaulted.

FOUR

❧❦❧

MASSAQUOIT SAT HUDDLED next to the fire he had built in the wigwam, where he had found a half-rotted sack of maize, which he pounded in a mortar and then mixed with melted snow to form a paste that he was now boiling in an earthenware pot on the fire. He heard the footsteps in the snow approaching the wigwam from the north, the side of the clearing facing the forest and opposite the way leading to Newbury. The direction from which the steps were coming, and the realization that only one person could have found him so soon, told Massaquoit that he had nothing to fear from this visitor.

Wequashcook shook the snow from his beaver hat as he stooped to enter the wigwam, which was still sheathed in its summer covering of light reed matting. Nobody had been back in all the time after the disastrous fight in the swamp to replace it with a sturdier layer of bark. As a consequence the temperature inside the wigwam, even with the heat provided by the fire, was not very much higher than the frigid outside air. Wequashcook made an exaggerated shivering gesture, hunching his shoulders and wrapping his arms around his chest. Without waiting to be invited, he crouched next to the fire and extended his hands, palms down, over it.

Massaquoit offered a barely perceptible nod, and then looked toward the samp, boiling in the pot.

"Yes," Wequashcook said.

With a wooden spoon Massaquoit ladled out a heaping portion into an earthenware bowl and handed it to Wequashcook. He then served himself. They ate, in silence, with their fingers, as soon as the samp had cooled sufficiently. Massaquoit licked his fingers.

"I trust you do not have English at your back," he said.

"I came from the forest," Wequashcook answered. "I traveled in a great circle." He bent over his bowl, scooped up a lump, and put it into his mouth. "I was in an English house one time," he said, "and they served this with honey in it."

"You did not come all this way to talk with me about cooking."

Wequashcook scraped the remaining samp from his bowl and then put it down.

"A band of English attacked your white woman's house. I saw them as I was coming back to Newbury."

"That is why I am here."

Wequashcook nodded.

"They were looking for you. They thought they could scare the white woman into telling them where to find you."

"I doubt they would succeed."

"They did not. She and her girl aimed an old musket at them, and then other English came."

"Who were they?"

"I was too far to see. After a while, they all left. And when they were safely away, the white woman shot the musket into the sky."

Massaquoit smiled at the thought of Catherine sending off her visitors with a musket shot.

"Why do you come here to tell me these things?"

Wequashcook, in a gesture that had become habitual when his conversations with Massaquoit reached this kind of juncture, ran his fingers over the scar on his head left there by Massaquoit's knife. But then he shrugged.

"I do not think I know."

Massaquoit studied the other's countenance, but all he could read there was stony perplexity, and he concluded that he could not provide a better answer himself for their troubled yet persistent relationship. Wequashcook had led the English to the fort in which Massaquoit's wife and young son were sleeping. He claimed then and ever after that he did not know that the English would so brutally attack and leave only ashes and charred bodies. But the fact was that it happened, and Massaquoit, whose wife was kin to Wequashcook, stopped his hand before he could kill the man he would never forgive or trust. Yet here Wequashcook was, sitting beside him, licking his fingers, having eaten the food Massaquoit had prepared for himself.

"The English will come looking for Indians," Wequashcook said. "Any Indian will serve their purpose."

"You are welcome to stay with me," Massaquoit said, and in his mind the offer, although sincere, also contained the alternative, that he would like to keep an eye on Wequashcook.

"I thank you," Wequashcook said, "but I do not enjoy your cooking that well, and I believe I can better protect my skin by getting closer rather than farther from the English."

"I understand you," Massaquoit said.

Wequashcook rose to his feet.

"I never doubt that," he said.

Massaquoit watched as Wequashcook stooped at the entrance to the wigwam, parted the mats that served as its door, and then pushed his way out. As he held the mats aside, the wind came rushing into the wigwam causing the fire to rise and then threaten to die. After he left, the fire resumed burning and Massaquoit stared into its flames. In his hand, he held the shiny metal object he had found in the snow. He knew that he must find its owner, and that it would have been a mistake to have asked Wequashcook to help him do just that.

As befits a man whose money comes from the sea, Samuel Worthington's large house overlooked Newbury Harbor. The house was set on a rise that gave way to the town dock that Worthington now owned after having bought it from Governor Peters, and from his front door he could see the sails of ships as they entered the harbor. The sight of a sail, in fact, was his chief joy, for each one promised to fatten his already bulging purse with profits from trade and from fees for use of his dock. He was in the habit of walking down to watch the unloading of any ship that came in, even those in whose cargo he had no direct interest, for all trade that flowed through Newbury Harbor was to his financial advantage.

Had he been looking at the harbor today, however, as Catherine and Woolsey struggled through the drifts toward his house, he would have seen only one ship, the one that recently brought Thomas and Frank Mapleton from Barbados, its hold long emptied, the hull held in the embrace of several inches of solid ice as Newbury endured the worst winter in the young colony's history. Catherine glanced at the ship.

"The *Helmsford* is not leaving this harbor anytime soon, and I imagine it is an unhappy sight to greet Samuel Worthington's eyes every morning, his ship useless to him until the spring."

"No doubt," Woolsey replied, "and do you not yourself await the *Good Hope*?"

"I expect it has found mooring in warmer waters."

"That young man's sister is on board. May the Lord help us find her brother beforetime, and well," Woolsey said.

Catherine ducked into a gust of wind, but nodded at her old friend's piety, which she shared to an extent, but she also felt that the Lord's hand was not going to guide the search for Thomas so much as young Nathaniel Worthington.

Master Worthington was looking neither at his ice-bound ship, nor at his arriving guests, whom he had glanced at through his window. Instead, he stared across the room at a savage wearing a beaver hat, standing stoically in front of the pistol aimed at him by Lionel Osprey. Wequashcook's eyes did not waver as they focused on the muzzle of the weapon, not three feet from his face, while Osprey moved the pistol in small circles, as though too impatient to hold it still.

"No, Lionel," Worthington said. "Mistress Williams and Magistrate Woolsey approach. We do not want to give them further cause to embroil me in trouble." He looked at Wequashcook. "And perhaps she can tell us, given her familiarity with the local savages, whether we can take this one at his word."

Osprey lowered his weapon, but kept it at his side.

"I am not in favor of trusting this one, whether Mistress Williams vouches for him or not. Remember it is your son and his safety we are talking about."

Before Worthington could answer, there was a knock at the door, and a couple of moments later, Catherine and Woolsey were ushered into the room by a middle-aged serving-woman. Woolsey looked from Osprey to Wequashcook and then settled his gaze on Worthington.

"Samuel, what have we here?" he asked.

"Why, a savage who has come to offer his service leading Nathaniel and his company after the other savages that killed old man Powell and took Thomas into captivity."

"You do seem to know a good deal more than anybody else concerning the circumstances of these unfortunate events," Catherine said.

"Indeed, Mistress, indeed I do," the merchant replied. "But to the point. Know you this savage?"

"Why, that is William," Woolsey said. "He is a praying Indian."

"Aye, I've seen him at meeting, although I am not sure how much he prays," Worthington said with an edge to his tone. "That is not my question, however. Do you know the man well enough that I may safely trust my son's safety to his hands?"

Wequashcook removed his beaver hat.

"I speak for myself, and this"—he pointed to the scar on his scalp—"speaks for me."

"And how is that?" Worthington asked.

"You seek the man you call Matthew, but who calls himself Massaquoit, do you not?"

"We do."

"It was his hand did this to me," Wequashcook said.

Worthington looked at Catherine and Woolsey.

"Know you anything of this?"

"No," Catherine replied. "Matthew does not tell me much of his friends. Or his enemies. Nor do I inquire."

Worthington paced back and forth for a moment, his brows furrowed.

"My son is anxious to find his friend Thomas, more for the sake of his betrothed, I believe, than for the lad himself, who truth be told, we found to be an unhealthy influence."

"If you cannot convince yourself to trust your son to William," Woolsey said, "no one would fault you for keeping him home and letting others, more used to these matters, pursue Thomas and his captors."

"My boy is adamant," Worthington said.

"Aye, that he is," Osprey added, "and we too are very anxious to recover Thomas. Is that not right, Master Worthington?"

The merchant turned a grim face to his man, and then nodded.

"For the sake of my son, of course," he said.

Wequashcook, who had been standing with his gaze fixed on the space between Worthington and Catherine, now stepped toward the door.

"If you do not want my services, perhaps you can hire Matthew to find himself." He replaced his beaver hat and offered a quick nod of his head, that could have passed for a bow, if one wanted so to see it.

"Stay a moment," Worthington said.

"I have stayed too long," Wequashcook answered. "But I understand your confusion. You cannot tell one savage from another, William from Matthew. I will watch for your English warriors to start out, and I will be there if you want me to guide." He strode past Catherine and Woolsey and through the door, shutting it sharply behind him.

Woolsey glanced at Catherine and she nodded.

"Samuel," he said, "I do not want to add to your difficulties at this moment." He looked at the closed door, which still held the attention of the merchant. "But," he continued, "Mistress Williams came to me this morning with a grievous tale about an attack on her house yesternight by men in your employ."

"I know of no such attack," Worthington retorted.

"And were you not there last night, accompanied by him"—Catherine pointed at Osprey—"with that very same weapon in his hand?"

"To be sure, we were there, to put an end to the foolishness you had yourself incited."

"What business had you with Mistress Williams?" Woolsey asked, directing his question to Osprey.

"Why, nothing at all, if it pleases you."

"Why came you then to her house in such a threatening guise?"

"I attended Master Worthington. These are dangerous times."

"Feared you Mistress Williams, then?" Woolsey asked, and the question brought a smile to Worthington's tightly pursed lips.

"Surely not," Osprey said, "even when she pointed that old fowling piece at me. But it was her savage we sought, and her savage that required my being armed, as any man can tell you."

"Just so," Worthington added.

"And those lads," Catherine said, "I suppose they were afraid, too."

"For that I cannot answer," Worthington replied. "I sent them, to be sure, to see if you would be so kind as to inform them where your savage might be found."

"Need you send so many?" Catherine asked. "Do they not hear well, or speak well? Are they halt or dumb or diseased in their faculties, that so many came on so simple an errand?"

"I sent only Frank. He will have to answer for his companions."

"And his behavior at meeting?" Catherine demanded.

"Why that, too, if it please you."

"It pleases me well," Woolsey said, "and more if the lad answers to me on the morrow."

Worthington shook his head.

"I intended," the merchant said, "for him to make answer to me, as it is myself that acts as his father, being as I am, his master."

Woolsey nodded.

"So be it, then."

The door opened and Nathaniel took a hesitant step into the room.

"Father," he said, "I have finished my preparations and spoken with Mother."

"If you can excuse us," Worthington said. "The boy leaves at dawn."

"We must be content," Woolsey responded.

He took Catherine's arm and together they walked out. Once outside, as they bowed their heads again into the cold wind, they saw a solitary figure standing next to a bare tree, his eyes, beneath his huge beaver hat, fixed on the house.

"Will he lead them, think you?" Woolsey asked.

"Yes," Catherine said.

"And your man?"

"I do not know, but I believe he will be somewhere close."

And the next morning as Wequashcook led the company of English under the command of young Nathaniel Worthington out of Newbury toward old man Powell's farm, Massaquoit was already there. The dead dog was gone, dragged off as the flattened channel in the snow indicated, by some hungry beast. The hands of old man Powell were also gone. But the tracks he had previously noted of two people heading off into the woods north of the house were still visible, as the snow had stopped falling and a frigid blast of arctic air had hardened the crust of snow, preserving all impressions in it as though they had been etched in stone.

Massaquoit hoped to obscure those tracks as he followed

them, for he wanted to catch up to the people who left those prints by himself, and not accompanied by whoever else might be joining the pursuit. However, when he managed to snap off a thick, low-hanging branch from a pine, which he intended to use as a sweep to cover the tracks behind him, a few futile passes with the branch soon convinced him that the tracks must remain frozen in place, guiding the steps of whoever found them, and he had no doubt that Wequashcook would find them if he chose to do the job for the English. On that point, Massaquoit did not attempt to predict, for long ago he had abandoned any confidence in deciphering the motives, and therefore the behavior, of Wequashcook.

The tracks were easy to follow, and they confirmed his first impressions. Two people had come this way at about the same time. The similar depth of the prints told him that, as they had been made and frozen in place under the same weather conditions. Still, it appeared that the smaller prints were outdistancing the others, and soon he saw why, for the larger tracks suddenly stopped and veered off to the left. The original pursuer, he of the large feet, had concluded that he could not catch the smaller, swifter individual, and had given up, making his way back in a large arc, as though he, too, aware of the dead man lying in the house had no enthusiasm for coming close to the body.

Massaquoit resumed tracking the one who had continued to flee. He breathed in deeply, enjoying the bite of the cold air in his lungs. It had been much too long since he had felt so comfortable with what he was doing. He had exchanged his breeches and jerkin for deerskin leggings and a cloak of beaver skins that he found in the wigwam in the swamp. For a moment, he let himself believe that the English had never set foot on his people's traditional lands, and that he was again a Pequot sachem, pursuing a stag for its meat, and not a human to solve a mystery only to convince these same English to leave him in peace.

For a long way into the woods on a path formed by a declivity between two stands of pine trees, the tracks were evenly spaced, telling Massaquoit that terror had given his human quarry considerable stamina to sustain a full running stride through what must have been the significant resistance of the snow. About a half mile into the woods, where the path narrowed to a mere foot and a half between the trees before disappearing where the two stands of pines merged, the spacing between the tracks narrowed as the runner, finally losing some of his fear, or the energy which it had inspired, slowed to a walk. Then, the tracks stopped next to a fallen log where the path ended. Apparently the boy, for that was who Massaquoit was quite certain he was trailing, had sat down to catch his breath and to gather his thoughts.

Massaquoit, too, paused at this place, so that he could try to imagine what the English boy was thinking. He was not as used to hunting humans as animals, whose habits were clear. The deer would find the same way to the stream where they drank, or the young trees whose branches they could reach when the snow covered the land. But what was he to think of a terrorized English boy running from the butchery that had just occurred at his master's house? He did not for a moment believe that the boy had killed the old man. The hole in the old man's head from a pistol or musket, probably shot at close range, and the botched job of scalping brutality suggested a white man pretending to be an Indian, and as for that, Massaquoit had a clue, he thought, in his pouch. No, the boy was running from whoever had shot that old man, then opened his head and cut off his hands, leaving them for a starving dog to try to eat with teeth too old for the chewing.

But where would that boy think to run? And then Massaquoit had the beginnings of an answer. The boy must have sought a place to hide when either he could run no longer, or when, sitting on that log, he realized the broad and obvious tracks he was leaving behind.

Massaquoit gazed into the woods, which closed in front of him. There were no obvious signs of continued flight, no tracks or broken branches. It was almost as though the boy had ascended from the log, and for a moment Massaquoit did gaze up through the trees as if he expected to see the English boy perched on a high limb. The sun blinking back at Massaquoit through the uppermost branches told him that it was late morning, and that he had several hours before he would need to find shelter for the night. Still, he kept looking up, for he felt a presence in that direction as though the boy's spirit were calling to him.

The path had ended at the log where the line of trees formed a tight arc. He started on the left side of the arc and studied each tree in turn, looking for any indication the boy had passed by. The snow between these trees was not deep, and in spots the frozen earth was visible. In one such place, he saw a vine seemingly ripped in two as though a foot that had caught in it had, in freeing itself, broken the vine. He could not be sure, but there seemed to be a footprint in the earth at that point. He noted this location, but then checked for other signs around the semicircle of enclosing trees. Finding no better clue, he returned to the broken vine and brought his own foot through it as though to become entangled, and then he continued in the direction his step took, deeper into the woods.

Catherine was not surprised when young Master Rowland knocked at her door at dusk, and then stood there, concern etched on his face as he tried to explain that his wife had need of her services.

"Aye, Master Rowland," she said to him. "I know well your Felicity's time has come. You have not left her alone?"

Daniel Rowland shook his head, and in so doing dislodged a chunk of snow that had been clinging to the broad brim of his hat.

"Goody Blodgett is with her, even now." The young man stopped, as though too embarrassed to go on.

Catherine put her hand on his arm.

"Your wife's father's quarrel is with my dead husband. None of it touches Mistress Worthington and me."

He shook his head.

"Nay, but it does. My wife's mother will not come to her daughter, and Master Worthington insists that Goody Blodgett tend to her."

"And yet you are here."

"Felicity speaks only of you. She cannot be content with Goody Blodgett."

"Then I must reward her faith," Catherine said.

Daniel's face relaxed into a half smile.

"You are coming, then?" he asked.

"Indeed. And shortly. Fear you not, but make haste back to your wife and tell her I follow you."

Daniel offered only an embarrassed nod before turning around and bowing his head against the wind, which was redistributing the top inch or so of newly fallen snow. Catherine closed the door and lifted her midwife's bag from the peg on which it hung. She probed the bag's contents, and not finding what she sought, raised her head with a perplexed expression.

Phyllis, who already had her heavy cloak on and the birthing stool in her arms, put the stool down.

"Well," she said, "and what do you not have that you are sure you will need?"

"Mistress Rowland is a delicate woman," Catherine replied. "I tended her leg when she bruised it falling from her bed. That was when she was no more than six or seven years old, when my John and Master Worthington still spoke to each other, at least in the way of business."

"A bruised leg, you say," Phyllis murmured, as though that long-ago hurt explained what was missing from the bag that Catherine still held.

"Yes," Catherine continued. "A bruised leg, but it was not a grievous hurt, and yet the child would scarcely sit to let me apply an ointment to relieve her pain."

"I see," Phyllis said, and now her expression brightened as she did understand the connection. "You will be wanting the feathers," she said.

"Indeed, I will," Catherine agreed.

Phyllis took the bag from her mistress and plunged her own, strong fingers into it, withdrawing her hand after a few moments, clutching three ragged gray feathers plucked from a goose that John had shot some years ago.

"Good," Catherine said. "Lay them on top of everything else in the bag."

Under a bright moon, they walked toward the Rowlands' modest house on a new way that branched off the main street that traversed Newbury Center. The way was exceedingly narrow, no more than ten feet separating the four houses, two on each side, that faced each other across it, and the constant snows of this winter had collected in this passage. An opening wide enough to accommodate one person had been burrowed down the middle of the way, and the snow had been beaten down to varying heights in paths leading to each of the houses, the depth determined by how frequently the residents had chosen to brave their way through the huge drifts. The snow in front of the Blodgett house was hardly packed down at all, as that family had apparently spent a considerable amount of time inside. The footsteps of Goody Blodgett were clearly visible on the surface of the snow that was still at least four feet high in front of her door. Her steps, therefore, had left deep impressions. Leading to the Rowlands' house, on the other hand, the snow was packed down and solid to a height of only a foot and a half or so, and it bore the muddled traces of many feet, evidence of the activity in that household as it prepared for the birth of the first child. Catherine pictured young Rowland pacing back and forth in that area before summoning the courage to ignore his powerful father-in-law by seeking her aid. She let her breath explode into the frigid air. Phyllis, who was plowing through the drifts a few steps ahead, balancing the birthing stool in her arms, turned to look at her mistress.

"What is it?" she asked. "Have we left something we need at home?"

"Master Worthington, it is," Catherine said, "and his long memory that attached to an ancient argument would have him place his daughter in the hands of Goody Blodgett."

"Oh, I see," Phyllis said, and Catherine knew that in this instance her sometimes slow-thinking servant was right with her.

"Go on with you," Catherine said. "Felicity and her babe cannot wait for us."

Phyllis strode ahead, and Catherine followed. Just as they turned onto the path leading to the Rowlands' house, they were overtaken by another woman whose labored breathing evidenced the haste with which she had been walking.

"And is it you, Catherine?" she asked.

Catherine turned to face Alice Worthington.

"Indeed, it is, Alice. Your son-in-law has just summoned us, and so we are here."

"And glad I am."

"I come in opposition to your husband's desires," Catherine said.

Mistress Worthington frowned.

"Aye, but he is not birthing a babe, and you know my daughter."

"That I do, and I trust I am prepared to help her."

"With the Lord's help," Mistress Worthington said, "she will not suffer overmuch."

Catherine started to walk again, when she realized that Mistress Worthington was not following.

"I will come by and by," she said, glancing over her shoulder. Catherine looked in that direction and saw the narrow-shouldered shape of a man making his way toward them. He nodded toward Mistress Worthington, and she sighed. "Samuel comes soon," she said. "I will wait a little for him."

Catherine followed Phyllis to the door, which opened before she could knock on it. Daniel stepped aside to let them into a small front room. A serving-girl stood uncomfortably by his side, unsure what to do as her master had preempted her responsibility to greet their guests. She bowed her head, and when Daniel was unable to do more than mumble something unintelligible, the girl pointed to a room on the left from which now could be heard a low but continuous moaning.

To the right was another small room, which apparently was going to be the nursery, for it contained a simple rope bed and a cradle. A candle burned on a table next to the bed, on which the bedclothes were rumpled, and judging from the tousled hair and half vacant eyes of the serving-girl, she had recently been roused, no doubt by Felicity's moaning as her labor began. Catherine motioned Daniel into that room.

"Sit you down to rest in there," she said. "There is no more you can do, and your servant will be needed to attend your wife. She will not be using that bed until after your babe is born, so now get you in there."

Young Rowland, however, did not immediately move.

"She is calling for you and her mother," he said.

"Well, I am here. I cannot vouch for Alice, but I do believe she will be here shortly."

"I was packed to join Nathaniel," Daniel said, "but then her time came."

Catherine followed the non sequitur.

"Your place is here with Felicity," she said.

Daniel nodded and walked into the room and sat down on the maidservant's bed. He ran his hand over the bedclothes, as if to see if they were still warm. When he seemed settled, Catherine strode past the serving-girl, and motioned for Phyllis to follow her into the room in which Felicity Rowland lay, her face ashen, her lips quivering, and her body tensed as though to ward off the next pain.

Goody Blodgett, a plump woman of thirty, sat on a stool next to the bed and stroked Felicity's cheek while making soft, cooing sounds. She looked up at Catherine with an expression of perplexed concern on her face.

"I have been here this last hour," she said. "She looked like she would be quick, but then . . ." She shrugged.

Catherine placed one hand on the young woman's forehead, and ran the other over the swollen belly, noting how low the babe seemed to be. She waited for a contraction, but after ten minutes none came.

"Have the pains stopped, then?" she asked.

Felicity nodded her head.

"How long?" Catherine asked.

Felicity shrugged.

"It was when I sat down next to her that everything stopped," Goody Blodgett said.

Catherine pointed to the corner of the room.

"Put the stool there, Phyllis," she said. "We will not be needing it for some time. Perhaps you and the serving-girl can go into the kitchen and see what there is for us."

"I fear, Catherine," Felicity said. She raised herself and leaned on her elbow as she looked past Catherine to the door. "And my mother?"

"Soon," Catherine replied.

"The pains began," Felicity said, "and they hurt so bad. Daniel could not bear to look at me, and he ran out not knowing where he went. I sent him to get Mother and you, but he came back with Goody Blodgett, and she it was who sent him out again for you."

Catherine glanced at Goody Blodgett, who nodded her assent.

"You understand," Catherine said to her, "that Felicity is comfortable with me here."

Goody Blodgett frowned.

"So she has said to me."

"I will need your help," Catherine said.

"Master Worthington himself—" Goody Blodgett began.

"If it is the fee you are after, you can have it," Catherine told her.

Goody Blodgett's face relaxed.

"You know my Jacob has been sick," she said.

"I do indeed," Catherine replied. She turned to Felicity. "Tell us about your pains."

Felicity winced at the memory.

"So bad," she said. "So bad."

"Where?" Catherine asked.

The question seemed to perplex Felicity as though she had not located the pains before.

"Why here, mostly," she said, pointing to the base of her spine.

"Ah," Catherine responded, "so is that the way of it."

"Yes," Felicity said. "Am I in danger?"

"No," Catherine assured her. "But the babe is lying against your backbone, and that is why it hurts you the way it does."

Felicity formed her face into a question, as a child will do when presented with some new and confusing fact.

"Is that bad?" she asked.

"It is why it hurts," Catherine explained. "It will continue to hurt you there until we can get the proper pains to start again. Those will bring the babe down where it belongs."

"I am too afraid," Felicity said.

"I know," Catherine said, her voice now almost a lullaby. She leaned across the bed to Goody Blodgett. "Tell my Phyllis we need that special tea. She will know what I mean. And if she is already into the beer, tell her that can wait, and attend to the tea."

Goody Blodgett bridled.

"I am not—" she began.

"No, you are not," Catherine agreed. "But I must stay with Felicity, and yet I need that tea."

Goody Blodgett rose slowly to her feet.

"Yes," she said, and she walked out of the room. Catherine watched her back, wondering whether it was more difficult to deal with the pride and financial need of an inexperienced midwife such as Goody Blodgett, or the stubborn vindictiveness of a man such as Master Worthington, when all that any of them should be concerned about was the terribly frightened young woman.

Felicity lay with her eyes closed. Perspiration beaded her forehead. Her breathing was shallow and strained, and every few minutes her face tightened as though responding to a spasm of pain, and yet, Catherine knew, her labor had stopped. That was worrisome to the degree that the longer this pause lasted, the more drained Felicity would be of the strength needed to push out her babe. Furthermore, Catherine knew that the child, too, was vulnerable as it worked its way down to the birth canal, a trip of only a few inches, but one fraught with potential difficulty. It

would be better, she knew, for mother and child to bring
the babe out as soon as possible.

To that end, she would use her tea made of valerian
root, and the feather. The tea would relax Felicity so she
could gather her strength. And then the feather would be
able to do its job. Catherine stroked the young woman's
forehead, and was rewarded with half-opened eyes and a
grim smile.

"My mother?" she asked.

Catherine looked about her as though expecting to see
Mistress Worthington in the room.

"She is on her way. I have sent Daniel out to fetch her
in. I do not know what she can be thinking about."

Felicity smiled a little more fully.

"Father always says how forgetful Mother is, but I do
not think she will forget me now."

"No, I think not," Catherine agreed.

Phyllis appeared in the doorway with a steaming dish
of tea. Its pungent aroma filled the small room. Catherine
motioned for her to come forward. Goody Blodgett followed her into the room, her eyes fastened on the dish.
Phyllis handed the tea to Catherine, and started to speak.
She looked at Goody Blodgett and closed her mouth.

"Drink," Catherine said to Felicity. "You need to rest,
and this will help you."

Felicity lifted herself and took the dish from Catherine.
She brought it to her mouth, but then jerked her head back
as she breathed the fumes rising from the liquid.

"I do not think I can," she said.

"What are you giving her?" Goody Blodgett asked, placing her hand on the dish to prevent Felicity from bringing
it again to her mouth.

"Just a root tea," Catherine told her, "that you would
do well to learn how to use on occasions such as this."
She bowed her head toward Felicity.

"I use blue cohosh to start the pains," Goody Blodgett said, and thrust out her chin.

"And well you do," Catherine responded, "but not for Felicity, not now. She is not ready."

Felicity shifted her eyes back and forth between the two women, and then stopped with her gaze on Goody Blodgett.

"I must drink, as Mistress Williams says."

Goody Blodgett let her breath escape loudly from beneath her clenched teeth, and then dropped her hand. Felicity brought the tea to her lips and took a small sip. She puckered, and then took another, larger sip, and finally gulped down the rest. She let her head fall back on the pillow, and closed her eyes. Catherine took the dish from her hands and stood up.

"Let us leave her for a bit. Then we must see if we can start her again."

Goody Blodgett was already on her way out of the room. Instead of going toward the kitchen, however, she headed for the front door, took her cloak down from a peg next to the door, flung it about her shoulders, and turned to face Catherine.

"I cannot be responsible," she said. "I do not know what was in that tea, but I did see the feather on the top of your bag, and that I cannot countenance. Blue cohosh is the thing, so say I, and so I shall report to Master Worthington, who, if you needs must know, has paid me well enough, and in advance. He will not be happy to find you here in my place."

"Master Worthington's happiness does not concern me," Catherine replied.

Goody Blodgett pulled the door shut behind her.

"She is in the kitchen," Phyllis said. "I did not want to say so before."

"I know," Catherine answered. "Tend to Felicity."

Catherine found Alice Worthington, her head inclined toward a candle on the table as though seeking its warmth. The serving-girl crouched next to an indifferent fire, trying to poke it into life. Mistress Worthington shivered and lifted a worried face to Catherine.

"How is it with Felicity?" she asked.

"She rests. Do you not want to see for yourself?"

"My husband," Alice began. "He will have no one but Goody Blodgett. I told him that I would see that *you* left."

"He is not here," Catherine said. "Goody Blodgett is gone. She decided her skills were wanting. And your daughter waits for you." She turned to the serving-girl, who still prodded the fire as though unsure what else to do. "What is your name, girl?"

The girl did not respond, but stood up so that Catherine could get a good look at her. She was perhaps seventeen or eighteen, with straight black hair, a dark complexion, and a sullen look on her face.

"I see," Catherine replied. "What name was given you?"

"After the English took me from the swamp, they said I am Elizabeth."

"Well, Elizabeth," Catherine said, "I expect you have seen a babe born before."

"I have."

"Then leave the fire to us, and go sit by Felicity in case she rouses."

The girl's face did not change expression, nor did she nod, but she left the kitchen.

"I worry," Mistress Worthington said. "It was Samuel's notion to give that captured Indian girl to Felicity and Daniel. I did not approve the idea."

"She will not hurt your daughter."

"I suppose you have some knowledge of them."

"Matthew does not tell me much of his people or his ways. As you recall, that is forbidden him."

"I do not take you for a person overly concerned about what the magistrates forbid."

"Nor you your husband."

"As to that," Mistress Worthington replied, "I am not as brave as you." She looked toward the door. "Samuel will be here soon, and he will have met with Goody Blodgett."

"Be that as it may, we must tend Felicity," Catherine insisted, "and the sooner the better."

Phyllis was stroking Felicity's hand as Catherine and Mistress Worthington returned to the birthing room. Elizabeth sat on the bed, cradling Felicity's head in her lap.

"How does she?" Catherine asked.

"She just awoke," Phyllis said, "and asked for her mother. Her pains seem to have begun again."

Alice Worthington strode to the bed.

"I am here, child," she said.

Felicity grimaced in response to a contraction, set her teeth hard against it, and then yawned. Mistress Worthington turned to Catherine, a question in her eyes.

"She is drowsy from the root tea I gave her. It is powerful, but she needed her rest. She was exhausted, and she is not strong, as well you know."

Mistress Worthington nodded.

"Now, we cannot wait any longer," Catherine said. "She has what strength returned to her as she is like to have." She retrieved her midwife's bag from the corner of the room where she had stowed it, and pulled out the feathers. Elizabeth started to get up as Catherine approached.

"Stay you there," Catherine said, and squeezed between Mistress Worthington, who had sat down on the bed, and Phyllis. She waited for another contraction, which followed within a couple of minutes. And then another came as Catherine watched. The room was silent except for the breaths expelled from the several women, and the sharp intake of air as Felicity felt the start of each new pain. Catherine lifted Felicity's shift and ran her fingers between her legs and into the birth canal. She probed until she could feel the opening in the cervix.

"She is open enough," she said, "but her travail is weak. Her pains are regular, but they are not strong. Alice, you must open her mouth for me. She may well resist anybody else."

"Is that necessary?" Mistress Worthington asked.

"It is," Catherine said, "and promptly."

Felicity opened her mouth in a loud gasp, and lifted her body off the bed, holding it rigid until the contraction stopped. Falling back onto the bed, she reached for her mother's hand.

Catherine motioned to Phyllis, who stood up and slid the birthing stool next to the bed. With her mother on one side, and Elizabeth on the other, Felicity slid her feet to the floor and stepped to the stool. Catherine was struck by how frail the young woman looked, and she recalled her as a child with long brown hair, trailing after her brother as they ran about the meadow behind their house, so thin that it seemed a breeze might lift her off her feet. And now as she tottered next to the bed where she had been lying, only her swollen belly gave her any token of solid substance, and even that was smaller than one would expect at full term, causing Catherine some concern as to the wellbeing of the babe beneath that small bulge. Other than her belly, Felicity's body was a series of sharp angles on a narrow structure, her hips barely wider than her shoulders, which did not extend too much beyond her pretty face and disheveled hair.

The stool had a high back and a flat-bottomed seat shaped like a U. Felicity eased herself down, and Catherine stood on one side, Alice Worthington on the other. Alice looked at Catherine.

"Yes, now," Catherine said.

Mistress Worthington brought her hands to the side of her daughter's jaws, and stroked along the hinge.

"You must open," she said.

Felicity shook her head, her eyes wide with confusion and fear. Her mother pressed a little harder on either side of her jaw, and her mouth opened slightly. Felicity moved her head back and forth to greater purpose, but her mother's hands remained firm.

"Just a little more," Catherine said, and waited while Mistress Worthington succeeded in opening her daughter's mouth a couple of inches. Felicity's eyes began to roll back in her head in terror, and then another contraction started. Catherine slid the feather into Felicity's mouth and pushed it down her throat. As the contraction built, Felicity gagged against the pressure of the feather.

"Good," Catherine said, and she pushed the feather down farther, while running her other hand over Felicity's belly. "I feel it moving down." She removed the feather, and Felicity bent over gasping for breath, her spittle dripping down her chin.

"That was good," Catherine said. "It will not be long now."

And then for the next several contractions, Catherine induced a gagging response in Felicity that increased the pressure on her diaphragm as she struggled for breath. Each time, Catherine held her hand gently over the young woman's belly, and nodded at the progress. Mistress Worthington had stationed herself behind the stool so she could cradle her daughter's head. Phyllis held her hand on the other side, and Elizabeth crouched in front of her, offering a rhythmical chanting sound that paralleled the rising and falling intensity of the contractions. Thus engaged, the women did not see Daniel enter the room.

"Master Worthington is approaching the house," Daniel said, "and Goody Blodgett is with him."

Catherine looked up.

"Then he may be in time to welcome his grandchild."

"What can I say to him?" Daniel asked.

"Why, anything," Catherine replied, "but keep him out of our way."

"But—" Daniel tried to continue, but Elizabeth increased the volume of her chanting, and Felicity, as though encouraged, moaned loudly. Daniel shrugged and left the room. Catherine felt the baby's head start to crown. She ran her fingers over the peritoneum, expecting it to be about to tear. To her surprise it felt tight, but not dangerously so. She raised herself and again applied the feather. This time Felicity did not need encouragement to open her mouth.

"That's it, my lovely," Catherine said. "Swallow until you cannot, and then a little more."

Felicity drew the feather down her throat and gagged. Catherine rested her palm on her hard uterus as it contracted even more powerfully. Felicity screamed in pain and then clamped her teeth into Catherine's finger. The feather fell to the floor. Catherine knew the baby was on its way out. She knelt in front of the birth stool with her hands ready to receive the infant as it slid out.

"Push, one more time," Catherine instructed.

Elizabeth raised her voice to a keening wail. Phyllis held one of Felicity's hands, and her mother the other. A loud rumbling of male voices forced itself into the birthing room, but none of the women so much as looked up. "Why, what do you mean?" the deeper voice asked. "She is unable to talk with you," the other, higher-pitched voice replied, then there was an angry stomping of heavy feet toward the door.

The baby slid down into Catherine's hands, and Felicity, with her eyes closed, dropped back against the arms of Elizabeth, who stopped chanting the moment the baby was expelled. The room was silent. Phyllis handed Catherine the knife with its blade newly sharpened, and Catherine cut the cord. Holding the tiny babe in her arms she understood why it had come out so easily. She could scarcely feel its weight. Cradling it in her right arm, she saw that it was scarcely longer than the distance from her elbow to her outstretched thumb. Its chest barely rose with its breath, so that for a moment Catherine thought it was stillborn.

Felicity snapped her eyes open and extended her hands.

"My babe," she said, but then dropped her arms as the afterbirth began.

"Oh," she said.

"It is not quite done," Catherine told her. "Just a little more."

She handed the infant to Phyllis and delivered the placenta. She waited nervously, anticipating as she always did at this point an explosion of blood, but to her relief the afterbirth slid out smoothly. She heard labored breathing behind her, and realized that somebody had entered the room while she concentrated on her tasks. She turned to see Samuel Worthington, his face red and beaded with perspiration beneath his wide-brimmed hat, which still carried a layer of snow from the new storm that had begun. Daniel's hand was grasped ineffectively around the large merchant's arm, unable to stay Worthington's movement toward Catherine and the newborn in her arms. Daniel dropped his hand and followed his father-in-law.

Worthington glanced at his daughter.

"How does she?" he asked.

"Well enough," Catherine said.

Worthington leaned over to view his grandchild. The snow melted and dripped, and Catherine turned the infant away.

"And the babe?" he asked.

"A fine boy, as you can see."

"A boy, do you say. Aye, that I can see for myself. But does it breathe?"

"Yes."

He pulled off his hat and handed it to Daniel.

"Let me see him, then," he demanded.

Catherine held out the child. Worthington studied its thin chest until he could assure himself that it was moving. There was no motion otherwise, as the babe's eyes remained shut, and it did not cry or stretch its tiny limbs. The merchant looked to Elizabeth, still cradling his daughter's head. And then he looked back down at the infant.

"I would not have that savage in this room. I heard her chanting as I approached the room. Casting a spell, I tell you, that is what she was doing. Casting her evil spell on this poor misbegotten babe." He turned back to Daniel. "I told you to turn her out if you saw any reason to suspect her."

"I saw none," Daniel said.

"The more blind you, then. See you not your child unable to breathe?"

Catherine brought the infant to her chest. It opened its eyes and offered a low cry. She cooed to it.

"It breathes," Daniel said, "and Felicity has come to depend on the attention of this Indian girl that you yourself gave to us."

Catherine smiled at the babe, but in her mind she was smiling at Daniel finally standing up to his father-in-law. Worthington grunted.

"Barely does it breathe, and I tell you that girl is the cause. She must be closely watched if she is to stay. Mark that she does not whisper under her breath in the presence of the babe, or make unusual gestures with her hands. I have heard that is how they cast their devilish spells." He turned to Catherine. "And as for you, Mistress, Goody Blodgett does inform against your methods with my daughter."

"Why, then," Catherine responded, "she is very much

mistaken. And I remind you that it was I who taught Goody Blodgett what she now knows about midwifery."

"Be that as it may," Worthington said, "I will hear more of this matter. And until I do, I forbid you to attend my daughter. Look to it, Daniel." The merchant held out his hand, and Daniel placed his hat in it. He stomped out of the room. After he left, Daniel asked Catherine in a barely audible whisper.

"Will the child live?"

"I must be honest," Catherine replied, rocking the babe in her arms; its eyes were shut again. "I do fear. But see to your wife."

Elizabeth backed away from the birthing stool, and Phyllis and Mistress Worthington stood aside as Daniel approached his wife. The women withdrew from the room to leave the young husband alone with his wife. Catherine carried the babe into the servant's room and placed it in the cradle. Elizabeth sat down on the bed next to the cradle and rocked it.

Sometime later, Catherine sat with Alice Worthington at the kitchen table, half-drunk tankards of groaning beer in front of them. Catherine noted the wrinkles on Alice's face, and recalled how once they had been able to share intimacies before their husbands' business differences created a wall between them that neither one had the energy nor motivation to breach until this evening. Now, facing the very real prospect that Alice's first grandchild might not survive until morning, the two women looked at each other, trying to recapture the basis of their friendship. Alice let out a sigh that filled the quiet room.

"My Nathaniel wanted so to be here for his sister. You remember how close they were as children, how he would pick her up when she fell, how frail she was even then."

Catherine saw again in her mind's eye the image of

young Felicity running as though carried by a breeze, and she nodded.

"Indeed, I do," she said.

"It is this business with Thomas that has made him so anxious he could not bide here even knowing her time was so close."

Catherine had followed the flow of Alice's words, anticipating that she would say "business with Indians," and so she had to shift her attention to the young man she had almost forgotten, the one who disappeared on the night that old man Powell was killed.

"And why is he so taken with that young man?"

Alice began to answer and then stopped herself. She worked the corners of her mouth as though attempting to make them form the right words.

"He is the brother of Nathaniel's intended, as I am sure you have heard."

"I have. But your face tells me that is not all there is to it."

"I never could fool you, Catherine," Alice said with a quick smile. "No, there is more, but I do not profess to understand all of it, as my husband took this matter into his own hands."

"And what matter would that be?" Catherine asked.

"Why, sending Thomas off to learn how to farm with that old man."

"Hmph," Catherine said. "He could have found a better mentor."

"Ah, but mentoring was not fully the point."

Catherine anticipated what Alice did not want to say.

"There were problems in the house, then," she said.

Alice nodded.

"Between Nathaniel and Thomas?"

"Yes," Alice replied, "but I can say no more."

"You needn't."

They did not speak for a few moments, and then Alice turned her head in the direction of the servant's room, where the only sound was the creaking of the cradle beneath Elizabeth's patient foot.

"Wait, and pray," Catherine said, and Alice closed her eyes and began to move her lips. A second later, Catherine felt her own prayer for the newborn well up within her, inarticulate and powerful, and she too closed her eyes and prayed.

FIVE

❧❧❧

THE TRACKS HAD disappeared in the hardened ground where no snow remained to bear their imprint. Massaquoit imagined himself the fleeing English boy, pushing his way through the thickening forest. Every twenty or thirty yards into the woods Massaquoit's feeling would be confirmed by a branch or torn vine, evidence that somebody in considerable and careless haste had passed that place.

After a while, he found himself in a small opening among the trees. A dried and frozen creek bed, through which a rill of water would again flow in the spring, emerged from behind the screen of trees on the left, crossed the clearing, and then dropped sharply to the right. He concentrated on that creek bed. The boy would now be tired but still fearful. His weariness might lead him to follow the creek bed down so that he could continue to make good speed while recovering his energy. But the drop there was steep, and might have posed too great a challenge. Massaquoit looked to the left where the creek entered the clearing. He remembered the strong feeling he had earlier, when he gazed up into the tree and could almost see the boy clinging to a branch, and he concluded now that fear would have driven the boy to go upward. People being hunted are more afraid of enemies coming down on them than those that might rise up from below. His own, bitter experience traveling through the low-lying mire of the swamp had taught him that. He remembered wanting, with something approaching desperation, to climb a tree in order to see what was coming toward him, and not be taken unawares by his pursuer. The boy would have been moved by the same emotions, and so Massaquoit turned to follow the creek bed as it worked its way back among the trees and toward an elevation from which it must start.

The grade was gentle for a quarter of a mile, and Massaquoit congratulated himself on making the right choice. He felt that the panicked boy had preceded him on this path, and before long he was certain of it as he stood next to a broken branch hanging over a sudden drop in the creek bed, a place where the boy must have stumbled and grabbed the branch to keep himself from falling. And there, ahead on the ground, was the amputated branch itself. From this point, the creek bed narrowed until it was no more than a couple of feet wide, as the grade rose sharply and then leveled into a rocky plateau. One rock, in particular, caught Massaquoit's attention. It jutted out from the side of the creek bed, offering a sharp protuberance, which would cut anything brushing against it with any force. And there, lying on the ground, beneath that protuberance was a piece of fabric. He picked it up, and recognized the homespun wool out of which the English shaped their clothing. The piece of cloth was an undistinguished gray, but on its edge was a dark red, almost black, stain of dried blood. The English boy, in his haste, had caught his leg on this rock, torn his breeches, and left some of his blood behind.

Massaquoit tucked the cloth into his pouch. Although the sun was shining, he now felt the cold wind sting his

cheek as he looked at the treeless plateau punctuated by a
scattering of huge boulders. The creek bed, here not much
more than a groove, crossed the plateau and then ascended
through the vertical rock-facing at the edge of the plateau.
He climbed onto one of the boulders and surveyed the area.

He could see the creek bed as it wended its way down
the hill toward the clearing just now visible through the
tops of the trees. He looked down the other side of the
hill and his eyes focused on a narrow line that worked its
way through the woods on that side curving to the north
and west, and he knew he was looking at a footpath used
by various local tribes, for hunting, war, or commerce. He
stared as far along the path as he could, and at the most
distant point he thought he saw a line of black specks,
looking like a file of ants against the white of the snow,
moving away from him, but he knew well that at this distance his eyes could be deceiving him. He lay down on
the boulder and shielded his eyes from the sun, which was
sliding toward the western horizon. The antlike figures
seemed to have gathered into a tight knot, which no longer
moved. The sun's rays came at him on an almost horizontal
plane providing a hint of warmth to his back, but his belly
felt as though it were freezing to the boulder. He had almost decided that his eyes must have fooled him, when he
saw a gray wisp float up from the edge of the path. Within
a few moments, the wisp thickened into a steady stream
of smoke lifting, he knew, from a campfire. So there had
been movement, and whoever the travelers were, they had
made camp and were now warming themselves by a fire
while he lay on cold stone tracking a frightened English
boy.

The more pressing question was who was at that campfire. The most frequent travelers along that path were Iroquois coming down from the north to trade or sometimes
to harass the English, as they had allied themselves with

the French to the north. Or perhaps it was the Narragansetts traveling in the opposite direction, probably more for commerce than for war. He felt alienated from both these tribes. The Narragansetts had fought alongside the English at the fort where his wife and son died, and he himself, as a Pequot sachem, had had skirmishes with them as they encroached upon Pequot hunting and trading territories. Whoever these travelers were, they would not be friendly toward him. Whether they might be responsible for the old English farmer's death was another question.

He stood up and stretched his arm toward the dying sun as though to embrace its feeble warmth. He looked to his left where the boulders gave way and the creek bed climbed the last steep incline to a crest on which grew one thin and scraggly pine. Next to it, just visible, was what appeared to be an opening into the side of the hilltop. The thought struck him that in that cave he might find his quarry, huddled and even now staring back at him. Well, he thought, let him sit and worry for a while. He could not go anywhere if indeed he was there.

He turned to study the direction from which he had come. He saw nothing, and yet he knew that if his eyes could search through the trees that blocked his view of the bottom of the hill he had just climbed, he would soon see a file of English, and at its head would be a man wearing a beaver hat, for he had no reason to doubt either Wequashcook's skill as a tracker, or the old Indian's inclination to make himself of use to the English.

He sat down on the boulder to consider his options. He could climb to the crest, approach the cave, and capture the boy, if he was there. But the boy who had just witnessed his master's death might not believe that Massaquoit was offering him protection. Then he would have a troublesome captive on his hands while he waited for the English to arrive. He could, on the other hand, go down to meet the English and show them where their prey was, but this idea did not sit well either. He did not want to give Wequashcook any help, nor did he trust the English to recognize his own motives. Perhaps he should take the boy back to Catherine and let her decide what to do. That would be difficult, for he would have Wequashcook breathing down his neck, but he concluded it was best.

He clambered down from the boulder and walked to the groove in the rock face. There was clearly no way to climb to the cave from this point, and he began to think more highly of the English boy for having found a hiding place so secure from a frontal attack. He worked his way to the left and found nothing but sheer rock, virtually impossible to climb. However, when he went to the right of the rock wall he discovered a gentler grade where his feet could find purchase and his hands openings to hold onto as he lifted himself up. From this angle, he could climb toward the top of the hill directly in a line with the pine tree that stood sentinel at the side of the cave opening. He started up, placing his foot on a flat surface in front of a fair-sized boulder. Once standing on that narrow platform, he hoisted himself to the top of the boulder. As he did so, he looked up just in time to see the sun, which was sitting on the rim of the hill, glint off something bright, and then he detected movement from behind the tree, heading toward the cave opening. However, he was now looking directly into the sun, and he could not be sure of what he thought he had just seen.

He continued climbing, glancing up at every opportunity to check for further signs of somebody or something at the top, but he saw nothing. He was still ten yards from the top when the sun slid behind the hill and he was immersed in sudden darkness. It would be foolish to continue without being able to see the ground beneath his feet. He had no intention of taking a roll back down the hill, caroming off those boulders he had just passed. And he was sure there was somebody, now alerted to his presence, waiting for him at the top of the hill. He would wait for dawn and proceed at first light.

He knelt so as to sense the contours of the ground immediately around him, and he was able to make out, a little distance away, a place where two boulders came together to form a natural shelter. He made his way carefully to that spot and crawled between the two large rocks. A fire was out of the question. The nearest firewood was down among the trees he had left, and besides he did not want to be quite so obvious announcing where he was, even if the most likely person to be waiting for him on the top of the hill was a frightened English boy. He curled himself into a ball and tried to convince himself that he was really quite warm.

He spent the night in a fitful sleep. Although his ears strained to detect any noise that might announce the advance of an attacker, he heard only his own quiet breathing and the soft rush of an occasional wind, which ceased after a while as the air froze hard and still around him. He awoke before dawn and waited for the first rays to illuminate the ascent to the top of the hill. As soon as he could see his foot- and hand-holds, he began again to work his way up. He climbed with his eyes scanning the crest, waiting for the movement he now deemed inevitable of the blade that had glinted in the sunset the evening before.

The last five yards were almost vertical. He stood on a narrow ledge a few feet above the last level stretch beneath the crest. He tried one way and then the other, but found no easy way to continue. Directly beneath the pine tree the rock face was nicked and gouged enough to provide places to put hands and feet, but it would be a slow and perilous ascent. He pushed his right foot as far into the first niche as he could, but did not manage to get more than the tips of his deerskin boots into the space. He reached as high as he could with his left hand and managed to grasp a jagged protuberance. He squeezed his palm down on that rock, even though it seemed his flesh would rip. He stepped up, swayed for a moment, and then found his balance.

He proceeded in this fashion, one shallow foothold after another, each time finding something to grab with his hand, until he could just reach the lip of the rock wall that gave on to the level terrain. He raised himself another foot so that straightening up, he would be able to see over the edge. But he did not do so. Instead, he remained in an awkward half crouch, his feet resting sideways on a narrow ledge, his hands digging into niches that permitted half his fingers to grab. There was another, wider ledge one step higher, but if he hoisted himself up on to that one, his upper body would be exposed over the top of the rock wall—so he waited.

When he heard and saw nothing after a few moments, he straightened up sufficiently to bring his eyes to the lip of the rock. He pressed his cheek against the cold stone and focused his right eye on the tree, which was now a few feet away. The sun was a little higher now, and its rays reached the left side of the tree trunk, casting a shadow to the right. Massaquoit studied that shadow. It looked a little thicker than the tree trunk itself. The front part of the shadow, closest to him, did not move, but there was a slight tremble in the rearward section. Yet, the air was calm, and the tree motionless.

He now stepped up to the wider ledge, his eyes on that shadow. He raised his head just above the edge, and looked past the tree toward the cave, but his peripheral vision was locked onto the shadow. His left hand sought and found a crevice it could grip with full force. He brought his right arm over the top slowly, and ran his hand over the surface as though seeking something to hold so he could lift himself up.

He sensed the motion before he saw it, and pulled his hand back just as the blade came down hard where his fingers had been a moment before. The blade clanked off the stone, throwing up a small shower of sparks. Massaquoit found the arm above that blade and seized it. His assailant tried to free himself but the force of his downward motion had thrown him off balance. Massaquoit yanked hard on the arm. At first, they were evenly matched, but then the attacker lost his balance and started to fall. Massaquoit pulled him down, and for a moment the man's dark face was even with his so that he could smell his breath and see the rage in the black eyes.

And then he was gone. His body hurtled over Massaquoit's head and bounced several times before it landed on the level terrain below the niche where Massaquoit had spent the night. His left hand still holding on so tightly that he had lost feeling in his fingers, Massaquoit leaned away from the rock surface to look down. The assailant was lying motionless, his head at an unnatural angle to his body, and Massaquoit knew that he did not have to worry about him any longer.

A fair-sized stone glanced off Massaquoit's shoulder, and then another dropped just behind his head. He looked up and saw that several more were rolling toward the edge and then over it. He put up his hand as a shield and waited for the thin cascade to stop. He raised himself to see where the stones were coming from, and he was just in time to catch a glimpse of yellow hair floating behind a body darting back into the cave. So, he had found the English boy after all.

He swung himself up and rolled onto the area immediately in front of the pine tree. He was still on rock, and it was coated with frozen dew, so he got to his feet slowly, grabbing a branch of the tree to steady himself. A couple of steps brought him onto an area of browned weeds made rigid by the cold, and they snapped beneath his feet as he walked to the cave. He kept his eyes on the entrance, but saw only dark shadows.

The entrance was an irregular opening no more than three feet high and less than that across. Massaquoit knelt down and peered inside. The sun was now high enough to shine over his shoulder into the interior, and there he saw, four or five feet into the cave and huddled against the back wall, a figure with head bowed, as though in supplication, arms extended palms upward. He waited for the boy to raise his eyes, but he did not do so. His body convulsed from time to time as he shivered violently; he was wearing only a shirt and breeches, which were torn at the knee of the left leg. Finally, he looked up and offered a tentative smile.

"Are you going to kill me?" he asked.

"I am going to take you back to the English."

The boy shivered again, so violently that he banged his head against the wall behind him. The he pointed past Massaquoit, through the cave entrance, toward the tree.

"They could not decide what to do with me. They argued. Then all but the one down there left."

"They did not know if you were worth taking along with them," Massaquoit said, "whether you could keep up with them, because they must know the English are looking for you. But because the English are looking for you, some of them thought you would be worth something in trade. That is what they were arguing about." He turned in the direction the boy was still looking. "That one must have been your new master. This morning he was going to kill you, but first he would test you to see if you were worthy. If you were not, maybe he would have spared you and

tried to see what he could get from the English for you."
Massaquoit held out his hand. "Come out into the sun."

"No."

"You will freeze."

"I am afraid."

"You must come back with me and tell the English who
killed your English master."

Massaquoit crawled into the cave. The boy turned away
from him, and Massaquoit seized his right arm. He backed
out of the cave dragging his captive, who offered no resistance. Once outside again, he lifted him to his feet.

The boy stood blinking in the sun. He wrapped his arms
around himself to try to stop the shivers that continued to
spasm his body. Massaquoit could now see the discolored
bruises on his face. His lips were swollen and his left eye
was partly shut.

"The man down there has a coat," Massaquoit said. "An
English coat."

The boy walked to the edge and looked down.

Massaquoit scrambled down to the dead Indian. He
turned him on his stomach so that he could remove the
coat. The fall had broken the man's neck, and his head
flopped and turned to look back at Massaquoit even as he
was on his belly. Massaquoit turned the head to face front.
He dragged the body to the base of a boulder. He gazed
up at the sun, which was climbing toward the south from
the eastern sky. He turned the body so that the sun was
over the dead man's shoulder at an angle, facing southwest. He propped the body against the boulder. Then he
knelt down and removed the coat, placing it on the ground
next to the body.

The boy had been peering over the edge.

"He won't need that now," he said.

Massaquoit looked up, his face humorless.

"He was not my enemy or my friend," Massaquoit responded. "His death does not come back to me, and his spirit knows this. I have left him with his back to the morning sun so he can travel to Kanta to meet his ancestors. He should travel there with something of his own, not a stolen coat from the English."

"Where is this Kanta?" the boy asked.

"Kanta is a god."

The boy snickered. "A god. How many do you have?"

"As many as there are."

"We have but one. The truc God."

"Have you seen this true god?" Massaquoit asked.

"Of course not."

"Is he an English god?"

The boy started to answer, then stopped.

"I suppose," he said after a while. "But that is a question for those wiser than me."

"Do you want to talk about your god and mine, or do you want to get warm?" Massaquoit asked. He picked up the dead man's coat. It was heavy wool, dark blue, with brass buttons. He ran his fingers down the row of buttons, stopping where one was missing. He felt in his pouch for the object he had picked up near old man Powell's house. He looked at it with his back to the English boy and then returned it to his pouch. He clambered back up to the boy and held out the coat.

The boy stepped back.

"Are you afraid of the coat?" Massaquoit asked.

"No. But maybe the man what used to wear it."

"Do you know who that was?"

The boy shrugged. "I thought I did, but it is a common kind of coat worn by many. And I am cold to the death."

"Then put it on."

The boy shivered once again and then reached for the coat.

"What do they call you?" Massaquoit asked.

"They what doesn't know better calls me Thomas."

"And those that do?"

He shrugged. "That's for them to know. And who do I thank?"

"Those who don't know better call me Matthew."

Thomas wrapped the coat about himself and after a few moments he stopped shivering.

"We must go back to the English," Massaquoit said. "When we find the English you can tell them what happened the night the old man was killed."

Thomas looked at Massaquoit as though seeing him for the first time.

"So that is the way of it, is it? They must think you did it."

Massaquoit shrugged.

"Well, as for that," Thomas said. "You might have. It was dark. I heard the old man screaming. I ran out. Somebody grabbed me. He hit me about my face, but he could not hold me. I got away and kept running. If it wasn't you, it was some other savage."

"But I was not there. And if I killed the old man, why would I not kill you now?"

"You can answer that one better than me," Thomas said. He seemed to have recovered some confidence with the warmth provided by the coat. He walked past the pine tree, dropped to the ledge and then to the ground next to the body. He glanced at the dead man, and then started walking down. Massaquoit followed and caught up with him.

"You are now in a hurry," he said.

"Yes, there is somebody I want to see. I expect he is with the English, coming to look for me, like the good lad he is."

Catherine arose from her sleepless bed and dressed hurriedly in the dark. The floor was icy cold beneath her feet, and her stomach complained, reminding her that she had not eaten a proper meal in two days. But she had already decided to skip breakfast, so as to make haste to the Rowlands' house. She was almost sure that when she got there she would encounter a scene of mourning, and that she might well have to help Felicity bury her child as she had helped to deliver it.

The sun was just rising as she repeated the walk she had taken the night before. The snow crunched under her feet, and the ice sparkled in the early light. She made what haste she could, moving in a rolling gait that somehow enabled her to keep her balance on the slippery footing. By the time she reached the Rowlands' house, her breath was forming frozen puffs of vapor, and a sharp pain jabbed her left side.

Standing in front of the house were Daniel and Master Worthington.

"Goody Blodgett is inside with my daughter," Master Worthington said, "so there is no need for you, Mistress Williams."

The ignorance and the arrogance of the man, Catherine thought. His grandchild's grasp on life was fragile, and there he stood placing that delicate life in the hands of a woman whose skill was, by common consent, a seed compared to the mature wisdom she herself possessed.

"Master Worthington," she said in a voice made calm and reasonable by her need to pass through this obdurate obstacle, "perhaps I can assist Goody Blodgett. It is possible my years may have taught me things beyond her experience."

"Aye," he said, "and that is what I fear. She has told me in truth how the birthing progressed under your direction, and she has said that what you did placed the babe in jeopardy for its life."

"Indeed, has she so said?"

"She has, and further I intend to take the matter of your fitness before the governor."

"As you wish," Catherine replied. "I will be happy to make defense of my actions then, but now my concern is solely for the babe."

The door opened behind Master Worthington, and there stood Felicity, leaning on her mother's arm. She was wearing only a shift, and she shivered in the sudden cold of the outside air.

"Father," the young woman said, "if it please you, step aside to permit Mistress Williams entrance." Her voice was faint, and she looked, if anything, thinner than she had been. Catherine wanted to get close to Felicity to talk to her, to examine her for signs of infection and fever that could kill her in a day, but it was clear that Master Worthington's substantial body, and even larger pride, would prevent her from approaching the girl. So, for the moment, Catherine contented herself with staring as hard as she could at the new mother. The wind kicked up in a sudden gust and pressed Felicity's shift hard against her thin body. Catherine could see the outline of her small breasts now, and she also noted how Felicity immediately pulled the shift away from her chest. So that is the problem, Catherine thought, and will Goody Blodgett have any idea how to deal with it?

As if he shared her thought at that moment, Master Worthington began, "Goody Blodgett—"

"She abides inside," Mistress Worthington said to her husband. "Please, Samuel, for our daughter's sake."

"I needs must talk with Mistress Williams," Felicity said.

The merchant's face reddened and his chest, beneath his heavy cloak, seemed to expand.

"Daughter, attend to your babe with the help of Goody Blodgett." He pointed to Catherine. "I do not grant entrance to this woman. There is no more to be said on that matter."

"But Samuel—" his wife began.

"Inside, I say. Wife, see to your daughter. If you both had done as I said in the beginning, we would not be standing here now in the freezing cold while the poor babe clings to life because of the evil ministrations of that woman." He jabbed his finger toward Catherine, and then placed a firm hand on the shoulders of wife and daughter to steer them back into the house.

Catherine stood long, until her feet numbed and her breath came with difficulty in the frigid air. She could not go inside, but neither could she will herself to leave. She felt a touch on her arm, and turned to find Phyllis standing behind her. Phyllis looked at the closed door and then back at Catherine.

"Master Worthington says I am a danger to the babe," Catherine said. "He will not let me attend his daughter or her child. He says Goody Blodgett can manage." She found herself sputtering, and stopped.

"He cannot say so," Phyllis declared.

"He did, I tell you, but I care not for the man's calumny, for I can recover my good name, but I do not think that babe will recover its life."

"You cannot stand here in the snow," Phyllis said.

"That I know," Catherine agreed, recovering herself.

"Are you going home, then?"

Catherine gazed at the plain face of her servant on which her emotions were always writ large, and saw the concern there now.

"I need to find out what is going on inside," she said, "and then I can go home."

Phyllis nodded her head, frowned, and then smiled.

"You can go home, now," she said.

"But—" Catherine began.

"I will find out for you while you warm yourself by the fire that I bade Edward tend to while I came after you."

"Master Worthington will not let you in, either," Catherine said. "He knows you as my servant, does he not?"

Phyllis shrugged.

"He may, I warrant, or he may not. But I am not so silly as to go in the front door."

Catherine understood, and began a smile that was interrupted by the chattering of her teeth.

"Elizabeth?" she asked.

"Aye, Elizabeth," Phyllis said, "and through the back door, if you please."

Catherine sat before the fire, rubbing her hands, watching Edward stoop over and poke the bottom log until it cracked, releasing a tongue of flame. The flame shot up in bands of red and yellow and she imagined the warmth she should feel, and yet the chill in her bones remained. Edward looked over his shoulder at her, saw her continuing shiver, and knelt again to his task, attacking the flaming log with greater vigor.

"Leave off, Edward," Catherine said. "The fire does well enough."

He stood up slowly, allowing his back to straighten at its own pace, and then walked out of the kitchen to occupy himself elsewhere in the house. Catherine knew that he used words sparingly, as though the effort of producing the sounds far outweighed any possible advantages speech might offer. Yet Phyllis spoke whenever possible, as though words brought her into communion with the human race, a feeling Edward neither experienced nor valued.

She watched him struggle to straighten his spine, and then amble out with hardly a look at her, not interested in questioning why his mistress had thanked him for the fire when she came in from the cold, and now seemed indifferent to the effects of his labor. To him, apparently, it was all one. He did as he was told without judgment or concern, and was happiest when he had finished a chore and could amuse himself with an activity of his own choosing, such as whittling a piece of wood.

Catherine's mind, though, did not stay long on the habits of her two servants. In fact, she permitted herself this distraction only because she could not stop herself from thinking of the frail babe she had delivered from its impossibly fragile mother. She could not long comfort herself with the illusion that Phyllis would return with the news that all was well. She tried, but could not convince herself, that Goody Blodgett would be equal to the task of helping Felicity and her infant through these crucial first hours. She had thought of asking Joseph Woolsey to intervene so that she could return to her proper place at Felicity's side, but had stopped at her house to warm herself first and to think of how she could approach her old friend with a request he would want to honor but would also bring him into conflict, once again, with Samuel Worthington. She did not want to put him in that position if she could help it. And so she sat, warming her flesh while her heart remained chilled, waiting for good news she had no reason to think would be forthcoming.

After a few more minutes of staring into the fire, she could no longer sit still, so she got up and walked to the shelves in the corner of the kitchen, where she kept jars, boxes, and bottles of her various remedies. She knew that the birth had gone well, that Felicity had not experienced any obvious problem, but that the babe was undersized and therefore in danger. Of course, Catherine recalled how Felicity had shuddered against the light pressure of her shift driven against her body by the wind, and she guessed that the young woman was going to have difficulty nursing her child. Once she verified that, she would summon Sara Dun-wood as a wet nurse. For now, she ran her fingers over the various remedies and settled on the powdered rhizome of yellow lily with which she could make a poultice. She took down the small jar and unstoppered it. She held it to her nose, assuring herself that it was still fresh enough to be of use, then set it on the table and made herself sit down to wait with what patience she could muster.

In an effort to shut down her mind, she lay her head on the table, and thus did not hear the steps coming into the kitchen until they were almost upon her. She looked up at Phyllis, whose face was red from the cold and whose chest heaved from the exertion of her hurried return from Fe-licity Rowland's bedside.

"Well, then, how do they?" Catherine asked without pausing for other greeting. Phyllis was equally direct in her reply.

"Very poorly, I'm afraid," she said. "The babe cries from hunger, and Felicity cannot give it suck. She says it pains her too much. Goody Blodgett has painted her breasts with honey, but it does no good. She knows not what else to do. Master Worthington mutters and paces about, and says he has business to attend to at his dock. And after that he will seek the advice of Minister Davis."

Catherine waved her hand briskly in front of her, as if by so doing she could remove Worthington not only from the conversation, but more importantly, from the situation he had helped to create, a situation that now threatened the life of his daughter and grandchild.

"Aye, business first, then God, and then perhaps his daughter's well-being. Speak not of that man to me," Catherine said. "Honey, you say, on her breasts?"

Phyllis nodded.

"She says she learned that remedy from you."

"Aye, that she did. But is it right in this instance? Honey

can soothe soreness, but perhaps Felicity's problem is graver than that."

"Goody Blodgett does not profess to know."

"I do not doubt it," Catherine said, permitting just a trace of satisfaction to color her words.

"She says," Phyllis continued, with an answering smile, "that as soon as Master Worthington leaves, she will make her way here to seek your counsel, for she cares more for that poor babe than his shillings."

"Has she come to that, then?"

Phyllis frowned. "I do not entirely trust her."

"We need not," Catherine replied. "But we do need her assistance in working around Master Samuel Worthington." She fairly spat out the syllables of the name. She pointed to the bottle of powdered lily rhizomes on the table. "And when we do, perhaps we can try a poultice of that." Phyllis nodded, but looked a little distracted, and Catherine realized she had more to tell. "How came you into the house?"

Phyllis's face relaxed and she took a deep breath.

"The shorter version of your story, if you please," Catherine said.

"I tell only the essentials, as well you know," Phyllis said. "The rest I share with Edward betimes, but as for that I could be talking to a stone."

"Go on, then."

"I went around to the back of the house, through snow as high as me, but when I arrived at the door, who was there but Elizabeth and she said she saw me through the window and understood where I was going. We understand our place, we do, and she was happy to see me, for she said her young mistress was ailing very much and the babe even more, while Goody Blodgett just stared from one to the other, sometimes saying something under her breath that sounded like a prayer, but Elizabeth, heathen that she is, cannot be taken serious on that. And we was sitting in the kitchen talking when Mistress Worthington herself comes in and her face is dark as shadows. She said Felicity will not leave off to give the babe her breast even though she cannot stop herself from screaming when she does, it hurts her so. Mistress Worthington said she knew not what to do, and then she asked after you, she did, and said she cared not what her husband said. Just then Goody Blodgett joined us, and we all sat around the table, nice as can be, never mind the poor girl and her child not ten feet away. Her husband came in, too, but seeing all us women gathered, got afraid and went out again. And then Goody Blodgett asked Mistress Worthington if you could be called in for your advice, and Mistress Worthington said that was exactly what she intended to do, and would I be so kind as to tell you all of this, which I have just done, so you could make your best haste there."

Phyllis stopped abruptly as though she had reached the bottom of her barrel of words. Catherine waited a moment, to be sure her servant had no more to say.

"That I will do. You must rest a bit, and then make your way to Sara Dunwood's house and bring her to Felicity. I expect the child has not had suck today."

"I think not," Phyllis said.

"It must then, and promptly. If Felicity cannot manage, Sara can."

"You could send Edward," Phyllis said.

Catherine rose to her feet and took her cloak from the peg. She placed the vial of powder into her midwife's bag.

"He cannot deliver the message to Sara as you can. You know how his tongue stumbles when he has to talk of things he knows nothing of, and it has been too long since he had anything to do with nursing mothers and their babes.

"He never—" Phyllis began.

"And that is why you must go."

Phyllis brightened.

"Right," she said. "You cannot trust such a mission to Edward."

Catherine was already moving toward the front door.

"I knew you would understand."

Phyllis's face darkened and she strode past Catherine. She stopped before the door.

"He has not been buried yet, has he?"

"No. You know well the snow is too deep and the ground frozen beneath it."

"I fear him."

"He is in a coffin, in his barn, where he will keep until the weather warms. He is not up and about."

"Not him, but his ghost. Especially, seeing that the body is lying there cold and alone."

Catherine took Phyllis's arm gently but firmly, and pushed her aside so she could open the door.

"Make haste then," she said, "and the ghost will not catch you."

"You shouldn't mock me," Phyllis said, but Catherine was already out the door, and did not turn back.

Alice Worthington and Goody Blodgett were standing in the doorway stamping their numb feet as they peered up the road, their eyes tearing from the cold wind, as Catherine arrived. Alice stepped forward and opened her arms in an embrace.

"My daughter, Catherine, she is in your hands and God's." She held her tight and then stepped back. "You know that Samuel has gone to the dock, why I cannot say, as his ship is stuck fast in the ice, and he has taken Daniel with him. The boy follows him about like a puppy. I thought his place was here with his wife and child, but Samuel would not hear of it."

"It is no matter," Catherine said, "and perhaps better that they are not here to trip over."

• • •

Felicity lay very still in the bed. Her face was flushed, and perspiration beaded her forehead in spite of the draft coming through the window frame. Catherine put her hand on the young woman's cheek, and it was very warm. She sensed Goody Blodgett standing behind her.

"What think you?" Goody Blodgett asked.

Catherine turned to see the conflicting emotions of injured pride, humiliation, and need fighting in the other woman's countenance. She did not immediately answer, but instead opened Felicity's shift. She could not restrain the half gasp that forced itself through her lips. The underside of Felicity's left breast was swollen red. The swelling caused it to look like a deformed sack, bulging on the bottom from a heavy weight. The nipple above the swelling was still covered with the dried and cracking layer of honey that Goody Blodgett had applied.

"I tried the honey, as you once told me," she said.

Catherine nodded.

"Aye, that you did, and that is to ease her pain when the babe sucks." She ran her fingers over the breast, which felt warmer than her cheek, working her way from the top down to the angrily inflamed area. That spot pulsed. She then palpated the other breast. The nipple was cracked beneath the honey coating, but the flesh was cool and it otherwise appeared normal.

"She has been able to give the child suck a little from that one," Mistress Worthington said. She was standing behind Goody Blodgett and peering over her shoulder. "But she has not much milk, and she cannot endure the touch."

A cry came from across the way, and a moment later Elizabeth entered the room rocking the babe in her arms. The infant's tiny fist grabbed at her breasts and its mouth worked in a sucking motion between cries that started as weak whimpers but soon grew into howls.

"I cannot give him what he needs. I can only rock him to sleep, but then he rouses, and you see he is hungry."

"I have sent for Sara Dunwood," Catherine said. "She is nursing her own babe and can wet nurse this one." She placed the tip of her forefinger on the abscess. Felicity writhed and bit down hard on her lips until she drew a drop of blood. She ran her tongue over her lip and swallowed the blood. She moved her head back and forth, trying to focus her eyes. "She is in danger," Catherine said in a hushed whisper. "The fever rages in her and will consume her. This must be lanced or she dies." What she did not say out loud in deference to the others, particularly Alice, was that she feared the young woman might die no matter what she did, and for a moment she indulged the anger that rose in her again at having been prevented from attending Felicity sooner. Goody Blodgett seemed to read her thoughts.

"I sent for you as soon as I could. You know how it was. I need the fee, and—"

"You thought you could manage as well as I."

Goody Blodgett lowered her head for a moment, and when she raised it her jaw was thrust forward although her eyes were wide with fear.

"I did. And Master Worthington said he would have no one but me attend his daughter."

"That he did," Alice said, "for he was set against you, Catherine."

"There is no time for any of that," Catherine said, "and it is of no matter." She reached into her midwife's bag and removed a small sharp knife. "Alice, comfort your daughter. Elizabeth, put the child in its cradle and set yourself on one side, with Goody Blodgett on the other."

The women arranged themselves as directed: Mistress Worthington at the back of the bed, her arms cradling Felicity's head, Elizabeth on one side and Goody Blodgett on the other, each holding one of Felicity's hands, while stroking her bare arm. Catherine clambered onto the bed. Felicity stirred, and opened her eyes, which at first started with fear but then relaxed in relief.

"Mistress Williams," she said, her voice no more than a hoarse whisper. "I am so weak."

"Aye, that you are surely, for you have the fever caused by a bad humor."

Felicity's eyes widened again in fear.

"If I . . . who will take care of—"

"Hush," Catherine said. "You will tend your babe, as soon as we tend to you." She put the fingers of her left hand over Felicity's eyes while keeping her right hand, with the sharp little knife out of sight behind her back. "Now then, you just lie back in your mother's arms. It won't be but a moment."

Felicity's body tensed as though she expected to be assaulted, but she let herself fall back into Mistress Worthington's embrace. Catherine brought the knife from behind her back toward Felicity's breast. The abscess was centered on the underside. Catherine placed the fingers of her left hand beneath the breast where it lay against the rib cage. Ever so slowly, with the least possible pressure, she lifted the breast to position it for her knife. But as soon as it was raised, Felicity stiffened, partly in response to the pain caused even by the gentle pressure of Catherine's fingers, but as much or more in anticipation of the pain that was to follow.

"Steady," Catherine said. "You must help me, Felicity, if I am going to help you." She looked at the three women surrounding her patient. "Steady her now, any way you can. She must not move."

Mistress Worthington, who had been stroking Felicity's cheeks while cradling her head, now moved her strong hands to her daughter's shoulders while Elizabeth and

Goody Blodgett each seized the arm she had been caressing. Catherine crouched over Felicity's midsection and lowered herself until she was just touching the young woman's belly. If she began to buck, Catherine would come down on her with her full weight. She lifted the breast again, and Felicity struggled against the hands constraining her. Catherine watched the spasm, knowing it would soon subside, and when it did she jabbed the knife into the abscess with a quick, certain motion. Felicity screamed in full voice, and thick yellow pus flowed from her opened breast. She tried to bring up her knees to dislodge Catherine, but Catherine settled her considerable weight on her thighs. She then probed a little further, as Felicity now offered a steady, low humming moan. A little blood joined the pus, so Catherine withdrew the knife. She waited until nothing else flowed from the abscess. The breast deflated as the pus oozed until it was of a size and shape more nearly like the other.

Catherine swung herself off the bed and retrieved her midwife's bag, from which she removed the jar of powdered lily rhizome. She looked at Elizabeth.

"You can let her go now, and bring us a wet and warm cloth."

Elizabeth nodded and whispered something in Felicity's ear that caused a weak smile to form on the young woman's lips. Catherine took Elizabeth's place at Felicity's side and stroked her arm with long, slow movements.

"It is over, now," she said. "We have expelled the bad humor and you will start to recover. I have a special poultice with me that will give you ease."

Elizabeth returned with a warm, damp cloth, and Catherine sprinkled powder from her jar onto the wound on Felicity's breast. She wrapped the cloth around the breast.

"Alice," she said, "can you sit with Felicity and see that the cloth remains in place?"

"Surely I can."

Catherine rose to her feet, feeling both relief and weariness. She had every hope that Felicity's youth would enable her to recover quickly. There was still, however, the problem of the babe, whose cries now reached them from across the hall.

"I will walk with the child," Catherine said, "until Sara arrives to give it what I cannot."

"Nor I these many years," Alice replied with a smile.

There was a knock at the door, and a few moments later the round, red face of Minister Davis appeared peeking into the room. White hair straggled from beneath his skull cap, and he walked in bowing his head.

"Master Worthington bade me come and pray with Felicity," he said.

"And welcome you are," Catherine said, "for I have done all that I can for her."

"He also said that I should take care to lift any spells the heathen girl might have placed on her."

"There are none such," Catherine said with a little heat.

"I did not think so," the minister replied, "but—"

"But you would not gainsay Master Worthington."

Minister Davis offered a slight shrug and knelt beside Felicity. He closed his eyes and then cast them heavenward. Catherine watched, thought about joining him, and then decided she would offer her own prayers to God, as something in her rebelled against her joining her thoughts to his at this moment. She entertained the idea, as sometimes she felt she must, that his God shared the name but not the character of hers. The God Minister Davis prayed to seemed more intent on coercing obedience, whereas her more benign deity filled her own heart with hope. She left the minister praying while she walked across the hall and picked up the crying infant, and as she paced the room with the babe in her arms, she felt her weariness depart.

•   •   •

A stub of a candle sitting on a low table next to the cradle flickered an inadequate light as Sara Dunwood sat nursing the babe. From across the hall came the low murmur of the minister's voice articulating words of supplication for the life of his parishioner. The murmured voice flowed like a gentle stream over smooth stones in the silence that filled the rest of the house, and Catherine felt herself being lulled by the counterpoint between voice and silence, and by the first faint stirring of hope that all might yet be well. The babe sucked hard on Sara's breast.

"Hungry he is," Sara said.

"You have come none too soon for him."

Sara shifted her weight on the stool on which she sat. She was a plump young woman of twenty-five with a pretty face marred by pimples and a missing front tooth. She kept her eyes fixed on the babe, a smile on her lips as she felt the strong tug. After a few moments, the child stopped sucking, its eyes closed, and she rocked it for a moment in her arms before placing it back in the cradle. She laced up her gown and stretched.

"Mine own waits for me, and I do not think Allan has much patience."

"Can you return this evening?"

"Aye, I can."

"I can send Phyllis to walk with you."

"I do not think she will want to come."

"Was she that afeard?"

Sara nodded and chuckled.

"She swore she felt the ghost of old man Powell riding on her shoulder. Then it ran off in the shape of a cat, and when she passed by his barn, she heard his coffin lid bang open."

"Does that not bother you?"

"'Tis the living what concerns me. That old man was more to worry about when he drew breath than he is now, lying stiff and cold, his wicked soul no doubt on its way to perdition."

"Why Sara, I tended his hurt hand not two days before he was killed. I found him like many old men, strangely fixed in their ways, but no worse than that."

"Ask the lad about that, then," Sara said.

"Thomas?"

"The same, the one now running from the savages that killed his master. Ask him about that hand, if he still has a tongue in his head or his head on his shoulders when he is found."

"I trust he will."

"Well, then, when he is found, and you ask him that question, see if he remembers coming to me own house and begging Allan to protect him from that old man's lust for him, how he was being used like some old men use a goat or a cow. His mouth was swollen and out of joint that night he came running to our door, it was. It weren't no dog what bit that old man's hand."

"I see," Catherine said.

"Well, then, maybe you can understand why young Nathaniel is so anxious to find him."

SIX

THEY HAD FOLLOWED the creek bed down to where it widened as the ground leveled. Massaquoit, who had been leading the way, stopped and held up his arm. Thomas stumbled to a halt at his side. The creek bed continued in an arc through a stand of pine on one side and maple on the other. At the point where it curved out of sight behind the pine, it entered the clearing where Massaquoit had stood deciding that his quarry would seek higher ground. Now he stood very still and listened. The wind blew silently through the bare limbs of the maples but whistled through the needles of the pine. After a few moments he was sure of what he heard.

"The English are very close now," he said.

Thomas had copied him, bending his head into the wind as though straining to hear.

"I did not hear anything but the wind," he said.

"That is because you heard only the wind, but not what it carried. We must wait here."

Thomas bundled the coat about him but still shivered.

"How do you know it is not the friends of that fellow you left lying in the snow?"

"They are gone, for now, but they may come back."
Massaquoit pointed toward the entrance of the clearing.
"The English are there. If you are so cold, and so certain
your friend awaits you, then go on ahead. I am not so sure
of my welcome among them."

"Not me either. I can wait with you."

Massaquoit stared hard at the young man. He had always flattered himself that he could read a man's heart in
his face, that he could sift through the man's words to find
the truth. But this young English posed a new challenge.
He could not read him.

"Then why do you suppose the English are so anxious
to find you?" he asked.

Thomas shrugged in a gesture that revealed only that he
found the question ignorant or irrelevant.

"A man can be of interest to others for many reasons,"
he said.

"But your friend, no doubt—" Massaquoit began.

"He more than the rest," Thomas replied. He straightened himself and began walking in stiff-legged stride toward the entrance to the clearing. "It is time for me to find
out."

Massaquoit took a step toward the boy, intending to stop
him, but then he just watched. He had seen a slight movement in the pines, just a flicker of shadow moving toward
them, and he had no doubt who was there, and that this
troublesome young man would soon be taken off his hands.
And so he watched Thomas walk away from him, slipping
every few steps on the icy ground, and then slowing as he
got close to the clearing. When he came abreast of the
place where the shadow had shown itself, a figure emerged
in front of him. Massaquoit saw the shrug of the young
man's shoulders as he confronted this figure, and then they
both made their way toward the clearing. After they had
gone a few steps, the figure turned around, tipped his large

beaver hat, and raised his hand with the palm facing Massaquoit. Then he threw his arm around Thomas, and resumed walking toward the entrance to the clearing.

Massaquoit understood the gesture, although he reminded himself that his level of trust in Wequashcook was only slightly higher than it was in the English. Still, Wequashcook's sign that he should stay back coincided with his own sense that he should proceed with caution. He waited until the two men were about to turn out of his sight before following them, keeping to the cover of the pines on the side of the creek bed, ready to melt into the frozen woods at the first sign of a pike or musket pointed in his direction. They made the turn and he could no longer see them, but if he strained his ears he could hear the crunch of their feet on the hard crust of snow. He adjusted his pace so that the sound of their feet remained constant, letting him know they were the same distance ahead of him.

Reaching the turn of the creek bed, he stood behind the thick trunk of an ancient pine and peered past it. He could see them again as they approached the entrance to the clearing, a space between two maples just wide enough to accommodate the two figures walking abreast. However, before they could walk through that space, a short, burly man confronted the pair. From this distance Massaquoit could not be sure, but the man looked like the one he had seen in the meetinghouse on the day he was forced to leave the service. The man gestured at Thomas and then seized the young man by the shoulders, ripping the coat off him. He held up the coat and raised his voice in words that Massaquoit could not understand, although he could detect the anger in them. The man threw off the cloak he was wearing and put on the coat. He pointed at the cloak, and Thomas picked it up and wrapped it around himself. The stocky man again gripped Thomas by the arms and shook him so

violently that Thomas's head snapped back and forth. He
shoved Thomas away from him. Thomas turned around and
pointed in Massaquoit's direction.

By the time the boy raised his arm to point, however,
Massaquoit had hidden himself behind the tree. He waited
there, listening to the angry baritone of the older man rise
in pitch until it was joined by Thomas's nervous tenor, and
for a few moments the air was filled with their duet, voice
pushing against voice. Then there was a loud snap followed
by a muffled thud, and Massaquoit knew without looking
that Thomas would now be picking himself up from the
snow. He heard a heavy tread followed by lighter steps
over the snow, and then there was silence.

Wequashcook would find him before long. Massaquoit had
worked his way to a little rise that overlooked the clearing. From there he could see the English camp. Toward the
rear of the clearing was a tent large enough to house three
or four men. Ranged around it in matching arcs, like two
arms, were smaller tents between which were two camp-
fires. Clusters of English soldiers huddled next to the fires.
Massaquoit's eyes, though, remained fastened on the larger
tent, where he figured the leader of the English troops must
be. After a while he saw a tall young man walk out of the
tent followed by the stocky man. They conversed for a few
moments. It seemed that the younger man was giving orders to the other, who then stalked off, shaking his head.
The young man went back into the tent, and Massaquoit
heard steps coming up behind him.

"You have found a good perch," Wequashcook said.
"They have been talking about you."

"That is why I am here."

"The English leading the troops was very happy with
the prize you brought him."

"But the other one seemed more interested in the coat he was wearing."

Wequashcook smiled.

"Of course. It is his coat. You must have found the one who took it from him."

"I did. He has no need of the coat."

The smile disappeared from Wequashcook's face.

"His friends will seek to avenge him."

Massaquoit shrugged.

"The English should not have been so foolish as to lose his coat," he said. "And the one who took it was going to take the boy as well."

Wequashcook squatted and pointed several hundred yards up the creek bed.

"We found the English lying in the snow, his head bleeding. If we had come a few minutes later, he would have no need of his coat either."

Massaquoit reached into his pouch and pulled out the brass button. He held it up so that it glinted in the sun. Wequashcook stood up, leaned toward it, and nodded. He held out his hand, and Massaquoit dropped the button into it.

"That coat," Wequashcook said, "has an interesting past. Where?"

Massaquoit had already decided that he was not prepared to share that particular information with Wequashcook.

"That is what I hoped you could explain to me," he said.

"But I know no more than I have told you. Perhaps in the struggle the button came off, if you found it near here."

"Ah, yes," Massaquoit said. "That must be what happened."

Wequashcook frowned. "I hope you do not take me for such a fool."

"A fool? No, that is not a word I would ever use to describe my old companion, who now serves the English."

"Only so that he can serve himself. But I have not told you what I came to say. I have convinced the English that you are that boy's rescuer, and that you pose no danger to him or to them. They are mostly satisfied. But it would help if you could tell them what I already know, but which they will not believe from my lips."

"That the boy stumbled on a trading party of Iroquois that is now on its way back to the French up north?"

"Yes."

"And why should they believe that truth from my lips more than yours?"

"Because you can tell them that you saw the Iroquois leave."

"There is the matter of the dead Iroquois."

"We need only convince them their mission is complete and they should go home."

"Yes," Massaquoit said, "but you and I know that the body will be found."

Wequashcook looked up, shaded his eyes from the sun, which was now just over the top of the trees.

"We have a little time, at least until the morning. We will tell the English they need a good watch while they sleep."

Massaquoit felt the sting of the cold wind that intensified the hollow in his stomach, and suddenly he decided he would rather take his chances being warm and fed even if it meant risking his life to secure the comforts of food and a fire among his enemy.

"I will stand with them," Massaquoit said. "I do not want to place my life in the hands of the English, who cannot see the bear that crashes through the woods in pursuit of them."

Wequashcook shook his head.

"Do you think they will trust you?"

"As much as you. But I am sure they will have one of their own watch with me."

"We find ourselves between two enemies," Wequash-cook said, and then he started walking down the slope toward the creek bed.

Or three, Massaquoit thought, watching the tall beaver hat bob in front of him as Wequashcook led the way toward the English camp.

Only a sliver of moon rose above the trees in a cloudy sky that seemed to promise more snow. Massaquoit stood outside the large tent, listening to the muffled voices that reached his ears through the canvas sides. The voices stopped, and Wequashcook slid out through the flap, straightened up, and beckoned him to come inside. The flap was stiff with a thin layer of ice that melted in Massaquoit's hand as he took his time following Wequashcook back into the tent. He had no intention of showing any anxiety or even interest. He was merely stopping by to do the English a service. It would be up to them to decide whether they would receive what he had to tell them with the same good faith with which he offered it. But at bottom, he really did not care. He wanted only to be left alone.

Inside, he found himself looking at the young English officer he had seen only from a distance. He was sitting on a low-slung rope mattress bed that was no more than a foot off the ground so that he peered through the knees of his long legs while his arms were wrapped around his shins. Standing next to him was the older, burly English man, whom he had first encountered in the meetinghouse. Crouching in a corner with a blanket around his shoulders was Thomas. His long blond hair hung swung as he moved his head to look up at Massaquoit, his face expressionless.

"Here he is," Wequashcook said. "Let my brother speak to you in his own words."

Lionel Osprey took a step forward so that he stood between Wequashcook and Thomas. He held his thick arm out with its palm toward Massaquoit.

"Your brother can wait a moment," he said.

"I want to hear what Matthew has to say," Nathaniel said. His voice quavered as he sought to inform it with an authority beyond his years and experience. Lionel bowed in a gesture that could be seen either as acknowledging the young officer's position or condescending to an inexperienced boy trying to be a man.

"And you shall, Captain, if it pleases you to wait until I hear from this one." Lionel pointed toward Thomas, who seemed to shrink back farther into the corner.

"Osprey, I think Thomas has had quite enough to deal with, do you not?"

Lionel ran his hand slowly through his thick hair, and then lifted it where it lay over his forehead. An angry red scar ran between and above his eyebrows.

"He is not the only one who has had his fill these past days," he said. "As you know well enough, I came very close to losing the top of my head."

"And you know who stopped the hand with the hatchet in it." Wequashcook's voice filled the tent for the moment. "It would be good for you to remember that."

"Aye. It was you. I confess it. But I am not sure that on another day you might have had that hatchet in your own hand." He walked to Thomas and heaved him up by his arms. "Now, lad, just a word from you." He pointed at Massaquoit. "Did that one over there capture you?"

Thomas shook his head.

"Did he offer you any violence?" Nathaniel asked.

Again Thomas shook his head.

"Are you not satisfied?" Nathaniel said to Osprey.

"As well as I can be. But I tell you, Captain, you are advised to trust none of these savages. Listen to me, sir. I have seen them and what they can do. Here and in Jamestown before, where I was with Captain John Smith."

"So I have heard you tell my father, many times."

"The iteration does not make what I say the less true."

"Do you have need of me?" Massaquoit asked. "I grow weary and cold standing in the entrance to your tent, like a poor dog waiting to be fed or beaten."

"You know what you are, then, do you?" Lionel said.

Massaquoit took the man's measure. In one way, he was not so different from men he had encountered before the English arrived, Indian men who asserted dominance with words. The difference with this English bully was that his vehemence was activated by the skin color of his adversary. In time, Massaquoit thought, I will make answer, but not now.

Nathaniel rose from his cot, a slow, almost languorous, unfolding of his long, thin body. His head brushed the ceiling of the tent and he had to stoop a little. He looked at Thomas, and his expression softened into tenderness.

"Thomas says you saved his life." He turned to the trio of Wequashcook, Osprey, and Massaquoit, who stood within an uneasy foot of each other. "William, of course, agrees with that account while Osprey, whose judgment I must respect, expresses doubts. He thinks that you, Matthew, are not to be trusted, that you have somehow, I know not how, placed Thomas, who is a sensitive youth, in your power and have thus gained control of his tongue."

"I can take you to where a dead Iroquois lies hardening in the snow, but—" Massaquoit began.

"Into a trap, I warrant," Osprey cut in.

Massaquoit continued as though he had not been interrupted.

"It would not be a good idea. His companions may have come back for him."

"The murderous dogs," Lionel said.

"Are they not the very ones we seek?" Nathaniel asked.

"No," Massaquoit said. "They are not."

"Traders," Wequashcook added. "Those Iroquois have finished their business and will be on their way back to the French in Montreal. Unless—" He shrugged as though hesitant to express the obvious.

"Unless," Massaquoit finished the thought, "they now seek him who killed their friend."

Nathaniel looked from one to the other as though weighing the credibility of each.

"We will set careful guard tonight," he said. "They may be traders as you say, and if so, they have nothing to fear from us, or we from them. Or they may be the ones who murdered Isaac Powell."

"It was no Indian killed that old man," Massaquoit said, and Wequashcook looked at him as though he had betrayed a confidence they shared.

"Do you mean that he cut off his own hand, and then tried to lift his own scalp, holding the hatchet in his bloody stump?" Lionel Osprey asked.

"At another time, in another place, I can speak of these matters, but I tell you no Indian killed Isaac Powell."

"So say you," Lionel sneered.

"I do," Massaquoit maintained.

"Leave us now," Nathaniel said, his eyes on the young man still on his haunches in the corner. He beckoned him to rise.

"Thomas stays here with me. To recover from his ordeal."

Massaquoit felt the short, stout English man coming up behind him as he stood on the same crest he had occupied

with Wequashcook that afternoon. In front of him, two nervous young English soldiers, no more than boys, stood
resting their long pikes on their shoulders, blades glinting
faintly in the weak light of the moon. The temperature had
continued to fall in the hours after sunset, and a stiff, bit-
ing wind had risen, chilling anybody not near a warming
fire. Massaquoit pulled his blanket about him, and observed
how English soldiers held themselves, so stiffly and crip-
pled with anxiety that it was unlikely they would be able
to react to an enemy, even one that strolled before them
with deliberate and slow-moving menace. The man now
breathing heavily after his climb, however, was another
story. Massaquoit fully realized the violent capabilities, and
talents, of Lionel Osprey, who now nudged his arm hard
enough to cause him to struggle to regain his footing on
the ice-encrusted ground.

"I can relieve you," he said, "so you can warm yourself with your brother in his tent."

Massaquoit pointed to the shivering soldiers. Neither had
turned at Osprey's approach, and only now did the one on
the right slowly swing around, his teeth chattering to challenge the newcomer.

"They are the ones who need to be relieved. I await the
dawn."

Osprey pulled his heavy coat tight about him as a blast
of frigid wind cut through the small group. The two young
soldiers struggled to steady themselves and to maintain
something like a military posture, even while their shoulders shook so hard they could scarcely keep their pikes
steady. Massaquoit turned his side to the wind and clenched
his teeth. He took note of how Osprey's thick hand held
his coat together at the spot where it was missing a button.

"I pulled that coat off a dead man," Massaquoit said. "I

would not wear it if I had nothing else and the north wind was blowing even harder than it is now."

"Savage superstition," Osprey said. "The dead mean nothing to me."

"His spirit—" Massaquoit began.

"You must have missed Minister Davis talking about how in his learned opinion you savages have no more soul than a hog."

"And no less."

Osprey squinted his eyes into a scowl.

"I must have lost my senses in this cold, to be talking theology with such as you."

"Still that coat does not warm you, although I have held it in my hand and it is a fine, heavy coat."

"It is no more than the wind."

"The wind, too, is a spirit. Along with those of the dead."

Osprey shrugged and stepped past Massaquoit to the two soldiers. He put his hands on their shoulders, turned them around, and pushed them, none too gently, in the direction of the camp. They started walking, slipping now and then on the ice as they balanced their heavy pikes.

"It's you and me then, Matthew," Osprey said. "I've sent those poor lambs home."

Massaquoit nodded. "If we both try to watch the night through, sooner or later we will not see anything. The cold and weariness will be a blanket in front of our eyes."

"Do you propose we take turns, then? And how do I know I can trust you?"

"Stay awake yourself, then," Massaquoit replied. "If they are going to come, it will be near dawn. I will sleep now."

While Osprey stared at him without comprehension, Massaquoit knelt before a snow drift of about six feet. He scraped away the hard crust toward the bottom, and then scooped out the softer snow behind it until he had carved out a space just large enough to accommodate his body. Wrapping his blanket around himself, he worked his way in. He closed his eyes and smiled as he heard Osprey's muttered cursing and the crunch of his shoes on the snow. He knew it would not be long.

Osprey, however, was more stubborn than Massaquoit had figured, and it was over an hour before he stood before the snow bank.

"Matthew," he said, "for God's love—"

Massaquoit rolled out of the drift and looked up at Osprey.

"No," he said, "not for the love of your English God." He stood up and beckoned for Osprey to take his place.

Osprey shook his head, but crawled into the space.

After a while, Osprey's breathing became regular, and then he began to snore. Massaquoit moved away from him into the shadow of the trees. He did not expect the Iroquois to attack, but if they did out of anger at the death of their comrade, it would be better for them to find this fat English pig first. He did not intend to wake him up to ask for relief. The wind was blowing from the camp toward the Iroquois. He found a thick oak and crouched in front of it so that its trunk sheltered him from the wind while his position still afforded him an unobstructed view of the possible breaks in the woods through which an attacking band might come. He waited, motionless and alert, willing his body to ignore the cold that made his bones feel brittle enough to snap if he moved too quickly. Just above the steady roar of the wind, he heard a faint howl. It continued for a few moments, seemed to move farther away, and then disappeared.

The snores coming from the sleeping Englishman had settled into a steady, low hum that barely reached Massaquoit in his position in front of the tree. The howl began again, this time louder and closer. It pierced the cold air, sending ripples of plaintive sound through the trees, and the wind rose in its own intensity to combine with the cry of the hungry animal. Wind and animal howl reached a crescendo and then stopped. After a few moments, the wind roared again, but the animal remained silent.

The wind died for a moment and the woods were silent, too silent, Massaquoit realized, for he did not hear the snoring of the Englishman. He stood up and stretched the cold-engendered stiffness out of his muscles. He listened hard. He heard a dull, crunching sound, and he knew that the English man had rolled out of his snow burrow and was coming toward him. He relaxed and waited for the steps to arrive. They passed a few feet away from him, and then stopped.

"Matthew," Osprey whispered. "Where are you?"

Massaquoit stepped toward the voice.

"Here," he said.

Osprey turned toward him, his arm extended, holding his pistol.

"Did you not hear it?" he asked.

"Of course," Massaquoit replied.

Osprey waved the pistol in the direction from which the howling had come. As if in answer, the animal began raising its plaintive cry.

"He's closer," Osprey said.

"I do not think so," Massaquoit answered.

Osprey steadied his pistol as though to fire it. Massaquoit stepped in front of him.

"Step aside," Osprey said. "A shot will keep the beast away."

"Maybe, but it will also tell any Iroquois scout exactly where we are." He pointed through a break in the trees to the east, where the first glimmer of the sun could be seen. "Leave the wolf to find the Iroquois."

Osprey nodded, and he started back toward the camp.

He had not gone more than ten steps when a shout came from that direction followed by more voices raised in a confused uproar.

Osprey urged his short legs into a trot. Massaquoit saw that the English man had again drawn his pistol and so he followed at a safe distance behind. They arrived in the camp to find soldiers rubbing their eyes and stumbling about, some with pikes or muskets, others unarmed. Half a dozen were gathered in front of Nathaniel's tent. Osprey headed toward them.

"Lieutenant," a soldier called to him. "Murder." He pointed toward the tent. Another soldier looked into the darkness beyond the tent. Osprey ran clumsily until he reached the second soldier, peered in the direction he was looking, raised his pistol, and pulled the trigger. The sound echoed through the camp and brought everyone to a stunned halt.

"Go see," Osprey said to the soldier. Without much enthusiasm, the soldier gripped his long pike, thrust it in front of him, and walked into the darkness. Osprey did not wait for him to report, but instead stooped and crawled through the flap.

When Massaquoit reached the tent, Osprey emerged.

"Have a look inside," he said.

Massaquoit waited for him to step out of the way. He pulled back the flap. Nathaniel lay on the floor. Blood ran out of the wound on his chest, leaving a dark red circle on his white shirt. A knife was on the ground next to him. A gray-haired soldier, with a full and unruly beard, pressed his hands on the wound. He looked at Osprey, and then held up his hands, palm out, to show the lieutenant how red they were.

"Do what you can, man," Osprey said, and the soldier again pressed his hands on top of the wound, which nonetheless continued to ooze bright red blood. In the corner, also bleeding from wounds on his leg and arm, was Thomas. He moaned as Massaquoit approached him, and then he lapsed into unconsciousness.

The back wall of the tent had been slit in two places. Massaquoit pulled the fabric apart. It spread only six or eight inches, and no more than a foot in length. The sun now lit the ground behind the tent. Massaquoit looked, but he did not expect to see the assailant, and he did not. He was about to let the torn fabric fall back into place when something dark lying on the white snow caught his eye. He shook his head and pulled the torn canvas together.

Osprey was at his shoulder.

"Did you see anything?"

"Nothing but the snow."

"There are tracks out there."

"Many tracks," Massaquoit said, "from many English feet. But I will go out and look more closely."

"That is the way, Matthew," Osprey said. "I have to tend these two."

Massaquoit walked deliberately out of the tent and circled to the rear. He made a show of kneeling at the point where the wall was ripped and looking at the footprints in the snow. Two soldiers watched him, and he rewarded them by lowering his head to an inch or two above the ground. One soldier nudged the other. Massaquoit got down on his knees and crawled about until the soldiers lost interest in him and joined the others waiting for news at the entrance to the tent.

Massaquoit stood up and without haste walked to the dark object protruding through the snow. He bent down and picked up a beaver hat. He looked around before standing up, and as he did, he slid the hat beneath his blanket.

SEVEN

JOSEPH WOOLSEY WAS waiting in front of the meeting-house as Catherine made her way through the drifts raised by the strong winds of the night before. She fought to catch her breath, and her lungs complained as she drew in the cold air. Phyllis, also breathing hard, labored behind her.

"Catherine, did you hear them all the night?" Woolsey asked. "People do say the witches held a sabbat in the woods last night."

"Do you mean the wolves?" she asked.

"I mean the devilish howling that everybody heard."

"I warrant even the devil would not venture out on such a bitter cold night," she replied.

"Catherine, it would be well for you not to utter such blasphemies," Woolsey said.

"Indeed, I heard such a noise that I was afeard and could not sleep the whole night," Phyllis put in.

"You must surely have dreamed your fear," Catherine told her.

"Why, I did not. I recall it very well."

"But it was I who did not sleep well last night, and as I walked by your room, I did hear you snoring."

"In fear, I say."

"Yes, no doubt," Catherine replied.

"It is time, I am afraid," Woolsey said, and he helped Catherine through the last drift before the steps of the meeting house.

They mounted the steps and paused before the door.

"I am indeed sorry for this," he said, indicating the door, and those waiting inside.

Catherine put her hand on the knob. The cold of the iron radiated through the thin cloth of her glove.

"It cannot be helped. I did what I ought to save the babe, as God is my witness."

"Aye, God, but He is not going to be called as witness."

The rejoinder, almost blasphemous by the strict Puritan standards of Newbury, surprised and amused Catherine, and she started to smile. But a more serious thought froze her lips.

"Is this not God's house?" she asked.

"Yes, of course," he responded.

"And who is inside today?"

"Ah, Catherine, well you know."

"Is it not passing strange how God's house is so quickly transformed into a place where man's justice is served?"

The thought furrowed Woolsey's brow as he tried to find a compartment in his well-ordered brain in which to place it. Failing to do so, he reddened and began to stammer a reply.

"Never mind, Joseph," Catherine said. "Another time, perhaps. They wait for us." She pulled the door open.

Inside, she saw Governor Peters leaning his long arms on a table placed in front of the pulpit. His heavy cloak was bundled about him against the chill of the drafty and unheated building. Catherine stepped toward him, and felt the cold wind blowing across the empty benches. Master and Mistress Worthington, flanking Daniel Rowland, sat on the frontmost bench, occupied during service by the most prominent male citizens. Their breaths hung in the air in front of their faces. On the same bench, but a few feet from her betters, was Goody Blodgett.

Catherine took a seat across from the Worthingtons. Catherine eyed each in turn and noted how Goody Blodgett would not meet her glance, while Samuel returned her stare with his customary arrogance. Alice Worthington's eyes expressed regret and impotence, and Daniel alternated looking at the governor and his father-in-law, as though unsure which of these masters he should obey this day if they chose to differ. Phyllis took a seat on a bench several rows back.

Woolsey held Catherine's shoulder for a moment before taking his place next to the governor at the table. Peters acknowledged his presence with a nod, and then held out his right hand, palm up, toward Samuel.

"Mistress Williams has arrived, in the company of my distinguished colleague, Magistrate Woolsey."

"And therein we have a problem," Worthington said, almost before the governor was finished. "For too long Mistress Williams has been shielding herself behind one man or another, first her husband, and now her husband's surrogate."

Woolsey took a deep breath.

"Worthington, you forget yourself," he said.

"Indeed, I do not." He shrugged. "But well enough. That is not our present purpose, which is to question Mistress Williams's practice of midwifery, to the extreme danger of my grandson, who even now clings to his life."

Catherine looked at her old adversary, not surprised, for she had long ago reconciled herself to the simple fact that Samuel Worthington was one of those creatures God endowed with a nature both stubborn and vindictive, as though to represent how base human nature could be when not admixed with His grace. From the moment she had recognized the fragile condition of Felicity's babe, she had known that Samuel would try to lay the onus on her. The sad thing, she realized, was that the man did not recognize his own bias, and believed he was acting in the interest of justice rather than from small-minded antagonism. At the moment, however, none of this mattered. Whatever his motivation, Master Worthington was making a very serious charge, against which she would have to offer a vigorous defense.

"And where is the child's mother?" Catherine asked.

"At home. This does not concern her," Worthington responded.

"Does it not? Was she not there when I delivered her babe?"

"She was insensible then, and now remembers nothing of that night."

"So says she?"

"Yes, and so I represent."

"Wondrous father," Catherine began.

"Mistress, your tongue," Governor Peters interjected.

"Wondrous father," Catherine repeated, "to so know the heart and mind of his daughter that he can so speak for her."

"No wonder, Mistress," Samuel said, "when a child is raised with a proper respect for her father, her governor, and her God."

Catherine started to comment on the order of worship but stopped herself. In this place, among these men, she was probably the only one to note the reversal of the usual notions of power flowing down from God, through the secular authority to the man as head of household, a hierarchy that had never made particular sense to her, although she recognized its pervasive influence.

"If it pleases you, then," Catherine said, "what charge do you impute to me?"

Worthington looked at Goody Blodgett.

"I know not these women's matters, such as birthing a child. To that, Goody Blodgett can testify. I can only affirm the result, which is a sickly babe I thought we would bury ere now, if it were not for Goody Blodgett's ministrations after Mistress Williams was discharged."

Catherine clenched her jaws to stay the words of rebuttal that rose in her throat. Instead, she looked to Joseph. Woolsey cleared his throat loudly, a mannerism that she knew announced his intention to say something portentous.

"Master Worthington," he said, "you claim to know naught of these matters, and yet you have concluded that Mistress Williams is the cause of your grandson's distress, and you rest your conviction on the word of another woman whose art is as mysterious to you as is that of Mistress Williams. Is that not so?"

Catherine relaxed her jaws and uttered a silent thank you to her old friend, who had raised his arm toward Worthington as he finished his question, and now waved his hand as though to encourage an answer.

"I speak only of the result," Worthington said. "Goody Blodgett can attest the cause."

"Goody Blodgett, then," Governor Peters. "Can you do so?"

Goody Blodgett rose slowly to her feet and looked at the powerful men who now demanded her testimony. She shifted from one foot to another, and when she spoke, her voice was barely a whisper.

"That what I seen Mistress Williams do is"—she paused as though to remember what came next in a prepared speech, and then continued—"contrary to the usual practices of midwifery." She twisted her face in concentration. "Causing the babe to be born before its time."

"And what were those practices?" Governor Peters asked.

Goody Blodgett blushed.

"I am unable to say."

"What, woman?" Woolsey demanded. "Come you here with such a charge, and you cannot say?"

"It would not be right and proper. It is fit I tell this to a woman who would understand me rightly."

"But," Peters interjected, "the only woman here is the one you accuse. Surely, you do not expect Mistress Williams to lend credence to your accusation against her."

"Pardon, sir," Goody Blodgett said with a thrust of her jaw. "She would if she spoke truth."

"And what would I say?" Catherine asked.

Worthington rose and held out a feather.

"This was on the floor after the babe was born. Goody Blodgett can testify to it being shoved down my daughter's throat to force her travail, a cruel and unnatural procedure that causes much harm." He looked at Goody Blodgett. "Speak, woman. The governor has demanded the specifics that are in your power to reveal, not mine. All I know is that my daughter, more precious to me than any but my wife and son, was delivered of a babe by Mistress Williams, and then fell into a fever that nearly put her in the ground, where I expect any moment to see the poor babe interred. The result, therefore, is clear. You must provide the cause."

Goody Blodgett, who had sat back down after her brief statement, relieved not to have to say more, now rose reluctantly to her feet.

"The truth is that the birth was not dangerous—" she began. Worthington looked at her as though his eyes were daggers, and she stopped. "Not dangerous until Mistress Williams arrived. And then she had Felicity drink a tea made from I know not what, but no doubt some evil potion, instead of the blue cohosh that all midwives know would bring on proper pains. And then the feather to cause gagging—why, I never saw such a thing before." She paused to gather her breath. "Then there is what she did to that poor girl's breasts, which I was treating right and proper with honey. There, now I have said it. Let it be there in the air in front of us all."

"My daughter," interjected Worthington, "cannot give the babe suck, and it languishes. Her breasts are ruined by Mistress Williams cutting them. I ask you, is it right and proper midwifery to cut open a woman's breasts?"

Governor Peters and Magistrate Woolsey stared hard at Catherine, and she had to think how little these men knew concerning these matters. Worthington, even if he spoke only out of genuine and immediate concern for his grandson, and not out of ancient grievances against her and her husband, still saw only a sickly babe whose mother could not nourish it. So, he looked for someone to blame, and she was available as a target for his anger. The other two men knew only that birthing was a dangerous business, sometimes for the mother and sometimes for the babe, and sometimes both died, and they were then bereft of wives and children. Further, they were men who saw God's heavy hand in all matters of this world, and this encouraged them even more to look outside themselves for the source of their losses. Blame the midwife, or some poor old hag that they could call a witch, or anybody but themselves, for they could not countenance the thought that an angry God was punishing them for their transgressions by taking their loved ones from them. No, much better to think that God was using their loved ones as innocent victims to show His displeasure with somebody handy, like the midwife, and then they could content themselves with their piety, and tell themselves that God had chosen to use this wife, or that babe, as a reminder of His terrible vengeance when His wrath was provoked by human frailty.

All of this, Catherine knew very well as she looked back

at the stern faces of her Puritan inquisitors, even that of her Joseph, whom she had known her whole life. He, too, would feel threatened and at sea when confronted by the mysteries of reproduction. And in his eyes, she saw a despairing look as he, along with the governor, awaited her answer. Well, then, she must educate them.

"She died else," she said with as much force and simple clarity as she could muster, short of shouting this truth to the high roof of the meetinghouse.

"Aye," Worthington said. "She surely would have died. From your ministrations."

Governor Peters, who had had his own disagreements with Catherine in the past and whose business interests were deeply entangled with Worthington's, leaned forward, his head tilted as though to hear more. He looked at Catherine.

"Does it please you now to give me leave to speak?" Catherine asked.

Governor Peters nodded his head slowly.

"All that Goody Blodgett says is true, true I used a tea to relax Felicity when she was worn to exhaustion with an unprofitable travail, true that after she rested I caused her to gag with a feather, an unusual procedure that Goody Blodgett in her limited experience would not have seen, and true that after the babe was born and Felicity's breast turned red and painful from bad blood, I opened it, which I did but to permit the bad blood to escape. And then she did mend."

"The honey?" Governor Peters asked.

Catherine glanced at Goody Blodgett. Even though the woman was impugning her reputation, and threatening her profession as midwife, she could not find it in her heart to be truly angry or vengeful. The woman was weak, in need because of her husband's illness, and she had been bought by Worthington. She turned back to Peters.

"A good remedy for certain problems. But not in this case."

"Would it not have sufficed?" the governor asked.

"It would not have. Indeed, I taught Goody Blodgett that remedy."

"Then perhaps you should have listened to your student," Worthington said.

Catherine was about to respond, when the muffled sound of drums worked its way through the walls of the meetinghouse, and all eyes turned in the direction of the sound.

"The troops must be returning," Governor Peters said. "I pray with fair news."

The drumbeat got louder and louder. All inside were quiet, their eyes on the door. It swung open. There stood Osprey, and next to him Massaquoit. Worthington took a couple of quick steps toward the door and stopped. He peered hard at Osprey.

"Nathaniel?" he asked.

Osprey turned and pointed behind him where four soldiers stood, each holding one corner of a litter on which lay the young officer. Behind him, on another litter, was Thomas. He tried to rise, but could do no more than support himself on one elbow as he stretched his other arm toward Nathaniel. Then he let himself fall back flat onto the litter. It rocked for a moment until the soldiers supporting it could restore its equilibrium. The soldiers carried both litters inside the meetinghouse and set them down on the floor. A rush of cold air accompanied them.

"Shut the door," Governor Peters ordered.

One soldier went to do the governor's bidding. He shut the door, and the litters were in darkness. Worthington made his way toward the litter where his son lay. He walked with uncertain step as though he knew that he did not want his eyes to confirm what he already feared was true. Before

he could reach his son's side, Osprey placed his bulky body
in his path.

"There was nothing we could do," Osprey said. "The
savages slipped into his tent. Cut them both up."

"Is he dead?"

"No, not yet," Osprey said. "But I believe he is beyond
help. I have seen many hurt like him."

"But my son," Worthington said, "my son." And he
pushed by Osprey, who stepped aside rather than offer any
further resistance. Alice followed her husband. Father and
mother stood looking down on their son.

"None of them lived," Osprey continued, as though he
had not been interrupted, and then under his breath, "nor
will he."

Worthington, though, was not listening to Osprey. He
was kneeling at his son's side, holding his hand, and pressing his ear to the young man's lips. He stayed in that position for several moments, and then his eyes filled with
hope.

"He still breathes," he said. He rose to his feet and
turned back to the governor and Woolsey, who were now
standing next to Osprey. "Call the surgeon."

"He is at Niantic," the governor said.

"Niantic?" Worthington's tone was incredulous. "When
my son lies here dying?"

"He was called to tend the sachem there, a goodly Christian man he is, even if he is a savage," Woolsey said.

Worthington got to his feet and grabbed Massaquoit's
arm.

"You, then, go. To Niantic. Bring back the surgeon."

Catherine, who had been left standing alone, pushed her
way past Osprey and approached the litter. Alice stepped
aside to let her lean over Nathaniel. She placed one hand
on his forehead, and the other on his chest where the blood
had dried on his shirt. She held her hand there until she

detected a faint heartbeat. When she lifted her hand it was warm with fresh blood.

"Can you—?" Alice began.

"I do not know," Catherine said. "But I can surely try."

"Have you not done enough to my family?" Worthington said. "Be gone with you."

Catherine looked at him, and then at Alice, who nodded for Catherine to stay.

"Phyllis," Catherine called, "hasten home and return with my comfrey poultice. You know where to find it."

"That I do," Phyllis said and she bustled toward the door, pausing just for a second to stare hard at Worthington, but just then Thomas moaned and the merchant turned in that direction. Catherine saw his expression harden. Massaquoit inched toward the door. He felt the tension among these English rising. Catherine noted his movement. "You go with her, Matthew."

Catherine kept her hand on Nathaniel's wound. Then there was a stir in the column of soldiers who still stood before the door. They separated to permit a young woman to pass. She was followed by another holding a babe wrapped in a blanket.

"Oh, Nathaniel," Felicity cried, and stumbled to her brother's side. She took his hand and squeezed, but the young man did not respond. She cast her eyes from her father, to her mother, and finally to Catherine.

"Father. You must permit Mistress Williams to tend Nathaniel. She saved my life." She looked toward Goody Blodget. "That one was more like to let me die."

"Felicity," Worthington said, "I told you to stay at home. You are not well. You know not what you say."

"I heard the drum. I looked out the window. I could not see who was being carried, and yet I knew. I summoned Elizabeth, and she carried my babe here, even though she knew she would earn your wrath for so doing."

"Aye, and that she has," Worthington said.

"Samuel," Alice said, "listen to your daughter. The surgeon is half a day away, and your son lies here. Go you and seek Minister Davis, and permit Mistress Williams to tend Nathaniel. I know well enough that she saved Felicity's life."

Governor Peters frowned.

"Mistress, why then did you not so testify?"

She looked at her husband.

"He forbade me, but I am not sure I would have held my tongue after hearing the untruths coming from Goody Blodgett's mouth."

Nathaniel's litter now lay on the table behind which the governor and Woolsey had been sitting. Catherine stroked his forehead with one hand while continuing to apply pressure to his wound with the other. The table was just long enough to hold the one litter, so Thomas was still on the floor. Catherine glanced down at him. His wounds were serious but not mortal, slashes on his left arm and leg, as though he had been trying to defend himself from a blade that hacked at him. His moans were barely audible, and saliva dribbled from his open mouth. Catherine covered him with a thin blanket, but still he shivered in the drafts of cold air that swirled about his thin body.

"He should be lifted off the cold floor," Catherine said, but Worthington shook his head.

"Leave him be. It was him that ran away. And my fool son had to go after him. Leave him be, I say."

"Samuel," Governor Peters said, "the boy may be the cause but perhaps he can disclose the attackers."

"Why, we know that," Worthington replied, "the savages, as Lieutenant Osprey says."

"Yet, we can profit by confirmation," the governor said, and without waiting for further reply, he motioned to two soldiers who lifted Thomas's litter and placed it on the foremost bench. Thomas lolled his head, opened his eyes, and grimaced in pain. Worthington watched with a scowl on his face.

"He will live," he said. He turned to his son and lowered his head.

A blast of cold air announced the opening of the meetinghouse door, and it was followed first by Massaquoit, who took one step inside and then stood aside, and then by Phyllis, who bustled in, a small jar clutched between her hands. She made her way straight to Catherine and held out the jar. Catherine looked at her own hand, still pressed on Nathaniel's wound.

"Yes, I see," Phyllis said. She pulled the stopper out of the jar and wrapped a clean cloth about her index finger, which she inserted into the jar and rotated until the cloth was well coated with the comfrey poultice. She handed the cloth to Catherine. Catherine tore Nathaniel's shirt, which she had been using as a compress against the wound running deep and wide across the young man's chest. She packed the wound with the poultice, pressing it firmly between the edges of the jagged skin. As she worked, she looked at his eyes. She knew the pressure of her hand in the wound should be causing pain, perhaps sufficient to produce a response, and perhaps that response would enable him to cling to life a little longer. She had no greater hope. She pulled his shirt back over the wound and then covered him with a blanket provided by one of the soldiers.

His eyes opened, bright and clear, and he began to move his lips.

"Thomas," he said.

"He is here," Catherine replied. "He is hurt, but not badly."

"Thomas," he said again, but he made no effort to follow Catherine's hand, which was pointing toward Thomas. "Thomas is . . . my friend. I love—" He stopped as though unable to continue, but Catherine noted that his breathing seemed, for the moment, a little stronger. Out of the corner of her eye, she saw Osprey advancing toward her.

"He should be quiet and save his strength, should he not, Mistress?" the lieutenant asked.

"He wants to speak, and we must let him," Catherine replied.

"My friend I love as I should . . ." Nathaniel said, his voice barely audible, and his chest heaved.

Osprey, now at Nathaniel's side, blocking Catherine, leaned over, and cupped his hand to his ear.

"What's that, lad?" he said. "What's that?" he said again, and his voice, louder than it needed to be, swallowed the sounds barely escaping from Nathaniel's lips.

"What says he?" Catherine demanded, but Osprey did not reply. There was silence and Osprey stood up.

"He has done, Mistress," he said.

"Thomasine," came from Nathaniel, and then he closed his eyes, his breathing barely perceptible now. Osprey stepped aside to permit Master Worthington to take his place at his son's side.

"Is there hope?" the merchant asked.

Catherine shook her head slowly from side to side.

"I think we have heard his last word, the name of his intended."

"Aye," Osprey said pointing to Thomas, "that one's sister."

The door opened again, and Minister Davis, his short, rotund figure well wrapped in a heavy cloak held before his face, hurried in. He took one look around the meetinghouse, over which a funereal silence had now descended, and stepped to Worthington's side. He looked down at

Nathaniel, squeezed the merchant's arm, and knelt beside
the young man.

"We must pray," he said. "The Lord is my shepherd,"
he began, and soon, one by one, the other watchers moved
their lips, repeating the words articulated by the minister.
Catherine, as was her wont, closed her eyes and concentrated her thoughts on a silent prayer of her own while she
mouthed the familiar words.

She kept one hand on Nathaniel's chest, feeling the feeble beating of his heart as it became fainter and fainter.
When it stopped, she opened her eyes, stood up, and motioned for Minister Davis to cease. She pulled the blanket
up over the young man's face.

Worthington's sob filled the meetinghouse. Alice's grief
shook her body, and she embraced Felicity. Elizabeth approached mother and daughter and held out the babe, who,
in perfect innocence, opened its eyes from its nap and
yawned.

Nathaniel lay covered by the blanket while his family sat,
heads bowed, on a bench in front of the table. Thomas was
drifting in and out of consciousness. When he was awake,
he moaned and tried to rise from his litter to approach
Nathaniel. He could not be made to understand that his
friend was dead. Catherine had dressed his wounds again.
He would be well enough in a few days.

He now awoke and sat up. His eyes were clearer, and
he seemed more alert.

"Nathaniel?" he asked.

Worthington pointed to his son.

"There. Dead."

Thomas looked at the still body and said nothing. Catherine watched him closely. She had expected an outburst of
grief, and so his silence was puzzling. For a moment, she
attributed it to the trauma of his wounds.

"It would be well for him to be put into a proper bed," she said.

"Not in my house," Worthington said.

"Take him to mine, then," Woolsey said. "I have more than enough room, and my serving-girl can make him comfortable until Mistress Williams can see to him." He motioned to the soldiers who had carried Thomas into the meetinghouse. "Pick him up." He did not wait for an answer, but walked to the door. The soldiers hoisted their burden up and followed. Worthington rose to his feet.

"Aye, take the quick one, and we will take ours home." He beckoned to Osprey, who motioned to the remaining soldier to take one end of the litter. The lieutenant walked to the other end, but before he could start to lift it, Worthington gestured for him to stand back, and the merchant took his place.

"I will carry my son," he said. "I could not keep him alive, but I will tend to him now."

Alice flanked the litter on one side, and Felicity, carrying her babe, the other. Elizabeth made to join them, but at a scowl from the merchant, she retreated to sit with Phyllis. The minister took his place at the head of the litter, and the small procession made its way to the door, which Massaquoit opened for them, and Minister Davis nodded as he walked out. Osprey had followed some distance behind the others, as though unsure what he should do once his master dispensed with his services. Massaquoit held the door ajar, and Osprey, with a shrug, walked through it. After he was outside, Massaquoit started to leave.

"Matthew," Governor Peters called out.

Massaquoit felt the hated English name as though it were a barb scratching his skin, and yet he stopped and turned back to the governor.

"I do not see William, your friend."

Massaquoit shrugged.

"I came here with the lieutenant."

"But William," the governor prodded.

"I did not see him."

"Was he not at the camp when Nathaniel was attacked?"

"I was with the lieutenant, keeping watch. I cannot tell you more."

"I see," Governor Peters said. He got up and made his way to the door, pausing in front of Massaquoit. "We will hear more of this, but this is not the time."

Massaquoit watched him walk out into the darkness. He had his hand clenched around the object he wanted to give to Catherine for safekeeping. He expected to hear the heavy door clunk against the frame as it was shut, but he did not. Instead, he heard a murmur of voices, one of them surely the governor's. He thought he recognized the other, but he was not certain. He hesitated; then the idea struck him that it did not matter who the other person was, and further, whether that person saw him deliver the object to Catherine. In a way, that might turn out to be a good thing. He approached Catherine and held out his hand.

"Take this," he said. As he spoke, he felt a cold breeze strike his back, and he knew the door had been opened wide enough for somebody to look in. He glanced toward the door, and then turned back to Catherine. He opened his hand and gave her the brass button.

Then he walked down the aisle to the door, which was now almost fully shut. As he walked out, he heard footsteps crunching the crust of the snow, and he saw a short, squat figure disappearing into the shadows. He smiled to himself and walked off.

EIGHT

THIS TIME WEQUASHCOOK was waiting for Massaquoit in the deserted camp in the swamp. The weather had warmed, and the melting snow had penetrated the top layer of soil, turning it into muddy slush. Massaquoit saw a thin spire of smoke rise from the wigwam, and he slogged through the mire toward it. Wequashcook acknowledged his presence with the slightest lifting of his eyes and then resumed his position huddled about the fire, his blanket pulled over his head. The skinned body of a bony rabbit was roasting on a makeshift spit above the fire. Massaquoit tossed the beaver hat toward him.

"Without your hat you are like the turtle with his head sticking out of his shell," he said.

Wequashcook now raised his eyes and stared steadily at Massaquoit.

"I am thinking that I would crawl into a shell if I had one." He put his hat on and pulled it down over his ears. "It is not much to warm a head that might soon be at the end of an English pike or sitting on a post somewhere."

"That is why I have come to see you. So we can both keep our heads, although if it comes to that I will not seek a shell. The English will find out my head does not come cheap."

"Ah—" Wequasheosh shook his head. "Still the warrior, when that time has long past."

"No, not a warrior. Just a man. Like you were once."

Wequashcook stabbed the rabbit with his knife and removed it. He sliced a piece of its flank and held it out to Massaquoit.

"He was very thin, already dead and frozen when I found him, but his meat will still taste good to a hungry man."

Massaquoit waited for the charred flesh to cool, and then he bit into it. It was chewy and sour tasting and yet he savored it, for as usual he could not remember when he had last eaten a full meal. Wequashcook watched him eat, and then sliced off another piece for himself. For several moments they worked their jaws around the tough flesh without attempting further talk. A piece of the stringy meat caught between Wequashcook's teeth, and he pulled it free. He looked at it, as though contemplating whether to try chewing it again, then tossed it into the fire, where it sizzled and then twisted in the flame.

"Tastes bad," he said. "It must have been an English rabbit." He offered another slice of meat. Massaquoit took it.

"I have something to tell you," Wequashcook said.

"I hope so. I have gone to much trouble to hide your hat from the English after finding it outside the tent where that young man was killed."

"You do not think that I . . ."

"No. I do not think you would be so stupid, but I wonder that you were so careless."

"I felt it come off and blow in the wind toward an English soldier. He did not see it, and I waited for a chance to retrieve it. But then other soldiers came running and I slipped away. Before I did, I saw you and the lieutenant."

He paused, and then a sly smile formed on his thin lips. "I was confident you would recover my hat for me. You have had an interest in it in the past."

"Yes. It seems that when you misplace it, it is up to me to find it and return it."

"That is because you are the reason that I wear it. Maybe we should say we are brothers."

Massaquoit shook his head.

"I do not think so." He waited. "You have something to tell me?"

"You must find the young English, the one who tried to fight you in the meetinghouse, and then the one I saw later carrying a torch with his friends and come looking for you at your English woman's house."

"Why must I find him?"

"Because I saw him look out of that slit in the tent."

"Out?"

"You see what I am talking about. Yes, out. Then he squeezed through the opening and moved some distance away, so it would seem he joined the others when they came running. It was at his feet that my hat was taken by the wind, but he was not looking at the ground. His eyes were on the tent and then behind him at the other English. He was in that tent when the English were attacked."

"And you just happened to be outside."

Wequashcook's face darkened.

"Put aside your suspicions while I tell you a plain tale."

"Speak, then."

"You know that the English boy, the one they call Thomas, the one you brought back into the English camp, was staying with the English officer in his tent."

"Yes. The English seemed very desirous of getting him back."

"The English officer's father hired me to bring him back, and you, too, if I could."

"You were very ambitious."

Wequashcook shrugged.

"It is better that I came after you than the English alone, or with some other guide."

"You are traveling a good distance from the tent where you lost your hat."

"Not at all. For I felt I must see to the English officer's safety. If I could bring him back to his father, I would then be able to do business with the father. Once Thomas was in the tent, I was never far away. The English did not seem to care. They felt I was on their side for having brought the boy back."

"And you saw something?"

Wequashcook shook his head.

"I heard first. Three voices, at first not very loud, but then getting louder. Thomas and the officer."

"And the other?"

Wequashcook closed his eyes in concentration as though he were again hearing the voices.

"I cannot be sure. It was higher than the others, almost like a boy. I came closer and knelt at the back wall of the tent. Their voices were muffled by the canvas of the tent and the wind was picking up and blowing in my ears. I pressed my ear against the tent wall. Then the voices stopped and something came hard against the tent. I was knocked to the ground. When I got up I heard grunts and from time to time one or the other of them fell against the tent wall causing it to bulge out at that place. I was going to run to the front to see if I could stop what was going on, but before I could, a knife blade came slashing through that tent wall, not more than a hand away from my face. Then that English soldier poked his head out. I threw myself on the ground when I saw the canvas part, and he did not see me. After a few minutes, he ran out the front, and circled to the back of the tent. All the noise had finally awakened the English soldiers and I heard their feet crunching across the snow. That is when I ran away."

Massaquoit picked up the last piece of the rabbit, a pitiful, thin slab of flesh. He ripped it in half with his fingers and gave one piece to Wequashcook and bit into the other. When he was done chewing, he licked his fingers.

"You have not told me," he said, "what words you heard, or what you saw."

"I could make out only one or two words. Names. Maybe the same, maybe not. Sounded like 'Thomas' and then maybe the same name longer. I do not know who spoke it. Maybe both. For I heard it more than once."

"And did you see anything in the tent before the boy ran out?"

"I looked through the slit for only a second, just long enough to see Thomas with a knife in his hand, bleeding from his arm and his leg, and the officer lying on the ground. The boy was standing over both of them."

"And then?"

"Then I thought it wise to put some distance between me and whatever was going on in that tent, for you know as well as I that the English would blame us even when they kill each other. And as I hurried away, I almost ran into that young English soldier. I am sure he recognized me, but he did not try to stop me. He ran to the tent, looked in through the slit, and then went around to the front as other soldiers arrived."

"He will have an interesting story to tell," Massaquoit said.

Wequashcook nodded.

"Of course. That is why I am here, eating rotten rabbit and talking to you."

The Newbury cemetery sat on the crest of a low hill behind the meetinghouse. The hill was just high enough to provide an unobstructed view of the harbor a short way beyond the Worthington house. A huge maple, reaching over a hundred feet and spreading almost half that distance, occupied the side of the crest closest to the water. As a founding member of the community, Master Worthington had made clear his intention that his family, when the time came, would be interred in front of that tree, perhaps thinking that he and his descendants would therefore always be near the harbor that had provided his family with its substantial wealth.

It was toward this place, marked by a newly dug grave that a procession of townspeople now headed. They followed the coffin, a box crudely fashioned out of pine, balanced on two poles held beneath it. On either side of the pole supporting the front of the coffin were Lionel Osprey and Frank Mapleton. The rear pole was held by Master Worthington and Daniel Rowland. It was a terrible day to be outside for any purpose, as after a brief warming spell, a sharp cold wind along with a mounting snowstorm had begun to blow in off the water from the northeast. Worthington, who had waited impatiently for an opportunity to bury his son, had summoned Minister Davis as soon as the ground had thawed on the first warm day, and the funeral was planned for two days hence. However, on the appointed day, the weather turned sharply cold again, and a steady snow once again filled the air so that Catherine, just a few paces behind the coffin could barely make out the features of the pallbearers. Minister Davis, at the front of the line of mourners, had disappeared into the white wave driven by a frigid wind. Woolsey held onto Catherine's arm, not so much to guide her steps as to help him with his own as they trudged along. Immediately in front of her walked Alice and Felicity. Felicity, still weak, clung to her husband's arm, but she had already refused her mother's suggestion that she return to the warmth of her fire.

The procession had started from the Worthington house, worked its way to the town center, and now paused before the meetinghouse. Minister Davis walked to Master Worthington's side.

"What think you?" the merchant asked.

The minister looked up through the snow to the lowering gray sky.

"Let us proceed directly to the graveside," Minister Davis said.

"My thought as well," Worthington replied, "but keep you in mind what I have said to you."

"Have no fear," Davis said. He resumed his position at the head of the procession, and the mourners, who had stood uncomfortably huddled against the wind, now moved in a straggling line, around the meetinghouse and up the gentle slope of the hill toward the burial ground, which at this early period in Newbury's history contained no more than a dozen graves.

Eventually, the son's grave would be marked with granite in a manner commensurate with his father's wealth and social position. But all that waited to receive him today was a fresh and jagged scar in the brown earth standing out in stark contrast to the abiding crust of snow. As the procession neared the new grave, the sound of shovels scraping frozen earth rose into the frigid air. Snow hurled up from the grave blended with that which was pelting down. The sound and motion stopped, and the sexton, a burly man of about forty, red-faced and sweating in spite of the cold, climbed up and out of the newly dug hole, followed by his twelve-year-old son, thin as his father was wide, both of them fairly covered in wet snow that clung to their cloaks and the wool hats pulled down almost over their eyes. They had been laboring to shovel out the new snow as fast as it fell so that Nathaniel's cold body would not be received by the even colder snow. Now, they hoisted their shovels to their shoulders and retreated beneath the maple a respectful distance from the grave as Minister Davis took his place and prepared to speak.

The pallbearers made their way past the minister to the grave's edge. As their hands were occupied with holding the poles supporting the coffin, they could not shield their faces from the driving snow, and thus they proceeded rather like moles in a burrow, feeling their way with their feet over the uncertain ground. The sexton, sensing the possibility of an embarrassing and dangerous misstep by one or the other of the pallbearers beckoned to his son and they hurried back to stand next to the grave, the father in front, and the son on the side toward which the pallbearers were edging. Lionel stood firm, but Frank Mapleton's foot slipped at the very edge of the grave, and only the sexton's stout arm and quick reaction prevented all from tumbling in. For a moment, Frank leaned awkwardly against the sexton's chest while maintaining his tenuous hold on his corner of the coffin. The sexton pushed against him until he straightened, and then added his own strong hands to the front of the coffin, while his son grabbed hold of the rear, and all then managed to slide the clumsy box into the grave.

The wind had picked up and now howled through the branches of the maple across the otherwise barren field of the cemetery. The mourners shook against the cold and huddled toward each other for protection. Worthington looked toward the minister.

"Begin, if you will, Master Davis."

The minister pressed his hands together, and lifted his head. As he did, a sudden and strong gust rushed against him, and he stepped back, almost losing his balance. He steadied himself and looked again at Worthington.

"Go ahead, I say, from the book of Samuel. I will have those words spoken over my son."

Minister Davis nodded, but his eyes looked past the merchant to a figure emerging from behind the maple tree. Worthington followed his glance.

"He has no business here," Worthington said. "Osprey."

The lieutenant was already in full stride toward the tree where stood Thomas, leaning on a cane fashioned from an oak branch to support his injured leg. He did not move as the lieutenant approached, but shifted his eyes back and forth as though torn between his desire to witness the interment of his friend and his fear of the merchant's wrath as expressed in the threatening posture of Lieutenant Osprey. Osprey raised his hands as though to seize the young man, who crossed his arms in front of his head, as though expecting a blow. But just as the lieutenant lunged, he stopped and dropped his arms to his sides, his eyes looking past Thomas. Thomas uncovered his head, looked behind him in the same direction as the lieutenant, and then he retreated behind the tree and disappeared into the falling snow. Osprey returned to the knot of people.

"Now," Worthington said, "he is gone and cannot pollute this rite. Let him return to Sodom whence came he."

The minister's face tightened in disapproval.

"We are burying your son," he said. Worthington looked toward the tree behind which Thomas had disappeared and made no answer. The minister lifted his eyes. " 'And the king said unto Cushi, Is the young man Absalom safe?' " he intoned, his voice struggling to rise above the wind. Catherine, although she was no more than a couple of feet away, and although the minister's voice, a strong and resonant baritone that on Sundays rose from his plump body and filled the meetinghouse, could barely hear the words that were swallowed by the onrushing wind whose whoosh carried to the ears of the mourners only the cold message of the insensible winter storm. Again, Minister Davis paused. Worthington strode to him and lowered his face to his.

"Proceed, I say, or I will do the office myself. Do you not have the words in your memory locked?"

"I do," Davis said, although he had to clench his jaw to stop his teeth from chattering.

" 'And the king said unto Cushi,' " he repeated, " 'Is the young man Absalom safe? And Cushi answered, The enemies of my lord the king, and all that rise against thee to do thee hurt, be as that young man is. And the king was much moved, and went up to the chamber over the gate, and wept: and as he went, thus he said, O my son Absalom, my son, my son Absalom! Would God I had died for thee, O Absalom, my son, my son!' "

The wind, as though out of respect, ceased for the moments it took for Minister Davis to recite this passage, and as his voice now reached all the mourners it was joined by that of Master Worthington, who said the same words except each time the minister said the name of David's son, the merchant cried out the name of Nathaniel, his own child now in the grave at his feet, and when the words were uttered, the merchant bowed his head to his chest.

The mourners turned back down the hill, in their minds the words they had just heard, but in their ears the sound of shovels of dirt mixed with snow now thudding against the coffin. Catherine walked at the head of the procession, as the Worthington family and Minister Davis lingered at the graveside watching the sexton and his son ply their shovels. As she walked, she occupied her mind with speculations designed, in part, to keep her thoughts from the cold that clenched her bones. She thought of Thomas, and she thought of the merchant's choice of biblical passage, and she remembered how Absalom had risen against his father. She wondered why Worthington had chosen such a text. Was it because in pursuing Thomas, Nathaniel had rebelled against his father's wishes? Or was it only the heart-wrenching cry of King David, grieving for his dead son that seemed fitting to Worthington?

Why, she asked herself, as she trudged down the hill, had the merchant conjoined a reference to Sodom to his father's lament over his dead son? If Worthington were David, and Nathaniel Absalom, where did Thomas fit? For although she could not yet figure out these connections, Worthington's insistence on that passage being hurled into the teeth of what was now clearly a late winter blizzard must carry some significance.

Colliding with these nebulous speculations in her mind was the hard roundness of the object entrusted to her by Massaquoit. That button, and the man who had lost it, now pushing his sturdy body, head bowed into the wind, like a ship's prow cutting a high sea, must be the key that would enable her to weave together the various strands now so stubbornly separated in her mind.

No more than fifty feet from the grave, on the bottom of the far side of the hill, Thomas huddled beneath the lowest branches of a spruce. The wet snow layered the limbs of the tree so that they drooped to form a screen behind which Thomas had been led a few minutes earlier by Massaquoit, who now knelt beside him.

"They are now gone," he said.

Thomas, who had been watching the snow continue to coat the branches over his head, did not respond.

Massaquoit pushed his way through the branches and began walking toward the grave. Thomas picked up his crude cane, brushed off the snow that covered it, and followed. When Massaquoit stopped a short distance from the mound of earth now covering the grave, and itself being covered by snow, Thomas continued. He stood leaning on his cane, looking down at the earth. When he came back to Massaquoit his face was set in a determined expression.

"I must leave this place," he said.

"The English wanted you back, and now they want you gone," Massaquoit said. "It is strange."

Thomas shook his head.

"Not at all." He pointed to the grave. "He wanted me. No one else."

"I see," Massaquoit replied. "Where will you go?"

He shivered and pulled his coat about him.

"To the south. To where it is warm." He paused, struck by a sudden thought. "Perhaps I will stop on Long Island, or one of the harbors along the way. I must try to intercept my sister on her way here, expecting to be married, to tell her that her husband is in the ground. It would be a kindness for me to do that, do you not think so?"

Massaquoit noted the change of tone in the young man's voice, from his usual sneer to something approaching concern. Still, a wicked little smile played on his lips.

"I think it would," Massaquoit said. "Will she continue here, anyway?"

Thomas shrugged. "I do not think I can speak for her."

Massaquoit took his arm, above the elbow, and squeezed.

"May you find what you seek," he said, "you and your sister."

Thomas's eyes seemed to respond to the pressure on his arm, but then he pulled away.

"As for that," he said, "I do not know that I will go so far away that I might not return in warmer weather."

"That might not be wise," Massaquoit said.

"It might depend," Thomas replied, "on whether I have the proper attire."

He drove his cane through the six inches of fresh snow until it reached the ground beneath, stepped forward with his good leg, and then dragging the injured one behind, he walked off into the snow, his back to Massaquoit and the grave.

•   •   •

Two days later Catherine sat at her desk, an account book open in front of her, but her attention drawn to the stream of melting snow falling from her roof onto the ground. Every few moments a large chunk would come down, shattering against the side of the house and sending a spray against the window. She was content for the moment to ignore the figures that indicated that the severity of the winter had flattened her income for the past two months, ignoring that unpleasant fact while she watched the snow explode, as though she were finally witnessing the loosening of winter's grip. It was two days after the funeral, and the weather had again turned warm, perhaps as a prelude to spring.

In her preoccupation, she did not immediately take note of the person approaching the house. When she did, she snapped back to the immediate moment, for she recognized the substantial shape of Matilda, the black servant of Master Worthington, filling the walk as she hastened toward the door. Catherine did not wait for a knock, but opened the door.

"Is it Felicity?" Catherine asked. "Or the babe? I can be ready in a moment."

Only the whites of Matilda's eyes were immediately visible as she had a dark, heavy cloak bundled about her head and shoulders so that her skin merged with the color of the garment. She pulled the cloak off and shook her head.

"No. It is none of them. It is the mistress herself that sends me to fetch you. She say that she cannot rid her bones of that chill from the cemetery and bid me tell you to come right away with that special tea you give her sometime."

"But—" Catherine began, but then caught herself.

"Has she the fever, then?"

"She seem well enough until the master leave the house and then she take to her bed and tell me to fetch you."

"Tell her I will be there very soon. With the tea."

Matilda nodded, drew her cloak around her again, and left. Catherine closed the door and walked back through the front room to the kitchen, where Phyllis was stirring the stew in the iron pot suspended in the fireplace.

"I will be needing the ginseng tea," she said. "Alice Worthington has sent Matilda to have me come with some."

"But did you not send me to her the day of the funeral with instructions that she should drink her fill of it? And did not I myself give her enough roots to last for a month, if she drank the tea every morning and night?"

"Indeed you did."

"Then—"

"Then go find my stock so I can bring her more, as she bids me."

"But—" Phyllis began, and then shrugged her ample shoulders. She took a step toward the door that led to a small room off the kitchen where Catherine dried her herbs, but then stopped.

"You know I do not fancy handling these roots."

"And that is why I want you to fetch them now, to see they are just the roots of a plant we plucked from the ground ourselves."

"So you say," Phyllis muttered and walked into the room. A few moments later, she emerged, her arm fully extended, holding a handful of the roots.

"Look at them. Just like little devil imps." She dropped them on the table. "Little imps with legs, and a little head, and just a stump of an arm here and there. I tell you I fancy I heard them scream in a tiny little voice when I took them off the rack." She looked back. "I think I can hear them even now, them that I left on the rack, crying out after their fellows, they are."

"Nonsense," Catherine replied. She picked up the roots,

so much like a human figure. "Roots, only roots." She put on her cloak, and then turned to her servant.

"Well, come along, then. The air might clear your head of these thoughts."

They hastened along the road that led to Newbury Harbor. Just as they reached the path that branched off it to climb to the knoll on which the Worthington house sat, Catherine stopped to face the water. She heard a cracking sound, like thunder in a summer storm, only today proceeding from the cracking asunder of the ice that had brought shipping to a stop all winter. Now, as she gazed at the bay, she could see expanding lines of black water pushing between blocks of ice, and toward the shore, blue waves reflected the sun and rolled toward the beach. On the dock next to the *Helmsford,* a knot of men were busy hoisting boxes up to the deck of the ship, and she was fairly certain that Samuel Worthington was standing among them, waving his arms about.

Matilda, still wearing her cloak, opened the door and led them into the hall. Catherine peered to her left into the well-furnished front room in which the fireplace offered a roaring fire well in excess of what the warming temperatures seemed to demand.

"I do not think I will feel warm again," Matilda said.

"Perhaps in the summer you will forget these cold days."

"Only I forget if I am back home in Barbados," Matilda replied. "Then I can forget all this snow and ice."

"I have the roots for the tea," Catherine said. "Perhaps you can boil some water. Phyllis can assist you."

Matilda held out her large, strong hand, into which Catherine placed the roots. Matilda studied the roots, a puzzled expression on her face.

"Yes," Catherine said, "I am sure you have made tea from such as these before."

"Ah, yes, I have. Mistress waits for you in her room up there." She pointed to the stairs that led to the second floor. She looked at Phyllis. "We bring the tea up there when it ready."

Alice Worthington was sitting up in bed, a cotton shawl wrapped about her shoulders.

"You do not look too poorly," Catherine said, as she pressed her hand to Alice's forehead.

"Indeed, I do feel better." She looked out a window that faced the harbor.

"I saw the men loading the *Helmsford* as I came by the road," Catherine said.

"Did you see Samuel there?"

"I believe I did."

"He knows I sent for you."

"I am glad of it."

"When Felicity and Daniel offer the babe for baptism, they will name him Nathaniel. That has softened Samuel's heart a little."

"And yours?"

Alice shook her head from side to side.

"The Lord's will be done," she said, "but never will my heart be whole again. That is, in part, why I wanted to speak with you."

There was a knock at the door and Matilda entered carrying a tray with a bowl of steaming tea. Phyllis followed with a second tray, on which sat another bowl.

"I thought Mistress Williams might want some," Matilda said, with a nod toward Phyllis. "It is from her roots that I make this tea."

"Bring mine here," Alice said, and Matilda set the bowl on a table next to the bed. Phyllis handed her bowl to Catherine.

"It really is very good," Alice said with a smile, after they left.

"Ah, yes," Catherine replied, "but you had a fair stock and brought me here to tell me something."

Alice put the bowl down on the table.

"It is not easy for me to tell you this. Especially after I did not defend you as I should have against my husband's accusations."

"You could not," Catherine replied. "I well understand."

"I dared not," Alice said. "But in part because I did not do the right thing then, I feel I must now."

Catherine studied the sorrow in her friend's eyes.

"You need not," she said.

"But I do." She got out of bed and walked to the door. She beckoned Catherine to join her, and when she did, Alice pointed down the hall to a closed door.

"That was Nathaniel's room," she said. She walked toward the door, but stopped at a narrow staircase that led to the attic. "When his friend Thomas first came here, he slept up there. But after a while, that was not good enough. He said it was too cold, that the wind came through the cracks in the wall. Nathaniel agreed with him. We did not see any harm when Nathaniel asked that another bed be placed in his room. Samuel had Matilda drag down Thomas's bed from the attic and place it next to Nathaniel's. But you see, I soon came to realize that they were using only one bed. Thomas's was never slept in. I kept this to myself until I confronted Nathaniel, and he just said they had become very close. Finally, I told Samuel. He was going to have Thomas brought before the magistrate for his unnatural attentions to Nathaniel, but I convinced him that Nathaniel would join Thomas before the whip, or worse."

"And so," Catherine said, "you had Thomas sent away."

"It seemed a good idea," Alice replied. "Isaac was getting old, and he needed help farming Samuel's land. Samuel thought Thomas could be made useful if he learned hus-

bandry, and Nathaniel could still see him. At a distance."
Alice strode to Catherine and threw her arms around her.
"And now see how it has turned."

"Hush," Catherine said. "You could not have known."

As Catherine and Phyllis left, they saw Master Worthington coming up the road, flanked by Lionel Osprey and Frank Mapleton.

"He won't be here long, that one," Phyllis said.

"The lieutenant?"

"The boy. Matilda told me that his things are packed, and Master Worthington will have him on his way. On that ship in the harbor if the ice melts, or overland up the valley if it does not, but he will be gone."

"I will not be sorry of it," Catherine replied.

"Me neither," Phyllis concurred.

The three men were now directly in their path. Worthington stepped aside with an exaggerated bow. Osprey and Frank followed his lead and moved to the extreme edge of the road, which had been narrowed by melting snow banks on either side.

"A good day to you, Mistress," Worthington said, and then offered a quick nod of his head toward Phyllis.

"And to you," Catherine replied. "I have visited with your wife."

Worthington waved his hand in a dismissive gesture.

"She fancies that you can cure her of her grief."

"I do not think so."

"Come, come, Catherine," the merchant said. "My son is dead, no fault of yours, but my grandson lives and Alice believes I have you to thank for his life. And I grow weary of our quarrel."

"As do I."

Worthington expelled his breath slowly through clenched

teeth, as though in that manner he was releasing his long-held animosity.

"Then permit me to ask you a question concerning Nathaniel's death."

Catherine did not want to close the door of truce that the merchant opened, but she remained wary of his sincerity.

"I do not think I can help you with that, Samuel, as I saw him only as he was about to die."

"Of course," Worthington agreed. "It is your judgment I seek. Tell me what you think of what young Frank here has told me. About Nathaniel and that sodomite Thomas."

"I do not think I want to hear such talk," Phyllis said.

"Why, go to, then," Master Worthington replied. "I talk to your mistress."

Phyllis sucked in her breath loudly and looked down at her feet, but did not move away.

"As you wish, then," Worthington continued. "The lad here tells me that shortly before the attack in which Nathaniel was killed, he heard those two quarreling, and here is the odd thing, do you hear, they were arguing about a woman. He is sure of that."

"And how is he sure?" Catherine asked.

Frank glanced at the merchant, who beckoned him forward.

"Tell Mistress Williams," Worthington urged, "but first your apology."

Frank looked as though he would rather have his teeth pulled from his mouth, but he shuffled toward Catherine and bowed.

"I am much grieved that I disturbed you some time back. It was only a prank."

"You can blame it on his youth," the merchant added.

"I accept his apology," Catherine said slowly, "in the spirit with which it is offered."

"Tell her now, lad," Worthington said.

"As Master Worthington says, I heard Nathaniel and Thomas. I was outside their tent, keeping an eye and an ear on them, like, and I hears one or the other keep saying, something like 'she's coming, and what then are you to do when she's here,' and the other replies something in the manner of 'why nothing more than you' and other such."

"Does this 'she' have a name?"

"I believe I heard one of them say something like 'Thomasine.' "

Worthington leaned forward and said in a hushed whisper, "That is Thomas's sister, who was to marry my Nathaniel. What think you, Catherine?"

"I do not think it strange that two men so connected might talk about the woman that binds them."

"But arguing, most fiercely, were they not, Frank?"

"Yes, as I believe."

"As for that, I do not know what to say."

Worthington looked disappointed.

"Pity," he said, "for I know how shrewd you are. I thought perhaps you could cast some light."

"I regret I do not meet your expectation."

Worthington shrugged.

"Ah, but there is another matter. Frank?"

Confusion spread over the young man's face for a moment, and then he seemed to remember.

"There was somebody else what saw something," he said. "That savage friend of your savage."

"The one they call William," Worthington added. "I am most anxious to talk with him."

"He was lurking about that tent, I can vouch for that," Frank said. "It may be he knows something, or did something."

"Know you where he can be found?" the merchant asked.

"No," Catherine replied.

"He is a special friend of your Matthew, is he not?"

"As for that, I cannot say. Nor do I know where Matthew is now. I do not chart his movements. Or his friends," Catherine said.

"Pity, then," Worthington muttered. He bowed his head toward Catherine, as though to speak in confidence.

"To tell you the truth, I fear for the lad, as long as this William is about."

"I do not think you have aught to fear."

Worthington leaned even closer so that Catherine could smell his breath, sour from decayed teeth.

"Ah, but if this William spied my Frank, and further if this William perchance had aught to do with the attack on Nathaniel?"

"Then you and Frank would indeed have reason to fear him, but I do not think any of your suppositions are sound."

"Maybe so. But just to be sure, I am sending the boy on an errand to Barbados." Worthington brushed at his eye. "One that my Nathaniel should have done." He stepped back and motioned for his two companions to follow him toward the house.

"Passing strange," Catherine said when they were out of earshot.

"He called you by your given name," Phyllis said. "I never heard him do so."

"Nor I, these twenty years. I cannot believe he has abandoned our quarrel. I can only wonder why he sought my advice on a question I obviously would know nothing about."

"He says he values your wisdom."

"I trust him not. I think I am being offered bait, but to what purpose, I cannot now imagine. It does make one wonder."

"Indeed, it does," Phyllis replied.

They followed the road away from the harbor, through the town square and then on toward Catherine's house. As they approached it, they saw gray puffs of smoke rising from Massaquoit's wigwam. He was standing, arms crossed, as though waiting for them.

"Edward told me where you went," he said. "I must talk with you about the young English who mocked me at your meeting."

"Why?"

"Wequashcook has given me reason to seek him out." He pointed toward his wigwam. "I have started a fire so that I can invite you into my house."

"Why, Mistress Williams can do no such thing," Phyllis said.

"But of course I can," Catherine retorted. "Go yourself to tend to our supper, Phyllis, and I will be in before long."

"Why, such a thing," Phyllis muttered, but she strode toward the house.

Massaquoit pulled back the flap to his wigwam and Catherine stooped down to make her way inside. There she felt the warm air from the fire, and in its dim light she saw squatting next to it, Wequashcook. Massaquoit came in behind her and closed the flap behind him.

"Wequashcook can tell you our concerns," Massaquoit said.

And so Catherine forced her balky knees to bend so that she could sit across the fire from Wequashcook.

"I am listening," she said.

NINE

W EQUASHCOOK DID NOT begin speaking right away. He studied a large log that cracked with a sputter, tossing sparks into the air. Slowly he raised his head. Catherine was unsure whether there was a protocol to be observed in Massaquoit's house. Perhaps, she thought, she should speak first, and so she did.

"Master Worthington is anxious to talk to you."

Just the trace of a mocking smile formed on Wequashcook's lips.

"I do not think I am as anxious to speak with him," he said.

"His servant, Frank Mapleton, who was with the English soldiers, says he saw you near the tent when Nathaniel Worthington was fatally wounded."

"That is true," Wequashcook said. "And I also saw him there."

"Master Worthington believes you might have had something to do with the attack on his son." Catherine waited for Wequashcook to respond, but she saw an expression in the old man's face that indicated he would not dignify such a preposterous charge with an answer. "Or that you might know more than you have already said."

"Now, that is a more reasonable idea," Wequashcook said, "but the truth is I have little to say."

"And yet something," Massaquoit encouraged. Wequashcook looked steadily at Catherine.

"You do me dishonor," Catherine said, "to question my motives."

Wequashcook shrugged. "I am no longer so interested in honor, but in breathing."

"Continue," Massaquoit said.

"As I have told Massaquoit, I saw the one called Thomas lying on the ground with the wounds you yourself have tended, and the other, the merchant's son, bleeding too much blood. I knew he could not live. And Worthington's man Frank Mapleton was there, too. That is what I saw. Before that I heard names, the same name, but not the same."

"Thomas, but not Thomas," Massaquoit said.

"Oh, that would be Thomasine," Catherine said. "She is Thomas's sister, who is coming here to marry Nathaniel."

Wequashcook looked at Massaquoit.

"All these years, and still my ear cannot understand these English names," he said.

"But what were they saying about Thomasine?" Catherine asked.

"I cannot say," Wequashcook replied. "Their voices were loud with anger. I heard that name. That is all."

"It is strange," Massaquoit added, "that this Thomasine's brother and her man were saying her name as they fought with each other."

"Yes," Catherine replied, "that appears odd, but there might be a simple explanation."

Wequashcook shrugged.

"That is for you, as an English woman, to figure out. I

cannot do more." He closed his eyes in thought for a moment, and then stood up slowly, stretching the muscles of his back and his legs.

"Now I think I must go to talk with Master Worthington."

"But," Catherine said, "you said you had no desire to speak with him."

"I have less desire for him to send his dogs after me. No, I will talk with him."

"He may put you in jail."

"I do not think so." Wequashcook stooped to go through the flap door. He looked back at Catherine.

"If Master Worthington decides to put me in jail, I hope I can trust that you will talk with him on my behalf."

"Surely," Catherine replied.

Wequashcook nodded and slipped through the flap.

Catherine started to rise, but her legs refused to cooperate. Massaquoit extended his hand, and helped her. She felt dizzy for a moment, and remained holding his hand.

"Thank you," she said. She looked toward the flap through which Wequashcook had exited. "I do not think Master Worthington will put Wequashcook into jail. They are too much alike, each seeking to outwit the other."

"In that case," Massaquoit suggested, "I would not wager against Wequashcook."

"Nor would I," Catherine agreed. "And thank you for inviting me into your house."

Massaquoit tilted his upper torso toward her in an awkward bow.

"Is not that what you English do?" he asked.

"Yes," she said.

"Before you leave, there is one more thing. I wanted to tell you, alone. You remember that button I gave you?"

"Of course."

"I found it outside the house where the old farmer was killed."

"Oh, the lieutenant," Catherine said.

Massaquoit tried not to show his surprise.

"I took note of his coat," Catherine said. "I saw that it was missing a button. You have said that Indians did not kill Isaac."

"The old man was shot with an English pistol. The scalping was only done to hide the bullet hole. It was made to look like Indians by those who do not know how we take scalps."

Catherine shuddered.

"Are you sure?"

"Yes. No Indian would have left the job half done like was done to this old man."

"What if he was interrupted?" Catherine asked.

"That is possible, but I do not think so."

"Then you suspect the lieutenant?"

"He was there at that time. Otherwise the snow would have buried that button where I would not have seen it."

"That he was there does not mean he killed Powell."

"No, it does not. The only one, besides the lieutenant, who knows what happened is Thomas and he is gone."

"Pity," Catherine said.

"But he may be back."

"That would not be wise."

"So I told him, and yet he said he might well return."

"If he does, we must talk with him before Master Worthington, or Lieutenant Osprey, can." She looked at Massaquoit, wondering if she could give voice to the thought that lingered in her mind, an itch that demanded to be scratched.

"It is possible someone else knows what happened to Isaac Powell," she said slowly, as though expecting to be stopped.

Massaquoit held up his hand.

"You do not need to say what is on your mind. I, too, wonder about Wequashcook. He was there when I found Thomas, and when Nathaniel was killed."

"And maybe he was there as well when Isaac Powell was attacked," Catherine suggested.

"Perhaps," Massaquoit said. "I do not trust him."

"Nor I Master Worthington."

"Two snakes, then," Massaquoit said, "one English, one Indian."

"And two men dead, another fled, and Thomasine, widowed before she was married."

"There is one more thing I can tell you. I do not know if it is important. I found the old man's hands next to a dead dog that had dragged them away as food. I saw the bandage you had put on. I also saw the dog's mouth. He had no fangs."

Massaquoit sat alone in his wigwam before the fire. He heard the wind rush by, and he sensed the drop in the temperature. Winter had returned that afternoon after Wequashcook and Catherine had left. It did not seem right that the warmth of his hospitality had been so rudely displaced by the return of the North Wind, who hurled his frigid breath against the wall of Massaquoit's wigwam.

He poked the fire with the end of a charred stick, which he then threw into the flames. The fire flared and he tossed another log onto it. His wood was almost gone. He had three more logs, just enough to last through the night. He wrapped himself in his blanket and curled up as close to the fire as he dared. Though his flesh warmed from the flame, he still felt a cold chill that had nothing to do with the temperature inside the wigwam.

• • •

In her bedroom, Catherine looked out into the black night that served as a stark backdrop to the heavy white flakes. She saw the smoke rising from Massaquoit's wigwam and wondered again why he refused her offer to wait out the storm in the comfort of her house. They lived next to each other, and yet there was a gulf that neither could bridge. She was sure she would walk across such a bridge, if it were there, but she was almost equally certain that he would not. She could not blame him for his feelings, but nonetheless they saddened her.

Still, they found themselves functioning as a team. She sought the truth of Nathaniel's death not so much for herself, but for her old friend Alice. Massaquoit seemed to have his own reasons, perhaps something to do with Wequashcook, as the two Indians, however unsure of each other, were both sure of their need to stand together against the English.

And several miles up the road leading out of Newbury lay the body of Isaac Powell, missing his hands, and his scalp half torn off. She did not think he had been buried yet, as there was no one, no relative, to seize the thaw as the Worthingtons had done for Nathaniel. No, in all likelihood, Isaac lay beneath a blanket of snow, in death much as he had been in life, a lonely and alienated figure.

She paced the room, the floorboards startlingly cold beneath her bare feet. Massaquoit's last comment returned and raised an image in her mind. She saw the wound she had tended, and now she visualized the dog whose teeth could not have made that wound. She remembered how reluctant Isaac had been to permit her to treat it. Sara Dunwood had told her how Thomas had sought refuge from the old farmer's unwanted attentions. Both Alice and Samuel Worthington, one way or another, had made it clear that Thomas had been sent away to sever his relationship with their son. Her hand closed on the brass button lying on the table next to her bed. It, too, was cold, as cold as the certainty forming in her mind that there was a thread connecting Isaac Powell and Nathaniel Worthington.

The one individual who could explain that connection was Thomas, and he had disappeared. There remained only one path to pursue.

She was dressed before the sun fully rose. She peered out her window in her bedroom that faced east and saw that the day was going to be bright. A steady drip of melting snow from the roof told her that a warm wind had replaced yesterday's storm. It was the first day of April, and perhaps spring would arrive to stay.

The promise of good weather only increased her anxiety. It was as though the deaths that had occurred in the cold grasp of winter would linger after the snows had melted, casting shadows of suspicion and unrest on Newbury, even as the earth renewed itself. She went downstairs, and thought about heating some samp for breakfast to quiet her stomach, but her mind's unease was more insistent than her hunger. She threw her cloak about her shoulders and walked out into the sunshine, pausing for a moment to feel its warmth, and then walking as fast as she could manage through the yielding layer of snow toward Massaquoit's wigwam. No smoke now rose from the hole in its top, and she feared that he had already left, and with his departure the only hope she had to pursue her suspicions, since to do so required Massaquoit's energies and skill.

Inside his wigwam, Massaquoit finished dousing the remains of his fire with one or two handfuls of snow, which sizzled for a moment as it melted against the remaining log. He heard the familiar steps of the white woman coming toward him and rose to greet her. He found her standing almost knee-deep in a drift that had formed in front of his entrance.

"Your feet must be cold," he said.

"Yes," she replied, "but that is what I came to see you about. My feet cannot do what I must ask yours to do."

"Your request might well meet my intention," he said, "for I was on my way to the harbor to see if the *Helmsford* was set to sail."

"I am glad to hear it, for I am most intent to know whether Frank Mapleton sails on her."

"And you would like me to fetch him back to talk with you?"

"Yes."

"That seems to be what I do these days. Catch up and retrieve wandering English who other English want to talk to."

"You are good at it."

"I would rather hunt something I could eat."

"But will you do me this service?"

He nodded his head slowly as though to emphasize the deliberateness of his decision to do as she asked.

"But not only for you."

"Ah, I see. For Wequashcook as well."

"For him, and all of us."

She noted the edge in his voice and so she simply replied, "I will wait for you."

The road to the harbor was rapidly turning into slush that made walking difficult even for Massaquoit's strong legs. His deerskin boots kept him dry, but they were soon covered in wet snow and pieces of ice so that he felt as though he had to bring his feet up from below the ground for each step. Still, he made good time, and although he was short of breath when he arrived at the hill overlooking the harbor, he was relieved to see that the *Helmsford* was still at anchor beside the dock, and that there was no sign of anybody getting on board.

He stood next to a young oak tree, no more than twenty feet high. One substantial branch diverged from the trunk at a height he could just manage to reach if he stretched himself full length. He grasped the branch and pulled himself up. The branch was wet, but free of snow, as it faced the east and the sun was now falling full force onto it. He slid along the branch until he was sitting in the crotch formed by its intersection with the trunk.

The gulls were up and circling the still dark waters. They swooped and cried to each other as they searched for food. A sailor appeared on the deck of the ship and tossed the contents of a pot into the water. One gull, and then another, and finally all of them dove to whatever scraps floated on the surface. They landed on the water and menaced each other with thrusts of their bills as they snapped at the morsels of garbage. The spectacle, as natural as it was, filled Massaquoit with unspeakable sadness.

For half an hour, the lone sailor, who had now disappeared back into the bowels of the ship, and the cantankerous gulls, were all that rewarded Massaquoit for his efforts to reach the harbor. But then, coming from different directions he saw a lone figure, pulling a sled, on a footpath that approached the harbor from the east, and two others on the wider path that came down from Master Worthington's house. It did not take him long to make out the distinctive beaver hat on the head of the lone figure. Wequashcook seemed to look in his direction and nod. Massaquoit studied the other two figures. One was short, seemed to walk fairly easily through the snow, and carried a sack over his shoulder. The other appeared to be laboring more with each step, and was taller. As they neared, Massaquoit could see that the taller figure was wearing a full-bodied greatcoat and wide brimmed hat, while the shorter one was bare-headed. So, it seemed, Wequashcook was coming to make his peace with Worthington and to see Frank Maple-ton off.

Something in the scene unfolding in front of him struck Massaquoit as wrong, and then he realized that the squat, powerful figure of Lieutenant Osprey was not at the merchant's side, as he almost always was except on those occasions when the soldier had been sent on a mission. Worthington looked in his direction, and Massaquoit pressed himself flat against the trunk of the tree. He looked about him, half-expecting to see the grinning face of the lieutenant staring back at him behind a pistol clenched in his hand. But the tree was in a clear space, and all he saw was snow, and the only impressions in it those made by his own feet.

He turned back toward the ship in time to see the shorter figure start to climb a gangplank that had now been lowered to the dock. The gangplank was a crude affair, not much more than a couple of rough boards nailed together. The ship rolled a little as a wave lifted it, and the figure struggled to keep his footing. His right foot came down on the side of the gangplank, and his body started to follow it into the black water between the dock and the ship. As he fell, he uttered a loud cry. He managed to grab the gangplank with his left hand. A sailor, not moving with any great haste, made his way toward the man, seized his shoulder, and then helped him back to his feet. Massaquoit could not see the sailor's expression, but his head moved in a jerky motion that suggested he was either agitated or enjoying the spectacle of a landlubber almost tumbling into the water.

Massaquoit noted Worthington's indifference to this incident: the merchant turned his head only once, when he was attracted by the cry of the man as he began to fall. Then he had turned back to Wequashcook, and bowed his head toward him in earnest conversation. That indifference, along with Osprey's absence, struck Massaquoit as very odd indeed. The shorter man was now standing on the deck, moving his arms in excited gestures toward the gangplank. The sailor who had helped him nodded and then pointed toward a door. The man disappeared behind that door.

Wequashcook and Worthington were still talking. The merchant walked over to the sled, which Massaquoit could now see was laden with a pile of goods covered by a heavy cloth. Wequashcook lifted up the cover and Worthington knelt to examine the items. The sun glinted off the metal of axes and pots and knives and other trade goods that could be exchanged for furs or perhaps wampum. Wequashcook pulled the cover back over the goods. He waved toward the deck of the ship, and two sailors came down the gangplank. Each took one end of the sled and they began hauling it up the gangplank. Worthington offered his hand to Wequashcook, but the Indian bowed without taking it. The merchant shrugged, nodded his head, and then turned back up the path leading to his house. Wequashcook watched the merchant leave, and then yelled something to the two sailors who were still struggling to bring his sled aboard. Once they succeeded, and the merchant was out of sight, Wequashcook strolled, as though aimlessly, to the base of the hill beneath Massaquoit. He looked around, then up at the sun to test its warmth. He made his way up the hill, stopping beneath the tree.

"You make one ugly bird," he said to Massaquoit.

Massaquoit lowered himself from the branch. He landed in knee-deep slush, and raised a spray of snow that reached to Wequashcook's face.

"And what kind of bird are you?" Massaquoit asked.

Wequashcook raised his hand to his face and wiped the melting snow from his cheek and chin.

"One who knows when to fly and when to nest," he said.

Massaquoit looked toward the ship.

"You are about to fly, then."

Wequashcook shrugged.

"My trade goods are on board."

"The young English, he is on board too."

Wequashcook shook his head.

"The young English who almost took a swim is some kin to Master Worthington. The one you seek must be elsewhere."

Massaquoit studied the other's face. He had been duped. The question was whether Wequashcook was part of the show.

"No, I did not know," Wequashcook said. "I saw you perched in your tree when I came here to make my peace with Worthington. He is not a man I want to have as an enemy. But he likes money above all other things, so when I offered him half the profits from my trading goods, he was happy to oblige me."

"He thinks you may have had something to do with the killing of his son."

"I told him that I did not. He seemed to accept my word."

"Maybe he waits for you to make some money for him, and then he will decide that he does not believe you."

Wequashcook smiled.

"You are beginning to think like the English."

"They did not invent deceit," Massaquoit replied.

"No, but perhaps they have perfected it. But consider this. The ship sails for Barbados. It will stop at Long Island so I can trade my trinkets for wampum from the Montauks. Master Worthington knew I would meet him this morning, and he brought along somebody who looks like Frank Mapleton, in case somebody like you was watching."

"Why would he go to that much trouble?"

"When you find this Mapleton, you can ask him yourself."

"Did you tell Master Worthington that I sought this boy?"

"I did not."

"Are you going to Barbados?"

"I do not know. But if you want to find that boy, you should look that way." He pointed to the north, away from the harbor and up the river valley. Then he made his way back to the ship and climbed up the gangplank.

Massaquoit watched the preparations for the ship to get under way. The wind blew gently off shore, just enough to fill the sails, which were turned to catch it. The anchor was lowered onto a platform attached to two longboats, which then rowed out a hundred feet into the harbor. An officer tossed a piece of wood onto the water and nodded as the outgoing tide carried it away from shore. When the longboats reached their position, the captain emerged and barked an order. The sailors aboard the longboats tilted the platform so that the anchor dropped into the water. The anchor cable ran through hawsers toward the bow of the ship and then to the capstan on the quarterdeck. The sailors on the longboats signaled the anchor was in place, and others on board threw their shoulders against spokes on the capstan. Massaquoit could hear the men grunt and the heavy anchor cable grate as it wound about the capstan. Ever so slowly, the bow of the ship began to turn, and then as it gained a little momentum, and the wind continued to push into its sails, it turned faster until it now faced the open water.

By noon, the anchor had been hoisted up again, the longboats returned to the ship, and the *Helmsford,* having been turned to face the mouth of the harbor, began to glide over the placid waves toward the sound that separated Newbury from Long Island. Beyond was the Atlantic Ocean and Barbados. Wequashcook was aboard. That part of his story might be true. As for the rest, Massaquoit would accept it as long as nothing contradicted it.

The ship was now reduced to a square black dot on the horizon. Massaquoit went down to the water's edge and found the path, just emerging from the melting snow, which hugged the river as it headed north. If Frank Mapleton was not on board the ship, he would be some miles ahead on this path. And with him, in all likelihood, would be the powerful little English officer who had left his brass button outside Isaac Powell's farm.

As he walked, Massaquoit felt perspiration gather in the corners of his eyes and begin to trickle down his cheeks. Each time he took a step, his foot sloshed down through melting snow that was rapidly becoming a layer of icy water. The sun shone on the river, turning the waters from black to blue, and streaking them in places with gold. He almost expected to hear the song of returning birds, but it was too early for that.

It did not take him long to find two sets of impressions, side by side, that had been left by individuals walking at a fast pace some time before. He judged the speed by the generous space between the footsteps and the time by the fact that the impressions, which should have been deep in the slush, were barely visible as the snow had almost melted enough to obscure the tracks. Soon there would be no way he could track his quarry. He would have to trust the word of Wequashcook, whatever his motives might have been for pointing him in this direction. Yet, somehow he felt that he would overtake Frank, and in all likelihood, lurking somewhere near when he did, would be Lieutenant Osprey. If Massaquoit was following a baited trail, he had flashed his own bait for the lieutenant when he permitted Osprey to see him hand the officer's brass button to Catherine that night at the meetinghouse when Nathaniel died.

Within an hour, he could barely see the tracks, as the sun now well overhead rapidly melted the snow, creating dozens of rivulets that crisscrossed the path in intricate patterns, obscuring all other indentations and lines. When the path passed in the shadow of a pine, the snow crust retained its integrity for a few feet, and he could sometimes find a footprint or two that encouraged him to think that those he was following had indeed passed this way. But even those occasional tracks eventually disappeared, and in some places the snow gave way to a soft mud whose surface was virginal.

To his left was the slowly flowing river, released from the ice of winter. To his right were the dense woods where the snow still lay deep between the sheltering trees. The woods offered no path branching off the one he traveled until several miles farther on where a narrow way cut through the trees to the village of praying Indians at Niantic. He did not think that Frank would have stopped there, but perhaps he, himself, should.

He almost missed the path leading to the village, for he had been concentrating on the ground in front of his feet, hoping to find at least one more set of footprints on the ground, which was now largely mud, and only occasionally still covered in snow. He looked up just in time to see the marker tree whose trunk had been trained to grow almost at right angles to the ground so that it pointed to the entrance of the path. He approached the spot with great care, examining the ground for any sign of some other person's feet, on the slim chance that Frank, either because of fatigue or hunger, or just contrariness, had decided to visit these Christian savages. But no such tracks were visible, and so he started toward the village.

He had not walked fifty yards when he saw a wisp of smoke curling up between the trees. He slowed his pace so that his steps became virtually soundless, and worked his way behind the trees that lined the path. He moved so that a tree always stood between him and the point at which the smoke rose. He strained to detect voices, but heard none. He peered around yet one more tree, and found that he was looking into a small clearing, no more than ten feet around at the edge of the path. In the center of the clearing sat an Indian boy of about twelve or thirteen in front of a fire, holding a small animal on a branch, serving as a spit, over the flame. On the ground next to him was a bow, with an arrow ready on the string.

Massaquoit picked up a handful of snow and shaped it into a ball. He threw the snowball so that it splashed against a tree to the left of the clearing while he approached from the right. The boy dropped the branch and picked up his bow in one very fast motion. He sighted the tree on which the snowball had landed. Massaquoit approached him from behind. The boy heard him at the last moment, and as he started to turn, Massaquoit held his arms so that he could not bring the bow around to menace him. The boy struggled briefly, but furiously, against Massaquoit's far superior strength.

"I mean you no harm," Massaquoit said. "But I did not want you, mistakenly, to harm me."

"Let me go, and we can see who wants to hurt who," the boy responded.

Massaquoit released his grip on one of the boy's arms, and with his free hand he seized the top of the bow. Then he loosed his hold of the other arm. The boy stepped back with the bow still in his grasp. He dropped the arrow, and Massaquoit relaxed enough for the boy to free himself. Massaquoit placed his foot on the arrow just hard enough to drive it most of the way into the snow. The boy looked down at the fire.

"My dinner is burning."

"Then you must rescue it," Massaquoit replied.

The boy picked up the branch and showed it to Massaquoit. On it was skewered a skinned, headless and tailless squirrel. The skin on the upper body was charred black, and the short forelegs were twisted together as in supplication. Massaquoit took out his knife and held out his free hand. The boy passed the stick to him. Massaquoit cut the squirrel in two. He gave the burnt half to the boy and kept the other for himself.

"It is polite," he said, "to offer your guest refreshment." He pointed to the half animal in his hand. "And the offer should be the best of what you have."

Massaquoit heard steps behind him. They were barely audible, made by somebody being very careful, as he had been, or by another child. He whirled about. Standing in front of him was a boy, a year or two older than the first. He was holding a bow aimed at Massaquoit's chest.

"You do not need to instruct my brother," he said.

"Somebody should," Massaquoit replied. "Put down your bow. My name is Massaquoit. I seek only information." He handed the good half of squirrel back to the first boy. His brother lowered his bow, but held it in front of him in a position that would enable him to raise it again in an instant.

"We know your name," the older one said. "You were the sachem the English chose to live while his brothers died."

Massaquoit felt the rage rise in him, a red fury that deprived him of any response but to put his hands about the insolent neck of the boy who would so distort the truth. How to convince this stripling that he would have preferred to die a thousand times rather than live as the sole survivor of English treachery? He took a step toward the boy, whose face spread in a grin that showed he was pleased to have found the button that would evoke Massaquoit's anger. The boy raised his bow and pulled its cord half back, an arrow now aimed at Massaquoit's heart. His brother reached for his bow, but Massaquoit put his foot back on it. He thrust his knife hand out in front of him, and crouched.

"I do not think you dare," he said.

As the older boy started to pull the cord to its full tension, Massaquoit dove at his feet and rolled against his shins. The boy pitched forward as his legs were taken out from underneath him. As he fell, he released the arrow, which shot harmlessly into the snow. The boy landed on his knees, but before he could regain his footing, Massaquoit was behind him, his knife pressed against the boy's throat. The boy struggled for a moment until Massaquoit pressed the blade a little harder into his flesh. His brother retrieved his bow and strung an arrow.

"That is not wise," Massaquoit said. "Put it down. You are boys. Do not again tempt the anger of a man."

"Do as he says."

Massaquoit had not heard the approach of the woman who now stood behind him. She was in her thirties, wrapped from head to toe in a heavy blanket, but her head was uncovered, revealing shiny black hair that reflected the sun. Her dark brown eyes shone even brighter, with an intensity that seemed almost palpable. The boy lowered his bow, his face still darkened into a prodigious scowl. The woman strode to Massaquoit and put her hand on the wrist holding the knife. She had small, delicate fingers, yet they exerted considerable pressure. He looked hard into her eyes, but she did not turn away, or ease the pressure on his hand. He pulled the knife away from the boy's throat. She released his wrist, and he stepped away.

"Massaquoit," she said, "do you not recognize me? And is that why you threaten my sons?"

He studied her face, her long, slender nose, high cheekbones that seemed almost to push through her skin, and her delicate lips. He still felt her small hard fingers on his wrist. Then he remembered.

"Long ago," he said, "I saw you in Uncas's house."

"I was a girl then. I looked at you, but you did not see me."

He recalled the visit to the Mohegan sachem. He had left the wife he had recently married home, and his heart was with her while his head was preoccupied with his failed attempt to secure an alliance with Uncas. It was no wonder he paid no attention to this woman at that time, but looking at her now, he realized that in other circumstances he most certainly would have noted her.

"I am Willeweenaw," she said. "I married a Mohegan. He was with Uncas at Mystic."

Massaquoit felt his stomach tighten at the name he had tried so mightily to erase from his memory. She reached her hand toward him, as though to touch the sorrow in his eyes, but then she let it drop and her expression hardened.

"My husband came back from Mystic, and he did not speak. I pleaded with him. Then another man, who was also at Mystic, told me how the English set the village afire, how some of the Mohegans like my husband tried to stop them, but how others were happy to join the English. My husband sat silent for two days, and then he wrapped a few of his things together in a bundle and he walked off into the woods. I have not seen him again."

"Did you not follow him?"

She looked at her two sons.

"He left me with these two, and no food. Their hearts are filled with anger. At their father. At me. At the people in our village. At the English. He knows where we are if he chooses to return."

"Perhaps you should not blame him. What happened there—"

"I do not fault him. I do not forgive him. We live here

at Niantic. I have accepted the English god, but my sons' hearts are still too hardened."

"That is not a bad thing," Massaquoit said, "if it permits them to be proud."

She walked to her younger son and knelt down to pick up the two halves of the squirrel that he had dropped. They were coated with a mixture of snow and wet mud. She held them toward Massaquoit.

"Pride does not fill an empty belly." She gave the good half to Massaquoit. "Here, you are on your way somewhere. Leave us." She glanced down the path that led to Niantic. "I do not think you are welcome there."

He felt the sting of her words while he recognized their truth, that there was no place where he could feel welcome, except, perhaps, in the house of Catherine, the woman who had saved his life when he desired most to die.

"Thank you," he said. He had little appetite for the meat of the squirrel, but he felt he could not refuse it. "I have a question."

"The ones you seek—" the younger brother began, and then stopped, his eyes on his mother.

"Go ahead," she said. "If you don't tell him, he might feel that he must enter our village to ask others."

"The ones you seek," the boy continued, "left the trail a little ways farther on. We saw them get on board an English boat that was waiting for them in a cove. If you hurry, you might catch them. The wind and current are against them. They will not be making much speed."

"Then I will not tarry," Massaquoit said. He looked at Willeweenaw. "Perhaps I will visit you in Niantic."

She shook her head firmly, but he noted that her eyes softened just a little.

"Go on your way," she said.

He began to retrace his steps down the village path to rejoin the trail heading north by the river. He heard steps running hard after him, and he turned prepared to defend himself. The younger brother, breathing hard, stopped in front of him.

"If the wind changes and blows upstream, you will not be able to catch up with them on foot," he said.

"Then I must hope it does not."

"If you take me with you, I can help you."

Massaquoit studied the boy's face. Anger still flashed from the dark eyes, and he realized that the boy's rage sought a target, and any target would do, Indian, English— it didn't matter.

"Your mother—" Massaquoit began.

The anger flowed from his eyes in a dark wave that turned his face into a hard scowl.

"Why do you think you found me alone in the woods? I do not ask my mother's permission."

"I see," Massaquoit said, and as he did, his eye caught movement coming at him from the village path. In a moment, Willeweenaw and the older boy appeared. They stopped a short distance away.

"I see that Ninigret has found you," she said.

"He wants to help me," Massaquoit said.

Willeweenaw shrugged.

"He does what he wants. Try to bring him back safely. If you do not, I will not have lost him, for he has already left me."

She did not wait for an answer, but put her arm around her older son and turned back toward the village.

"Do you not want to join your mother and brother?" Massaquoit asked.

"No. It is as she says."

Massaquoit looked at the boy, and he saw his own son, who would never reach this one's age. Massaquoit took the boy's arm.

"Keep your anger in your heart," he said, "but do not let it burn you. If you can do that, you can come with me."

Ninigret nodded and almost smiled, but then he formed his face into the hard lines that Massaquoit knew were the boy's way of hiding his uncertainty, if not his fear. They started walking, the boy taking two quick steps for each of Massaquoit's long strides.

"In that same cove," the boy said after they had rejoined the trail that paralleled the river, "where the English got on board their boat, there is a canoe we can use. It is in some tall grass at water's edge. It is not hard to find, but the English did not see it. They looked only for their own boat. In the canoe are furs. I can offer to trade with them when we overtake them."

Massaquoit admired the boy's quick mind, for he saw where he was going.

"I will darken my clothes with river mud," he said. "They will see a dirty old man with a boy in a canoe. By the time we get close enough for them to see who I am, we will have the advantage of surprise."

"And then what will you do with them?"

"One I want to bring back. The other I believe wants to kill me."

"Can you tell me why this is?" the boy asked.

"As we walk," Massaquoit said, and quickened his pace.

TEN

~3G2G~

EDWARD STOOD IN front of Catherine, a shovel on his shoulder.

"It is time to prepare the garden," he said.

Catherine looked past him to the area where the garden would be planted. The snow had completely melted, leaving behind scattered pools of water.

"It is Sunday," she said.

"You well know I do not often go to meeting," he replied, with his eyes on the ground at his feet.

"Go ahead, then," she said. "May the Lord forgive you. I think your heart is pure, even if you seem not to have felt His grace."

A smile strove to establish itself on Edward's wrinkled face. He was nearing sixty, and had worked for Catherine for twenty years, and during that time she could remember no more than half a dozen full smiles on his face. On this occasion, the smile quit halfway to full expression and fell back on an open-mouthed grin.

Catherine looked past Edward to the path leading from town to her house, and saw a small knot of figures approaching. One person, a woman with babe in arms, detached herself from the others and walked ahead. She turned back, after a few steps, as though to motion the others to wait for her, and they stopped walking. As soon as Catherine could trust her eyes in identifying her visitor, she hastened down the hill to greet her.

"It is surely a welcome sight to see you," she said.

Felicity shifted the infant in her arms.

"It is such a fine spring day, and I was feeling so renewed that I could not but stop to call." She glanced at her mother, father, and husband, who waited at a respectful distance. Samuel Worthington nodded, but his expression was grave. Alice flashed a quick smile and a nod, while Daniel lifted his hand tentatively in a wave. Felicity followed Catherine's glance and then focused instead on Edward. "He seems happy to be working the soil."

"I long ago despaired of using the word 'happy' in connection with Edward," Catherine said, "but insofar as he can be pleased by something, you are right." She placed her hand on the black sleeve of Felicity's gown. "And, truly, how is it with you and your family?"

Felicity drew in her breath, hollowing her cheeks and giving her face a pained expression. She shook her head slowly from side to side. Catherine extended her arms, and Felicity handed the babe to her.

"Minister Davis will baptize him Nathaniel today," Felicity murmured. "I asked Daniel if he minded, and he said he did not, but now I do not know if it is a good thing. I say the name, and I think only of my brother."

The infant, who had been sleeping, opened his eyes, which were a startling blue like his grandmother's. He stretched his arms out of his blanket and yawned. Catherine rocked him in her arms.

"He looks fine," she said. "And I think it right and proper that the memory of your brother in your hearts should find living expression in your son." She handed the babe back to Felicity.

"I trust you are right. Mother seems to think so, but father remains unreconciled to Nathaniel's death."

As if on cue at the mention of his name, Samuel walked over to them.

"Come, Felicity," he said, "it is time. Join your mother and husband."

Felicity took Catherine's hand and pressed it for a moment, then strode to Alice and Daniel. Samuel pointed toward Newbury Center, and they began to stroll in that direction while he remained standing in front of Catherine. He cast a disapproving glance at Edward, and then at Massaquoit's wigwam.

"Where is Matthew?" he asked.

"Do you not know?" Catherine asked.

Worthington seemed taken aback.

"What mean you?"

"I believe he seeks your servant."

"I know nothing of that."

"Do you not indeed?"

"No, Mistress Williams, I do not. Look to your own servants. One working on the Lord's day, and the other, supposed to be learning about our Lord, out on some other business."

"I look into their hearts and like what I see there," Catherine replied.

"Wondrous vision you have," the merchant said. He waved a goodbye and hastened after his family.

The meetinghouse was filled for the first time since before the winter. Catherine took her seat on the first bench, next to Magistrate Woolsey. Across the aisle from Woolsey sat the Worthingtons, first Felicity holding her babe, then her husband, father, and mother. Phyllis made her way to the rear where she found Elizabeth sitting alone. Behind Elizabeth and the other servants was the hindermost bench on which sat the Indians. On this day, that group stretched from one side of the meetinghouse to the other, but a conspicuous space, wide enough to accommodate two persons, had been left in the middle. Woolsey, who was trying unsuccessfully to position himself against the hard wooden back of his bench right next to Catherine, followed her glance to the rear of the building.

"What do you make of that space left by the savages?" he asked.

Catherine knew where he was leading, but decided to let him get there by himself.

"Think you not," he continued, "that they hold places for Matthew and William?"

"Perhaps," she said, "or it may be the empty places signify their absence."

"Approvingly, think you?"

"That I do not know," she said.

The magistrate shook his head and again leaned back hard against the bench.

"Do not take me amiss, Catherine," he said in a hoarse whisper, "but I do more and more believe those savages back there would be happier in their own church in Niantic, and so would we."

"It is a long journey for them to come," she said in a natural voice, although she recognized this was not her friend's major reason. Still, her remark elicited a knowing nod, as though Woolsey accepted her ironic concession as agreement.

"There, you see as well as I do. Better for them and for us."

"Yes," she said drily, "now all we needs must do is raise the money for such a building, and salary for a minister, for it is clear the savages have money for neither."

"If it is only a question of coin—" Woolsey began, but interrupted himself as Minister Davis opened his huge Bible with a resounding thump, and cleared his throat. Next to his pulpit was an ornately carved wooden stand, which held a basin. The minister glanced at the basin and then beckoned Felicity and Daniel. They got up, their faces both a little red but aglow, and walked to stand in front of the minister.

"We begin today with the baptism of Felicity and Daniel Rowland's babe," Minister Davis said. "Master Worthington has begged my acquiescence in so ordering our service, in view of his daughter's frail health, that she might be permitted to leave after the baptism if her strength fails her." A small murmur arose from the congregation, containing threads of approval and dismay at the irregularity of the procedure. Worthington looked around, and the murmur ceased except for one stubborn source in a row just before the servants, where artisans and small property owners sat. The merchant continued looking in that direction until the meetinghouse was silent; then he turned his gaze to the minister.

Davis dipped his hand into the basin, as though to test the temperature of the water.

"Baptism among us is not as it is among the papists, who view it as a magical cleansing of original sin, for we well know that sin is inevitably and inextricably woven into our very natures." His voice rose as he warmed to his subject. "Yea, no water of baptism can correct our affections so that we are drawn to the good and repelled from evil. Only God's free grace can grant us that favor.

"Rather than the papist's superstitious ritual, which is more befitting a witch meeting than a proper church rite, we baptize our babes to place them under the proper governance of the church, so that the application of water to the babe's forehead is a kind of seal of the covenant between God's chosen community and the infant. It is no more nor less than that."

He again placed his hand in the water.

"Daniel and Felicity Rowland, do you offer this babe to the governance of God's church?"

In turn, the couple intoned their assent.

"What Christian name have you chosen for the babe?" he asked.

"Nathaniel," Daniel replied, and Felicity bowed her head.

"Felicity?" the minister asked.

"Yes, Nathaniel," she replied.

The minister removed his hand from the basin and ran his wet fingers over the infant's forehead. The child had been sleeping, but it now stirred, offering a small cry.

"I baptize you Nathaniel Rowland," Minister Davis said, keeping his fingers on the babe's forehead, "and I accept you into our community, with the full hope and prayer that you will grow under our tutelage to an understanding of your Christian identity, and that in due time you will feel God's grace working within you, and make your conversion known to us at that season so that we may welcome you in full fellowship and communion."

Little Nathaniel, now fully awake, scrunched his face, balled his tiny fists, and emptied his lungs in a loud cry. Minister Davis permitted just a flicker of disapproval to darken his expression, and then with a wan smile he lifted his hand from Nathaniel's forehead. Felicity looked at the minister, and Davis nodded. She and her husband returned to their seats, Felicity rocking her son as she walked, and he quieted.

Catherine experienced a mixture of feelings in witnessing this scene. She was pleased to see the babe and mother doing so well, for she had remained nervous that one or the other might still be in fatal danger. But Felicity had a little bounce to her step, and color in her cheeks, and the child seemed to be getting enough nourishment. And although Catherine could not find it in her heart to object to the babe's innocence being introduced to the church's governance, part of her could not rest comfortably with the prospect of the child's growing up in a religious environment presided over by Minister Davis, a pastor who seemed more fit for the law than shepherding his flock to Christ. The minister was a learned man, Catherine knew, but he was also, more than he would ever admit, a political creature attracted to the powerful congregants such as Master Worthington, and likely to give only passing notice to the lesser members of his church. And more, for all his learned words he seemed unable to touch her heart. And so, as he began his sermon, she permitted his language to swirl about her head, while she chose from it those morsels that would lead her into a private meditation on her Lord's ineffable mercy in saving Felicity and her child.

The dugout canoe was where Ninigret said it would be, sitting in mud in a marsh at the water's edge, covered with dried reeds. It was not hard to find if one were looking for it, but not visible if one were not. Ninigret tossed off the reeds and pointed to a small pile of fox and beaver pelts. They had been covered with ice and snow that had melted in the warming air, and they were now moist and pungent. Ninigret lifted the top one, a red fox, and held it for Massaquoit's inspection.

"Do you think I can trade this for an English gun?" he asked.

"I do not know. I have been shot at by English guns but I have never bargained for one."

Ninigret tossed the pelt on top of the pile.

"Maybe I will ask these English."

"Do not forget why we are pursuing them."

"I do not forget." He leaned into the canoe and brought up a wide-brimmed English hat. He tossed it to Massaquoit.

"I got that in trade," he said.

Massaquoit put on the hat. It felt odd, and he did not like the way it blocked the sun's rays. Still, he concluded it was wise for him to wear it. He knelt down and gathered handfuls of cold mud with which he splattered his clothing.

"You no longer look like a sachem," the boy said.

"Good," Massaquoit said. He placed his shoulder on the stern of the canoe, and Ninigret took a position next to him. They shoved, and the canoe slid over the mud into the shallow water. Massaquoit knelt in the stern, the boy in the prow, and they began to paddle. Near the shore, in the shade, there were still a few pieces of ice floating on the water, but after a few strokes the canoe was out in the full sun, and Massaquoit felt perspiration begin to gather on his forehead and in the corners of his eyes.

The boy looked at the trail, just visible now, at the edge of the river.

"They will be looking for one man, a warrior, coming along there."

"We need only a little surprise," Massaquoit said, and he leaned his weight into his paddle. "I grow impatient with their game." Ninigret thrust his paddle into the water and laid his full weight against it so that he almost lifted himself off the bottom of the canoe. The craft shot forward.

The wind, which had been blowing gently into their faces, now picked up in considerable gusts, so they were working against both it and the sluggish current flowing downstream toward Newbury Harbor. They continued paddling hard. Every once in a while, Ninigret would glance over his shoulder at Massaquoit and then ply his paddle even harder. Massaquoit could see the strain on the boy's shoulders and hear his breathing begin to labor, but he knew his young companion would not ask for a rest. He respected the boy's pride, and so he would not compromise it by asking if he were tired. Instead, after a half hour of steady labor, he lifted his own paddle out of the water. Ninigret looked back, took a few more strokes, and then stopped.

They floated without conversation for a few minutes. The wind and current conspired to point the canoe toward the eastern shore of the river. Massaquoit put his paddle into the water as a rudder to keep the prow of the canoe pointed into the wind. He took several exaggerated deep breaths and then resumed paddling at a slower pace. Ninigret joined his effort and again they began a slow progress upstream. Before long their labors were rewarded.

As they came around a bend toward the west, they saw the sail of the shallop a quarter of a mile upstream. The sail moved first toward one shore of the river and then the other, as the craft tacked. It was moving no faster than they were.

"I do not think they can see us," Massaquoit said. "We will keep this distance for a while."

"What are waiting for?" Ninigret asked.

"An opportunity," Massaquoit replied.

That opportunity arose an hour later, as the shallop tacked to the eastern shore, and then instead of changing its direction continued into a shallow cove. Massaquoit looked up at the sun, which was now beginning to slide toward the western horizon.

"They must be tired," he said. "Now is a good time to overtake them."

They were close enough to see a short man bent over the long steering oar while another furled the sail on the single mast. They paddled slowly toward the shallop, giving the two on board ample opportunity to take note of their approach. When they were within twenty yards, the short man, whose eyes had not left them as they neared, reached into his belt and withdrew a pistol.

"That is the lieutenant," Massaquoit said.

Osprey beckoned them to come closer with his left arm, while his right held the pistol leveled at them. Frank Mapleton placed himself next to Osprey.

"Smile at them," Massaquoit said. "Then show them a pelt, a good one." He pulled the brim of his hat down until it nearly covered his eyes. He paddled with exaggerated slowness while Ninigret raised himself to a crouch. The canoe rocked but steadied after a few moments, and the boy reached into the pile of pelts and held up the bright red fox fur. Osprey waved his arm more energetically, urging them closer. Ninigret looked back at Massaquoit.

"Do not fear the pistol," Massaquoit said. "He cannot hit anything that is more than a few feet away from him."

"I do not fear. I only wondered if you are ready."

"I am. The lieutenant will fight. The boy will run. You chase him, and leave the little English to me."

Ninigret turned back to Osprey. They were no more than ten yards away. Osprey stopped waving his arm, and instead held it toward them, palm outward.

"I see your bloody fur," he cried. "No need to come closer."

"It is good fur," Ninigret said. He pointed to the pile in the canoe. "More here like it, even better."

Massaquoit, his eyes down and hidden by the brim of his hat, dipped his paddle into the water and propelled the canoe slowly forward. He raised his eyes just enough to focus on the pistol in Osprey's hand. It was aimed in the general direction of the canoe, but not specifically at either himself or Ninigret. He stroked once more, and the canoe slid a little closer, although the wind-driven current threatened to force it to the stern of the shallop. He continued stroking, gentle little motions, just enough to turn the canoe toward the shallop and inch closer to it.

"I said you are close enough," Osprey called out.

Ninigret looked at Massaquoit and shrugged.

"My grandfather is very old. He does not hear."

Mapleton bent down and picked up something. The slanted rays of the sun glinted off the long barrel of a matchlock musket. He struck a match and lit the cord, and then aimed the clumsy weapon at Massaquoit.

"Maybe he can hear this," he said.

Massaquoit tensed. It was too soon for a confrontation. Ninigret knelt down in the canoe and cupped his hands toward Massaquoit.

"Old man," he shouted, "stop paddling."

Massaquoit lifted his head slightly as though waking from a sleep. He nodded vigorously so Osprey and Mapleton could see the obvious motion of his hat. He kept his paddle in the water, without stroking, just to use it as a rudder to keep the canoe pointed toward the shallop. Osprey put his hand on the barrel of the musket and pushed it down.

"Relax, Frank," he said. "We don't need any of that. It's only a boy and an old man what looks like he can't lift his head up underneath that hat."

"That is right, English," Ninigret said. "We want only to trade. These furs, all of them for that musket and the pistol."

"Why, now, that is a proposition," Osprey said, "but I think you are selling your furs too dear, or holding our weapons too cheap. But come a little closer."

Ninigret picked up his paddle. He looked back at Massaquoit, who nodded, and then they both stroked. The canoe lurched forward, but it was turned by the current. Massaquoit dug his paddle hard into the water while Ninigret waited, and then when the bow was again dead on to the shallop, he too pushed his paddle into the water. The canoe gathered speed. Massaquoit kept his eyes on Osprey, and he saw the lieutenant's expression change from casual indifference to concern and then to alarm, as he realized the canoe was approaching faster than was necessary to come alongside.

"Why, what mean you?" the lieutenant said. He leveled his pistol. He had a short sword in his other hand.

"Do not hesitate," Massaquoit said to Ninigret. "Go for the boy. Seize his musket."

Osprey leveled his pistol at Ninigret just as the canoe clunked against the side of the shallop. Mapleton lifted his musket, but the match cord was no longer lit. He grabbed it by the barrel, and prepared to use it as a club. Osprey pulled the lever trigger of the pistol. It flashed and went off. Ninigret ducked to one side as he saw the lieutenant fire. The ball whizzed by him and landed in the bottom of the canoe at Massaquoit's feet. Osprey tossed the pistol aside, and switched his sword to his right hand.

Ninigret rose from his crouch and grabbed the side of the shallop. Massaquoit seized the top three or four furs and hurled them at Osprey. As they came down on and in front of the lieutenant, he swung himself on to the stern of the shallop while Ninigret leaped aboard amidship. Mapleton took one swing with his musket at Ninigret, missed, and dropped the weapon. He pulled a knife from his belt, but as soon as Ninigret began to grapple with him, he dropped the knife, freed himself, and dove off the shallop from the far side into the shallow water. Ninigret followed him and they both half swam, half stumbled toward the shore through knee-high water.

Massaquoit dropped to the deck of the shallop, balancing himself on his right arm while he kicked out with his legs at the lieutenant. Osprey, still busy shedding the furs, lunged at Massaquoit. Massaquoit flung his hat in the path of the sword, and deflected it so that it grazed his arm at the same time his feet crashed hard into the back of Osprey's shins. His knees buckled and he fell forward. His weight now pushed the sword further into the soft wood of the shallop's deck. He had both hands on the hilt of the sword, grunting as he tried to free it. Before he could pull it all the way out, Massaquoit rolled to his feet and clubbed his jaw twice, hard, and the lieutenant staggered, letting go the sword, which fell to the deck.

"Aye, so it is you," Osprey said. "I am not surprised." He lowered his head and charged at Massaquoit, butting him in the chest, and crashing his fist against Massaquoit's cheek, beneath his eye. They fell against the side of the shallop and then rolled onto the deck. When they separated, Massaquoit was able to seize the sword, and in a moment, he had it against the lieutenant's throat.

"I do not want your blood," Massaquoit said. "I want only to talk with the boy."

"I am sure you do, and don't you know that is why I have been taking him away from you?" He made as though to get up, and Massaquoit pushed the blade a little harder against his flesh.

"Do not be such a fool," Massaquoit said.

Osprey relaxed his body so that he lay on the deck. Massaquoit lifted the blade and stepped back. He kept the point of the sword, however, poised above Osprey's chest.

"Do you see that you are my prisoner?" he asked.

Osprey's face darkened into a frown, then eased into resignation with a lift of his eyebrows.

"Aye," he muttered, "it is not the first time I have been so, although the first at the hands of a savage."

Massaquoit lowered the sword so that it hovered immediately above Osprey's breast, and he moved the blade in small circles like a wasp locating a target for its stinger.

He sliced through the lieutenant's shirt and then just enough skin to draw a trickle of blood.

"You must learn manners," Massaquoit said. "I am a Pequot sachem, no more savage than you."

"As you say," the lieutenant replied. He pressed his fingers against the shallow wound until the blood stopped. "Do you think you can let me up?"

Massaquoit fought the urge to further humble his adversary, and gestured for him to stand up.

"What do you want of me, then?" Osprey asked. He looked toward the shore, where Ninigret and Frank had disappeared into an area of tall marsh grass. "I do not control that one. Nobody does. Master Worthington thinks he does, but that boy minds only his own interest."

"Ninigret will bring him back soon enough. You and I have a brass button to talk about."

"I did see you give some such thing to that meddlesome woman."

"I intended for you to see me do that."

"It's only a button."

"Like one on your coat that I took off a dead Iroquois who took it from you."

"'Tis a common thing, a brass button."

"I found this button in the snow outside Isaac Powell's house. Right after he was killed."

"Why, I was there. I do not deny it. Like you, after the poor fool was killed."

Massaquoit suddenly felt weary of his interrogation. It was not his business after all. Let the English deal with their own. He was feeling more and more like a hired hand, and his pride rebelled.

"I will bring you back to talk to the other English. If you promise not to struggle, we can have an easy trip back. If not, I will have to tie you in a way that you will find uncomfortable."

"I can sit easy and enjoy the ride," Osprey said.

A splashing sound drifted toward them from the shore. Frank Mapleton waded into the water in front of Ninigret. Frank's hands were bound behind his back with a piece of thorny vine, which pierced his flesh if he attempted to free himself. The vine was also looped around his neck, forcing his head back so that he seemed to be staring at the sky as he walked, His foot slipped into a declivity in the riverbed and he stumbled face forward into the water. Ninigret watched as he struggled to regain his footing without the use of his arms for balance. Finally, Ninigret grabbed Frank's shirt and hauled him up. Mapleton gasped and spit out a mouthful of water.

"He runs better than he fights," Ninigret said when they reached the shallop. He pulled himself over the side. Then he leaned back over the side and grabbed one of Frank's arms. Massaquoit took the other, and they hauled the young man up. Frank tensed his body as he was lifted, trying to keep the thorns from pressing into his flesh, but as he tumbled onto the deck his arms were thrown back and the vine cut cruelly into his neck, which turned red as blood gathered in the gash left by the thorns ripping across his skin. He forced himself into an awkward kneeling position and dropped his arms as slowly as he could to relieve the pressure of his bonds. He cast a rueful look at Osprey.

"I see you did not manage much better," he said.

"Maybe I did not, but I did not find the water so inviting as you did."

"You were supposed to keep me safe from him," Mapleton said, and he swung his head toward Massaquoit.

Osprey shrugged.

"I did what I could. No man can fault my effort."

"No, not that," Frank sneered, "just the result."

Massaquoit found a place between the thorns on the section of vine running down the young man's back. He grasped it and pulled it just enough to show how much more damage he could inflict if he chose. Mapleton leaned toward him, and moved his head toward the stern of the shallop.

"Over there," he said in a whisper.

Massaquoit led him there while Osprey stared hard at Mapleton.

"Don't believe what he tells you," the lieutenant said. "His tongue knows nothing but lies."

"Speak," Massaquoit said when they were out of earshot of Osprey.

"Just this," Frank said. "I was the bait, you see, and that one over there was supposed to take care of you when you caught up. All the time, he keeps on talking of this button that he saw you give Mistress Williams, and how he cannot let you say where you got it."

Massaquoit listened without expression.

"Do you have more to say?" he asked.

"Only this. Now I have shown you my good intentions, do you think you can let me go? I fear what they will do to me."

For answer, Massaquoit motioned to Ninigret, who began to set the sail while Massaquoit led Frank back amidship so he could take hold of the long steering oar.

"We have the wind, and the river runs toward Newbury," he said.

Frank shuffled forward, and twisted himself so he could reach a pouch at his belt. Massaquoit watched as he stretched his hands against the bite of thorns into the pouch, and then pulled them out. He turned around so he could extend his hands behind his back while he looked at Massaquoit over his shoulder. His hands were filled with coins.

"Here's money they give me, to play my part. Take it. Say I escaped. Only Osprey could gainsay you."

"I have no use for your English money."

The wind filled the sail, and Massaquoit guided the shallop toward the middle of the river. Frank Mapleton opened his hands and let the coins drop onto the deck. He watched to see if Massaquoit would pick them up. When Massaquoit did not, Frank knelt down and, suffering the painful jabs of the thorns into the flesh of his wrists, he gathered the coins, one by one and dropped them back into the pouch. He stood and stared over the stern at the water and watched his chance for escape disappear.

ELEVEN

꧁꧂

PHYLLIS CAME HURRYING into the kitchen with a basket of eggs, her face flushed with excitement. She began talking before she was fully through the door.

"Peace," Catherine said, "put down your basket and quiet yourself so I can understand what you are saying."

"The *Good Hope,* Mistress," she managed to sputter as she placed the basket on the table. The basket rocked for a moment until Catherine reached across to steady it. "The sails have been seen just outside the harbor, and there is a fair wind onshore."

Catherine felt a flush of excitement. The ship was long overdue because of the severity and unusual length of the winter, and she had had no news of it for more than two months. It was coming up the coast from Barbados with a cargo of sugar and tobacco for which she had paid, to which she would add the codfish and lumber she had brokered for Woolsey, once the ship harbored in Newbury. Then, fully loaded, it would cross the Atlantic. If all went well, she and Woolsey would reap a very nice profit, perhaps too much so in the eyes of Minister Davis, who was not overly fond of merchants whose profits he equated with the biblically proscribed sin of usury.

The *Good Hope* had been delayed by storms off the Virginia coast, and the bad weather had trailed her northward, finally driving her into harbor between the forks of Long Island, where she found safety from the wind only to be trapped by ice floes off Shelter Island. Now, at last, she had taken advantage of the warming weather to complete her journey to Newbury.

Phyllis hurried ahead of Catherine on the way to the harbor. When they reached the hill that overlooked the water, Catherine could see that a crowd of fifty or sixty people were already there, with more arriving on the main road as well as the secondary paths. Almost all were curiosity seekers who had no actual interest in the ship or its cargo, but the arrival of any boat, particularly after a difficult winter, always generated a market-day air of excitement even among people who had nothing to buy or sell. She recognized several tradesmen in their leather doublets and breeches, such as the chandler, the blacksmith, and the shoemaker, all taking time from their businesses, which they left under the supervision of servants, to come down to the harbor. Other servants dressed in their coarse and dull-colored garments stood at the fringes of the crowd while some of the more affluent citizens in brighter-colored clothing occupied the area immediately in front of the dock. Chief among these, was Samuel Worthington, who, Catherine surmised, must have seen the sail from his hilltop home before anybody else, and he was not one to pass up an opportunity to evaluate a competitor's goods so as to plan how best he might compete. Off to one side, at the extreme rear of the gathering crowd, stood a small knot of Indians, some in their native dress, others in English clothes. Catherine and Phyllis walked straight through the crowd, and people stepped aside to let them pass until they reached

Worthington. The merchant turned his head and nodded. Phyllis continued until she was at the beginning of the dock.

"Good morning, Mistress," Worthington said. "It seems good fortune has attended you today."

"The ship approaches," Catherine said, "but you well know its success depends on what is in its hold."

"For that, Captain Gregory is as shrewd and capable a seaman as any merchant could favor," Worthington said.

"He is that," Catherine replied, "and very happy I am to have in my employ."

"Should you retire from commerce, I myself would be pleased to have his service."

"I am sure he would be pleased to hear so," Catherine said, and to terminate a conversation whose superficial courtesy she was finding increasingly irksome, she walked past the merchant, and joined Phyllis at the dock. The ship was now close enough for her to see Captain Gregory himself standing on the quarterdeck. The captain doffed his large brimmed hat to her, and she waved her hand in greeting. He replaced his hat, and then pointed to the fore of the ship. Catherine followed his eyes and saw what he was indicating.

Standing on the forecastle deck, and leaning over a rail that separated it from the bowsprit was the figure of a woman. From this distance, all Catherine could make out was her blond hair, and the bright red, verging on scarlet, of her bodice. Several sailors who lounged nearby seemed, by their gestures, to be engaged in animated conversation with her. The woman was holding a bright green hat with which she pointed at the crowned lion figurehead and then threw back her head. As the ship slowly approached the dock, she leaned further over the rail and threw her arms about the bowsprit, as though she would clamber onto it. A sailor grabbed the hem of her gown and pulled her back.

The woman's voice rose into a high-pitched giggle, which was joined by the deeper laughs of the sailors. She straightened up, put her hat on, and walked across the forecastle deck, past the capstan, and stood next to Captain Gregory. Catherine could not see his face from where she stood, but felt certain it must have turned red beneath his deep tan.

So that, Catherine said to herself, must be Thomasine.

Others on the dock had apparently been watching the woman's performance, just as Catherine had done, for she noted now how many of them were pointing either at the quarterdeck or the figurehead, and there was much shaking of heads and murmurings.

"That one," Phyllis said, "you don't suppose she's—"

"Thomasine, I should say," Catherine said. "Thomas's sister."

"She does seem to be enjoying herself. And the way she is dressed, I do not think is proper for Newbury."

"I wonder where it might be proper, indeed," Catherine replied.

As the ship slid and bobbed next to the dock, sailors fore and aft tossed down cables to the waiting dockhands who hitched them around the pilings. A gangplank was lowered, and standing on deck, ready to disembark, was Thomasine. As she stepped forward, another figure became visible. Wequashcook lifted his beaver hat for a moment to wipe his brow. He did not move as Thomasine posed theatrically for a moment at the top of the gangplank, as though she were an actress, and then started down. As she approached, the murmurings of the crowd rose to a rumble, and then, as though at the command of some offstage director, all voices stopped and she proceeded down in silence. Master Worthington, accompanied by Governor Peters, came abreast of Catherine and Phyllis. Wequashcook remained on board, but his eyes were on the merchant.

"Know you who she is?" Worthington asked Catherine.

"I do not know," Catherine replied, "but I can guess that she is your son's intended."

Catherine watched a frown form on the merchant's face as the memory of his son's death brought pain to his eyes while the appearance of Thomasine curved his lips into a sneer of disapproval and wrinkled his nose in distaste. The frown set hard on his face for a few moments, and then gradually relaxed, seemingly in relief at the realization that the woman now coming down the gangplank and obviously heading toward him would not be his daughter by marriage. Still, he inhaled deeply as though to steel himself for an encounter he knew would be difficult.

Thomasine paused at the bottom of the gangplank, again in a theatrical pose as though to provide the onlookers with a full opportunity to see her She had her brother's blond hair and thin body. Her hat was of green velvet, with a silver buckle, such as a young man might wear if he were someplace other than Newbury, where such ostentation was frowned upon unless, and then with grudging tolerance, displayed by somebody of wealth and position. Her bright red bodice was laced together with a matching silver cord that seemed to catch and play with the sunbeams. A lace falling collar revealed her pale flesh. Her gown was of vibrant green that matched the color of her hat, and it was tucked up at the hem to reveal just a flash of her underskirt. She studied the ground in front of her for a moment, as though to find a place suitable for her feet, and then walked toward Worthington and Catherine. She limped a little on her right leg, and she held a rolled document in her hands.

"I am Thomasine Hall," she said with an exaggerated curtsy. "You must be Master Worthington." She kept her intense blue eyes on Worthington, offering not even a moment's glance at Catherine.

"I am Samuel Worthington," the merchant said. "But my son . . ."

"Is dead, sadly," Thomasine continued for him. "My brother, whom I think you knew, met me at Shelter Island, where he sought passage on a ship south. He told me." She lowered her head for a moment as though the grief of her loss weighed it down, but when she again lifted her eyes, they were bright with determination. "That makes me his widow, then, don't you see, dear Father."

Worthington's face blanched and then reddened, and his lip quivered.

"How, now," he said. "The memory of putting my son in the ground is still an open wound. How presume you to offer such a jest?"

Thomasine made a clucking sound with her tongue.

"Father, you do me dishonor, for your son and I indeed were married in Barbados before he abandoned me to come north with my brother. I followed soon after as I could, but he left me without the means, which I have only recently secured."

"Married, you say," Worthington retorted. "I do not think it."

She held out the document.

"We had a lawful contract, witnessed by my brother, and"—she hesitated—"in it, he settles a piece of property on me."

"Yes?" Worthington prompted.

"The Powell farm. Which he said you were to give him on his marriage."

"But I never consented," the merchant said. "And you cannot have married without my agreement." He pushed down the document which she continued to hold in front of his face as though demanding that he read it. "Even if you say truly, and that I do doubt."

The hardness faded from Thomasine's eyes, which now were rimmed with tears.

"This is a hard thing to find such a welcome, so soon after finding out that my fine young husband is dead."

Worthington turned on his heel, took a step away from the dock, and then looked back over his shoulder.

"We will hear more of this, in the proper time and place, before the magistrate. Then perchance we can see what merit there is in that piece of paper you flaunt as though it were Scripture itself."

"And where am I to stay?" Thomasine called after him, but the merchant continued walking. She raised her voice to the onlookers. "Can nobody guide me to this Powell farm, to my house?"

Catherine took her arm. "I am Catherine Williams," She pointed at the *Good Hope*. "It is my ship you have arrived on, so I ask you to abide with me until better arrangements can be made," she said. "It is not fit for you to go to the farm now."

Thomasine looked at her, as if seeing her for the first time, but something in her glance told Catherine that the young woman had been perfectly aware of her presence even while she had focused her whole attention on the merchant.

"Why, that is most generous of you, Mistress Williams."

Phyllis leaned down to whisper in Catherine's ear. "Do you think it wise? What room do we have?"

"Yes, and ample," Catherine replied, and she began to walk back up the road toward her house. "Phyllis, please have a word with Master Gregory and have him send Thomasine's things after us, and then join us at the house."

Thomasine sat on a straight-backed chair next to Catherine's carved writing table, on which lay the document. Catherine moved the candle a little closer to the paper and bent over it. The hand was bold, the letters well formed, but still she had to squint to make out the words. Once she did, however, she looked up with a bemused smile on her face.

"So Nathaniel promised you that you could live at the Powell farm he was to receive from his father."

Thomasine hesitated.

Catherine held up the paper.

"Have you read what is contained herein?"

Thomasine began to nod her head, but then shook it sadly.

"So is that the way of it?" Catherine said. "You cannot read, can you?"

"I can, a little," Thomasine replied, "but he told me right enough, and I know he would not lie to me."

"I do not see why he would, either," Catherine replied, "but I cannot say I understand what he did. Why were you not to live together? I cannot imagine Nathaniel wanting to occupy Isaac Powell's house."

Thomasine's face darkened for a moment, either in confusion or anger, but then she smiled.

"Nathaniel was not sure of the welcome I might receive from his father. He was right to so conjecture, as I now know from having met Master Worthington."

"And . . ." Catherine prompted.

"And he wanted to be assured I would have a roof over my head while he made his peace with his father."

"I see. How prescient he was," Catherine said.

She looked down at the paper again, not trusting her memory, even after so short a time, to recall accurately the most startling statement contained in the agreement.

"And if he was to die, you were to have the farm?"

"Yes."

"Was he ill that he envisioned dying?"

Thomasine shook her head.

"It was no more than a husband's loving concern for his wife, and a recognition of the sudden dangers of this world."

Catherine pointed to a signature at the bottom of the paper.

"And this is the signature of your brother, Thomas, as witness?"

"It is. I can read names, some names, like mine and my brother's."

Catherine handed the paper back to Thomasine.

"I am no lawyer, but I do know Master Worthington is going to deny the legitimacy of the terms in that paper. He was not fond of your brother. He separated him from Nathaniel. But it is a strange coincidence that he sent Thomas to the very farm promised you in this paper. Still, I am certain Master Worthington will assert this paper is a fraud."

Catherine studied the young woman's face, now half cast in shadow as the light from the candle did not fully illuminate it. She expected a reaction, some sign of being nonplused, or indignant, but Thomasine offered only a cool smile.

"Nathaniel did not like to talk to me of his father. But Thomas spoke full well. I know what I must contend with."

She stood up.

"I am weary from my journey. It has been overlong."

"Phyllis will take you to your room."

Catherine heard the voices of the two women, Thomasine's tone lighter than her expression of weariness would have suggested, while Phyllis's voice was barely civil. Then she heard them climbing the stairs, and a door shut on the second floor. A few moments later, Phyllis came down and appeared in the front room where Catherine still sat at her table.

"I am ashamed," she said, "that we have taken that

woman under our roof. It is not polite to use the word that is most apt to say what she is."

"Would you have her sleep on the dock?" Catherine asked.

Phyllis shrugged. "It would be no concern of mine. But I warrant had we left her standing there, she would not long have wanted for a bed, or someone to share it with."

"Perhaps so," Catherine replied, "and thus all the more reason to have her here."

"Why, that is not my meaning, not at all," Phyllis said. "But it is mine."

If anything, Dorothy seemed to have grown thinner, and her face more tense, as though the warming temperatures of the arriving spring, which had softened the earth and smoothed people's dispositions, had served only to harden her, accentuating the angles of both her body and the edges of her taciturn nature. She offered Catherine and Thomasine an almost imperceptible nod of her head as she opened the front door, and with an only marginally more noticeable movement indicated that Master Woolsey was in the front room.

He was sitting in a rocking chair with a heavy woolen rug over his knees and a thick shawl about his shoulders. The windows were shut, although the day was more than comfortably warm, and the magistrate shivered beneath his wraps. He looked up as they entered the room, and Catherine saw that his eyes were bloodshot. She walked to him and pressed her cool palm to his forehead.

"I did tell him that I could go to fetch you, Mistress."

Catherine turned back to the doorway where Dorothy stood, her narrow face pinched into a scowl.

"But he would not hear of it," she continued. "So it is a very good thing that you have come on some business this morning."

"Joseph, what means this stubbornness?" Catherine asked.

"I was in the very act of sending Dorothy for you when she saw you coming up the walk. And that is the truth."

"I will bring you something for your fever," Catherine said. Thomasine cleared her throat and then coughed into her hands. Catherine cast a disapproving look at her. "This is Thomasine Hall. She is Thomas's sister who was to marry poor Nathaniel. She arrived yesterday on the *Good Hope*."

Thomasine was wearing an outfit only a little more sedate than the one she had on when she walked down the gangplank. Her bodice was dark green instead of scarlet, and a linen collar had replaced the lace. The gown was the same, but she had left her hat at home. The effect of these changes was to bring her dress more into conformity with prevailing Newbury custom, although it was still just beyond being entirely respectable.

"I saw the crowd going past my door to the harbor," Woolsey said. "I asked Dorothy to go there to be my ears, and she did indeed tell me of this young woman."

"She has a document that she says is a marriage contract signed by Nathaniel." Catherine glanced at Thomasine, who handed the rolled paper to her. "We did hope you could offer your opinion, but you are unwell and it can await your better health."

Woolsey shook his head.

"I am afraid not, as Samuel Worthington outpaced you to my door this morning, before I was even out of my bed. He did not inquire as to my well-being, nor did he listen when Dorothy told him of my condition, other than to say he would return once I was awake and dressed. I do not think he cared whether I had time to break my fast. That is why I am now dressed as you see me. Else I would have kept to my bed."

"I told him I would send Master Worthington away," Dorothy offered from the doorway where she still stood.

"Let me see the paper," Woolsey said. "Samuel comes any moment. Dorothy, prepare to welcome him."

Dorothy did not move.

"Go to, child," Catherine insisted. "Obey your master."

Dorothy stepped back from the doorway. Catherine handed the document to Woolsey, and he unrolled it, holding it on his lap and peering at the writing.

"A most strange document," Woolsey said after perusing it. "It says here that Nathaniel gave to this young woman Isaac Powell's farm as fee simple determinable, to revert to the Worthington family in the absence of heirs. Most strange that Nathaniel who stood to inherit considerable lands besides that poor farm should see fit to make such an arrangement."

"Strange it is, Joseph," Catherine agreed.

"And am I not a remarkable bearer of such a document?" Thomasine asked.

Before Catherine could answer, there was a sharp rap at the door, followed by Dorothy's quick step to it. In a moment, she appeared in the room followed by Worthington, and behind him, Wequashcook. The merchant strode over to Woolsey without acknowledging the presence in the room of the magistrate's other visitors. He grasped the paper, which after a moment's hesitation, Woolsey released, although his face reddened in displeasure at the rudeness of the gesture. Worthington read over the document, his lips moving slightly at each word while his face darkened.

"He did not have the farm to give," he said as he folded the paper and handed it back to Woolsey. He turned his hard eyes on Thomasine. "I tell you, young woman, I know what spell you cast on my son, if you did not write that paper yourself, although the hand appears to be his, but Nathaniel did not have my permission to marry."

Thomasine met the merchant's gaze with one of her own as steely, and with a touch of brazen impudence that suggested she was not one used to being cowed.

"And yet marry we did. With my own brother as witness on the marriage night that we retired to our bed as husband and wife."

"And was he in the room with you?" Worthington asked.

Thomasine hesitated for just a moment.

"If he was here, he could tell you right well that what I say is true."

"It matters not. He is not here. And if you played the whore with my son, why that is a basis for a whipping in Newbury."

"If," Woolsey said slowly, articulating each syllable with emphasis in the way he did when he wanted to be not only heard but heeded, "it is as the young woman says, she may indeed have grounds certifiable for her claim to be Nathaniel's widow."

Worthington wheeled and took a step toward Woolsey. The magistrate half raised himself from his chair. He settled back into it as Worthington stopped, contenting himself with a withering glare. The merchant looked toward Wequashcook.

"William here tells me that he found you in a tavern, hardly able to stand, that another had to make your introduction to him, and that is the only way you knew to board the ship that brought you here. Is that not so, William?"

Wequashcook nodded.

"There. That is all I have to say on this matter. You shall not have any part of what my poor son would have inherited."

"I will bring the matter before the governor," Woolsey said.

"Do as you please." Worthington strode out of the room, followed by Wequashcook.

Thomasine watched their backs, and then she offered a little bow to Woolsey and Catherine.

"Why, thank you, good sir, for so defending my interest. And you, Mistress Williams, have been more than kind. I will not trouble you further. Even today, I will take my things to the farm, just as my husband intended."

"That is not wise," Catherine said, "as you well know Master Worthington does not want you there."

"And yet," Thomasine replied, "although I have lived long by my wits, I do not think you can find many who would call me wise. So, now I ask that I may take my leave, for I have much work today." She curtsied, an exaggerated squat that almost brought her to a seat on the floor, straightened up, and walked out the door.

"Remarkable woman," Woolsey said as the door shut, and he and Catherine were left alone.

"She has chosen a most dangerous enemy, nonetheless, and I fear for her safety. Sara Dunwood sends word to me that she has the toothache. I think I can bring her a poultice of hops that promises some relief."

"Does not Sara live next to the Powell farm?" the magistrate asked.

"That she does."

"An interesting coincidence," he observed with a smile. He stood up slowly, and almost staggered. Before he could fall, however, Dorothy was at his side, supporting him with a firm hand on his elbow.

"But where . . . how . . . ?" he began.

"I was just at the door," the servant replied. "I knew it would not be long ere you did something foolish."

"Goodbye, then, Joseph," Catherine said. "I am content to leave you in such capable hands. I will report to you if I find anything amiss at the Powell farm."

She waited for Dorothy to help Woolsey climb the stairs, and then she left.

•   •   •

Thomasine and her belongings had been gone even before Catherine returned from her visit with Woolsey that morning. She had wasted no time in claiming her new homestead.

"I can walk with you," Phyllis said, as Catherine gathered her midwife's bag late that afternoon.

"It is just your idle curiosity. I know you are not so fond of a long walk along a muddy road."

"I thought you might want the company," Phyllis replied.

"Come along, then," Catherine said. "It is no use my having to report to you what you want to see with your very own eyes."

The sun hung above the trees that rimmed the road leading away from Newbury Center. In a cleared area just ahead, they could make out the squat outline of the Dunwood house. A cow grazed in a sparse patch of grass behind the house, and a hog rooted in the front yard. On the side nearest town, Allan Dunwood was at work laying out the rows and mounds of a garden. He waved to them as they approached and motioned for them to enter the house, where a little smoke curled from the chimney. Beyond the Dunwood dwelling rose the slightly more substantial shape of Isaac Powell's house.

"You go on ahead," Catherine said to Phyllis, "as I know you have a special interest in visiting there."

"But what should I say to her?"

"I am sure you can think of something," Catherine replied. "Now go on. If I do not meet you there before you finish your visit, stop for me here."

Phyllis walked on ahead while Catherine turned onto the short path leading to the Dunwoods' door. Inside, Sara was sitting on a crudely fashioned joint stool next to a plank table in the front room of her two-room house. A chimney ran up the center wall dividing the front room from the one in the rear, where the family slept. The front room served as kitchen, parlor, and all-purpose space. Two similar stools hung from pegs on the wall next to the fireplace in which smoldered a dying fire beneath a large black kettle. One child, three-year-old Judith, sat at her mother's feet while Sara nursed her brother, ten-month-old David. The legs of the stool were uneven so that it rocked as Sara shifted her weight to move the infant from one breast to the other. Judith watched the legs rise and fall back to the floor, and as she leaned forward to lay her hand beneath one leg, Sara placed her foot in the child's path. Judith's little face tightened into a scowl for a moment, but then she contented herself playing with the hem of her mother's gown.

"You see how it is," Sara said, glancing from the child on the floor to the infant at her breast whose cheeks were puffed as he sucked. Sara winced as she spoke, as if the effort to articulate words was painful.

Catherine poked around in her bag until she found the poultice. She approached Sara.

"Which is it now?" she asked.

Sara opened her mouth and moved her head to the right.

"That side," she said, "on the bottom near the back."

Catherine peered, but the interior of the house was dim, and she could not see well. She cupped Sara's chin with the gentlest touch and turned her face toward the window. She could now see a swelling on the gum beneath the rearmost molar. She applied the poultice with a wadded piece of rag.

"That should help," she said.

Sara offered a brave smile.

"I do hope so," she said. "I feel a little relief even now."

Catherine left the poultice on the table.

"Use it as you need. I can bring you more."

David had abruptly fallen asleep, and Sara pulled a cradle out from beneath the table and laid him in it. She buttoned her bodice. Judith tottered over to sit by her brother and watch him in his sleep.

"A few moment's peace," she said. "Did you stop at my new neighbor?"

"Phyllis did," Catherine replied. "I did not want to delay coming to see you."

Sara chuckled, her pleasant face alight with a knowing smile.

"I am sure most people in Newbury would like a closer look at that young woman, after the way she showed herself coming down from the ship, dressed like the scarlet harlot in the Good Book." Sara nodded toward the window through which her husband could be seen as he labored over a shovel, and then she leaned forward, as though to share a confidence, which she offered sotto voce. "I can tell you she caught the eye of more than one of the men standing there at the dock. Why, I caught my Allan staring at her when he thought I would not notice, and then he made a sound as though he disapproved, and yet he did not take his eyes from her until I nudged him with my elbow in his ribs. That brought him round, right enough."

"Phyllis has instructed her that she cannot dress in that fashion in Newbury."

"And that is a fact," Sara said, now in a normal voice. "Folks such as her and me cannot dress like such fine ladies."

"Even fine ladies," Catherine responded, "would be a little more sober in their dress than she was yesterday. But maybe she fancies herself so, as she says she married Nathaniel Worthington."

"More like Nathaniel would marry that boy," Sara said with a crooked smile. She stood up, stretched her back, and looked down for a moment at Judith, who was still gazing at David. Then she started as though just remembering something.

"I am afraid Phyllis will be disappointed. I recall just now my Allan saying he saw Thomasine on her way to town not so very long ago."

"That is a pity," Catherine said, "for I do believe I know where she would have been going."

"The public house, no doubt," Sara said.

The room darkened so that the only light came from the dying fire. Sara jabbed a brand into the fire and with it lit a candle on the table. Allan came in and bowed.

"Evening, Mistress Williams. It gets dark sudden like here when the sun slips behind those trees. I can walk back with you."

"That won't be necessary," Phyllis called from the door. Her face was grim with disappointment. "She was not home."

"Yes," Catherine said. "She passed this way on her way to town. Another time, perhaps."

"Go on into Newbury Center to the public house, and there you can find her," Sara said with a meaningful glance at her husband.

"Why, perhaps I should go fetch her, then," he said.

"Do that, if you like," his wife replied, "and you can just keep on walking with her to that old dead man's house."

"I have more poultice, if you need it," Catherine said. "Come, Phyllis, we must make our way home."

Halfway to their own house, on a road now in almost total darkness, lit only by the dim glow of a rising moon, they almost walked directly into two figures approaching them from town. A male voice muttered a curse, while the woman's voice only laughed, a high-pitched giggle that seemed moistened by whatever she had been drinking.

"Do you think it was her?" Phyllis asked.

"I am quite sure it was," Catherine replied.

"God forgive me for saying so," Phyllis said, "but it seems to me that Nathaniel was not so unlucky in his death as he might have been had he lived with that one."

"Phyllis, that is a most untoward observation."

"Yet it is what I believe. The Lord knows I mean no harm when I speak my mind."

"I am sure He knows, but I wish I knew how to teach you better management of your tongue that so often seems to run wild."

They walked in silence until Catherine's house rose in front of them on its hill. As she usually did, Catherine glanced past the house to Massaquoit's wigwam, looking for some sign that he had returned. The wigwam was just visible, a hemisphere, flattened at the top as though pressed down by a giant thumb. It at first seemed as deserted as when they had left earlier in the day, but Catherine thought she saw a puff of smoke rise from the opening she knew was at its top. She started to walk toward it, when Phyllis took her arm and pointed to the house. Edward was standing in the doorway. And next to him was Massaquoit.

TWELVE

⟡

"B UT SURELY YOU have not left them sitting out there alone?" Catherine said.

"I am not such a fool, or so careless," Massaquoit said. He sat at the table and looked toward the pot on the fireplace. "But I am very hungry."

"Matthew," Phyllis began, using the Christian name she knew he detested, and which she only said when she wanted to assert her sense that he had risen above his proper place in the household. "Matthew," she repeated, "Mistress Williams is not your servant, nor am I, to feed you when you come flying in like some strange creature of the night, a very spirit carried by the wind."

"Massaquoit," Catherine said in a gentle but firm voice. "Assure me that those men in your wigwam are secure, and Phyllis will be most happy to put a fire under that stew, as she and I and Edward also must sup."

"The one who has shown that he might run is securely bound. The other had given me his word."

"I see," Catherine replied.

Edward, who had been sitting in a corner to the side of the fireplace, snorted.

"Gave you his word, did he, and you trust in that?"

"No," Massaquoit said, "not entirely. Ninigret is a very capable jailer."

"He is but a boy," Edward argued.

"Perhaps you want to join him in his watch?" Massaquoit said. He turned to Catherine. "He has proven himself a very formidable warrior, beyond his green years. And I am certain he, too, is most hungry."

"Phyllis," Catherine said.

Phyllis took her time walking to the fireplace, and then knelt slowly to stir the fire into fuller life.

"Edward," Catherine said, "we have guests in Massaquoit's wigwam." She waited for Massaquoit to nod his assent. "Have them come in to join us."

"All of them, Mistress?" Edward asked.

"Surely," Catherine replied.

Edward went out the door, shaking his head and muttering under his breath.

"I am taking you at your word," Catherine said to Massaquoit.

"Do not fear. The wild boy is tamed and the man knows if he runs I will track him down again and not be so gentle with him as I was last time."

Catherine put her hand on the deep bruise under Massaquoit's eye.

"Gentle, indeed," she said.

The door opened again and Edward hurried in. Ninigret followed, one end of the vine wrapped around his hand, the other still about the neck of Frank Mapleton, who stumbled in after him. Osprey, unbound, came next and bowed to Catherine.

"Good evening, Mistress," he said. "I must request that you notify my master of my return."

"In good time," Catherine answered, "I will send word to Master Worthington. Are you not hungry?"

"That I am," Osprey replied, "but more for my freedom than to fill my stomach."

Phyllis motioned for them to sit at the long table of polished oak. At a gesture from Massaquoit, Ninigret loosened the vine from around Mapleton's neck, and they all sat on the benches on either side of the table. Phyllis laid the wooden trenchers in front of them and ladled in the stew. They ate in silence for a few moments, and then Catherine reached into her pocket and placed a brass button on the table in front of Osprey. Osprey put down his spoon, picked up the button, and nodded.

"What of it, Mistress?"

"Is it not yours?"

"Likely it is. I did lose such a one. I have already told him." He pointed to Massaquoit.

"He says he lost it in the snow outside the Powell farm. That is, after the old man was killed."

"That is right," Osprey said. "I found the man dead. I could not help him, and so I left. The button must have caught on something and come loose."

"I am sure that matter will be investigated more fully by the magistrates," Catherine said. She looked at Mapleton, who had his mouth no more than an inch or two above the trencher as he scooped up the stew.

"I don't suppose you want to repeat your tale, the one you have already told Massaquoit?"

Mapleton lifted his face. Stew dribbled from the corner of his mouth.

"I cannot see that it would do any harm." He rubbed his hand over his neck, which bore the imprint of the vine like a collar, punctuated every few inches with an indentation where the thorns had pressed into the flesh. "That is if I have nothing more to fear from these savages."

"You are in my house now," Catherine told him, "and I vouchsafe your safety while under my roof."

"In that case, I can freely tell you that I filled your savage with a story just so he would not harm me further as we floated down the river, for I did think he would otherwise drown me. But as for that, I have nothing more to say."

A loud knock came at the door. Edward opened it, and there stood Wequashcook and Master Worthington. The merchant strode in past Phyllis, who was seated at the foot of the table. His elbow glanced off her shoulder, but he seemed not to notice. He continued until he stood behind and between Osprey and Mapleton.

"These men are in my employ. I have come to take them home with me where I can properly tend to them after their adventure with your savage."

"And what do you know about that?" Catherine asked.

Worthington looked toward Wequashcook.

"My savage was at the harbor when yours arrived with these two as captives. That is all I have to know. I insist you release them to my care."

"But, Samuel, they are at supper as you can very well see," Catherine said, "and they are free to go when they please." While the merchant kept his eyes on Osprey and Frank, Catherine covered the brass button and slid it off the table into her pocket.

"Now will do very well, then," Worthington said. "They can sup at my table as well as yours, and they perchance will find a better dinner conversation there."

Osprey got to his feet and seized Mapleton's arm.

"Up with you, lad, our master has come to take us home."

Frank, however, seemed reluctant to leave.

"Can I not finish my dinner?" He smiled at Phyllis. "She does make an excellent stew."

Worthington nodded at Osprey, and the lieutenant squeezed Frank's arm until the young man got to his feet.

"Come on with you," Worthington said. "We have things to discuss." He offered Catherine a barely perceptible dip of his head, and walked out as directly as he had entered. Phyllis, this time, leaned away from him as he passed. Osprey and Frank followed. Ninigret began to rise as though to impede their progress, but Catherine shook her head. Then Wequashcook left, closing the door behind them.

"Was that wise?" Massaquoit said. "We did go to some trouble to bring them back."

"I could have resisted," Catherine replied, "but to what purpose? To have you and Ninigret fight again, only this time in my house? What would be gained if you succeeded in defending our guests? Worthington would have come back with a greater force." She leaned over the table toward him. "I should have thought you would see, as well, that we must let them do what they want to do."

"Perhaps you can instruct me," Massaquoit said.

After Phyllis had cleared the dishes, Edward had gone off to bed, and Ninigret left to build a fire against the chill evening air in Massaquoit's wigwam, Catherine and Massaquoit sat next to each other at the table. Catherine fingered the button.

"This places Lieutenant Osprey at the farm. As he says, but perhaps not when he admits."

Massaquoit nodded. "I am sure he killed the old man."

"Why do you so think?"

Massaquoit held out his hand with three fingers displayed. "Indians, the boy, or the owner of that button. Those are the choices."

"We know Indians were attacking nearby settlements," Catherine said.

"Yes, but they did not kill this man." He lowered one finger. "I found the boy. He had fled in terror. And I do not think he could kill anybody. He is not a warrior like Ninigret." He lowered a second finger.

"And I found him by following his tracks in the snow. First there were two sets of tracks. The second belonged to the man who also wanted to catch the boy, but he gave up the chase. He is the one who lost the button. He is the lieutenant." He jabbed his remaining upraised finger at the seat that Osprey had occupied during the meal. "But," Massaquoit said, "I do not know why he did this."

Catherine smiled.

"I do not disagree. And I can begin to provide a reason. I believe that Isaac Powell died protecting Thomas. Because he had also been having his way with him. The boy, not that dog, had bitten his hand. Then came somebody, you say the lieutenant, and Isaac is dead. The person who came after Thomas might now threaten his sister, for it is clear to me that she must be the key not only to Isaac's death, but to Nathaniel's as well. It all ties together. I see the knot. I have not yet unraveled the strands."

Massaquoit smiled.

"And you would like me to keep an eye on her."

"Yes."

He rose.

"You know, I think you are right. There is something strange about Thomas."

"Yes. And his sister as well."

"Master Worthington seems hard set against them both."

"He is. And I fear that has cost him his son."

Massaquoit found Ninigret sitting by a small fire in the wigwam. The boy looked up, his face a sullen mask.

"I do not like it here. It is worse than Niantic. We bring back two English to the English woman, and then another English comes and takes them away."

"Yes," Massaquoit replied. "You can go home. But I was hoping you might help me just one more time."

Ninigret brightened.

"Are we going to capture those two again?"

"No. But if you come along with me, I will explain as we walk."

Ninigret was on his feet in an instant, his blanket about his shoulders, and outside the wigwam, all in one blurred motion. Massaquoit joined him.

"Where we are going we might feel the spirit of a dead English."

"Did you kill him?"

"No. An English woman is living there."

"Is she not afraid of the spirit?"

"I do not think so. But come, we will see."

By the time the pair passed the Dunwood house, the moon was fully risen. The faint glow of a candle could be seen in a window, and they heard a baby cry. They continued until they were standing on a rise within twenty-five yards of the Powell farm, which was in darkness. Massaquoit squatted. After a moment's hesitation, Ninigret knelt beside him with a question on his face.

"We wait and watch," Massaquoit said.

A breeze stirred, carrying a chill to them, a brief reminder of the winter cold. Ninigret shivered. He pointed to a freshly dug grave not far from the house.

"The dead English is now in the ground, but I feel his spirit," he said.

"That is just the wind. The spirit waits in the house where he was killed."

An hour later, Ninigret was lying stretched on the ground, bundled in his blanket. Massaquoit heard voices drift toward him from the house. At first they were barely audible, but then they became louder and angrier. A figure came hurrying through the front door. Massaquoit jabbed his elbow into the boy's ribs, and he started. The figure of a man lurched down the road to Newbury Center.

"He has been drinking," Massaquoit said. "He will be easy for you to follow. See where he goes."

Ninigret nodded and waited until the man, moving slowly and stopping to rest from time to time, had gone a safe distance ahead, and then he started after him, walking behind the tree line that edged the road. Massaquoit watched him dart between the trees until he lost sight of the boy in the shadows. He turned back to the house. For a short while there was no sign of activity, no candlelight in a window, no noise or movement of any sort, and yet he sensed a presence. He wondered if he were feeling the spirit of the dead farmer, and although he had told Ninigret that the chill night breeze was only the wind, he was beginning to doubt that opinion.

Then the squeaking sound of a badly hung door being forced past its frame rose from the house. Massaquoit stared hard in the direction from which the sound came. A figure of flesh and bones emerged from the house and headed down the same road as the other had taken, toward Newbury Center. The figure was wrapped in a full-length dark cloak that covered most of its head except for a narrow band of blond hair. The person walked quickly, but unsteadily, veering from one side of the narrow road to the other. Massaquoit watched it disappear into the shadows. There was only one road to the town center, with occasional paths branching off to farms or isolated houses. Ninigret and the man he followed would not be far ahead. Massaquoit trusted the boy would be able to observe both, since it seemed clear that the second person would soon overtake the first. He decided to brave the spirit of the old farmer, which he knew still hovered about the house, and see what he could discover inside.

The front door had been left ajar. Massaquoit entered

and sensed the spirit. Still, he made his way into the front room, where he had found the body of Isaac. In that room the spirit presence was very strong. He waited for his eyes to adjust to the darkness. Just enough moonlight coming in from the one window on the side of the house enabled him to study each object, the table on which sat two mugs smelling of beer, the two chairs, a narrow bed with its linen in disarray, and the remains of a dead fire in the fireplace. When he was certain that he had seen all there was to see, he walked to the rear of the room to open a door leading to a narrow storage area.

Here, between a rusty shovel and a dirt-encrusted rake, and next to a nearly empty barrel that still held scraps of salted beef, was a chest. Massaquoit scraped out the meat scraps and dropped them into the pouch he wore about his waist. Then he lifted the lid of the chest, but it was too dark for him to see what was inside. He ran his fingers down the sides and felt cloth bunched into piles on the bottom. He pulled the chest out of the storage area to the window in the front room where the moonlight illuminated its contents. He knelt and lifted each item in turn, and as he did so, his eyes opened first with wonder and then with a dawning recognition.

Ninigret returned within the hour. Massaquoit was back on the rise outside the house. The boy came hurrying toward him, apparently anxious to report what he had seen.

"There were two," he began. "The first man was having great difficulty walking. He stumbled and fell a number of times. I do not think he would have noticed if I had walked beside him, but I stayed behind the trees."

"And then along came the second," Massaquoit said. "I saw that one leave the house."

Ninigret nodded.

"Halfway to town, the second one overtook the first. All

I could see was a little yellow hair. They walked together. I followed. When they approached the town square, I stopped behind the last tree before the square. There is a house there where the English go to drink their beer. They went inside. I waited. They did not come out, and so I returned."

Massaquoit squeezed the boy's arm.

"That is good," he said. Ninigret smiled, just for a moment, enjoying the praise, but then, as though ashamed of his boyish weakness, he resumed his usual sullen look.

"What do we do now?"

"We wait. One or both may return."

And one did, only she did not look like the ones who had left the house a couple of hours before. It was well after midnight when a lone figure, wearing a cloak loosely about her shoulders came up the road. Massaquoit and Ninigret observed Thomasine walk into the house and close the door behind her.

"Is that the second one you saw?" Massaquoit asked.

Ninigret did not immediately respond.

"I cannot be sure," he said after a while. "I thought it was a man with a cloak over his face. I am sure only of the yellow hair."

Massaquoit nodded at the beginning of a confirmation of what he had seen in the trunk.

They waited the remainder of the night, taking turns, one sleeping, one watching, until the sun rose. A rooster crowed in the distance, and a hog came out from beyond the house and started to root, pawing the ground with its front hooves and burying its flat snout in the dirt. Every few moments, it would lift its head and eat what it had uncovered.

"I, too, am hungry," Ninigret said.

Massaquoit reached into his pouch and pulled out the salted beef. He divided the scraps evenly and gave Ninigret his portion. He put a scrap into his mouth and began chewing. The meat had the texture of leather, well cured, and a very strong salty taste. But it felt good going down into his stomach. Ninigret watched for a moment and then he too began to eat.

"We will wait here," Massaquoit said, after he finished his first piece. "To see who else comes, or follow her if she goes out again."

They ate in silence. And then they waited.

By the late afternoon, Ninigret's impatience was visible. He could not remain still. Several times he had sneaked to the house, crawling on his belly through the mud where the hog now lay. Massaquoit did not try to stop him. He was sure that the woman inside would still be sleeping off the beer from the night before, and besides the boy was being careful enough, approaching the house from its blind side, where there was no window, and then working his way around past the closed front door to the other side. There he peered through the window for a while, and then returned the same way he had come. Each time he offered Massaquoit the same report.

"She is in her bed. She hardly moves, but I do see that she is breathing."

And each time, Massaquoit had the same answer.

"Then we wait until she rises, or someone comes."

After his last return, Ninigret paced about. Massaquoit looked past the boy, and then he grabbed him by the shoulders and pulled him down until they were both lying flat on the ground. Ninigret began to protest, but Massaquoit pointed up the road toward town. Two figures approached, one short and wide, the other a little taller and thinner. They took no precautions against being seen until they were within a few yards of the path that led to the house. Then the shorter one motioned the taller one to continue while he took a position behind a tree.

Frank Mapleton approached the house in a crouch. He headed directly toward the window through which Ninigret several times had observed the sleeping woman. He stood up next to the window and peered in for a few moments. Then, without bothering to resume his crouching position, he trotted back to Osprey, who stepped out from behind the tree. The two conferred for a few moments, and then began walking toward the house. Osprey had his pistol out. Mapleton carried a thick club.

Massaquoit motioned for Ninigret to circle the house. The boy moved off, running with his body almost horizontal to the ground. Massaquoit watched him cross an open space and then find the cover of the trees. Massaquoit then crawled down the rise on his belly through the dried stalks of dead weeds that rose a couple of feet. He made no more noise than a snake slithering through tall grass. The weeds stopped in the front yard, where the hog, sensing the intrusion, was rising slowly to its feet and staring with its close-set eyes at Osprey and Mapleton. Massaquoit waited until he was sure that Ninigret must have had enough time. He rose to his feet and roared as loudly as he could as he charged toward the two men. They turned toward him, and Ninigret leaped out from his position at the side of the house.

Osprey raised his pistol at Massaquoit. Massaquoit darted to left and right. It would be a very difficult shot. The lieutenant decided not to spend his one bullet on an impossible target. He screamed at Mapleton and pointed him toward Massaquoit. Frank raised his club and Osprey hurtled toward the house. Ninigret threw himself at the burly lieutenant, but Osprey shoved him aside and entered the house. Ninigret rolled in the mud outside the door, then recovered his balance and got to his feet.

Massaquoit charged Mapleton. The boy waited until the last moment and then swung his heavy club at Massaquoit's head. Massaquoit leaned away from the blow and ducked, but still the club thudded against his shoulder, knocking him to one knee. Mapleton lifted the club again.

"This time, you savage bastard, this time," he said, his eye wide in anticipation of crashing his heavy weapon down on Massaquoit's skull.

Massaquoit made as though to rise to his feet, but as Mapleton started to swing the club, Massaquoit instead rolled into the boy's legs. Mapleton staggered, and the momentum of the club caused him to turn so that he half fell with his back to Massaquoit. Massaquoit jumped up and brought his fist down hard on the nape of Mapleton's neck, and the boy collapsed, dropping his club. A shot rang out from inside the house, and then two bodies locked together rolled out the door. Massaquoit seized the club.

Osprey disengaged himself from Ninigret and tossed his pistol aside. He pulled a knife out of his belt and stabbed at the boy. Ninigret evaded that thrust, but as he backed off, he stumbled against the hog, which had stood its ground as the humans fought around it. Massaquoit reached Osprey just as the lieutenant was bringing his knife down on Ninigret's exposed chest. Massaquoit managed to deflect the blow, but the blade still caught the boy's arm, and his blood spouted. He fell onto the back of the hog, which was now sufficiently disturbed to move on with a streak of Ninigret's blood on its haunches.

Before Osprey could lift his arm again, Massaquoit brought the club down on his wrist. He yelled in pain and dropped the knife. Ninigret picked it up. Massaquoit drove the end of the club into Osprey's soft belly, and the officer fell back inside the house, gasping for breath. Ninigret leaped on him with the knife in his hand.

"No!" Massaquoit called out. Ninigret started to bring

the knife down, but then let his arm relax and drop to his side. He stood up, but kept his foot on Osprey's neck. The lieutenant's face was red, and he was still struggling for breath. Massaquoit motioned for Ninigret to go back out to Mapleton. Then he walked to the fallen officer.

"You should have shot when you had a chance," he said.

Osprey lifted his upper body and tried to get up. Massaquoit brought the club down on the side of his head. He measured the force of the blow. He did not want to kill the man. Not just yet. The club bounced off Osprey's skull, just above the ear, and he slumped to the floor. Massaquoit waited. The officer did not move. Massaquoit stepped over him. He picked up the lieutenant's pistol and put it in his belt.

The woman lay on the floor moaning. She was wearing only a shift, and it was stained red where her blood was seeping through from the wound below her knee. Her face was white. She looked up at Massaquoit, and then fell back to the floor and lost consciousness. Massaquoit ripped off a piece of her shift and tied it as a bandage around her wound. He watched as the makeshift bandage reddened with blood, forming a widening circle. When the red circle stopped expanding, he picked her up and placed her on the bed.

Outside, he found Ninigret sitting on Mapleton's chest with the knife blade pressed against the young man's throat. He went back inside to the storage area and found a length of heavy rope, took it out, and tossed it to Ninigret, who bound Mapleton's hands behind him. Massaquoit dragged Osprey out, and took the other end of the rope. He rolled Osprey onto his belly, and tied his hands together with the free end of the rope. Mapleton rose to his feet and took a couple of tentative steps as though to try to run, but the lieutenant's dead weight served as an anchor to stop his progress.

Massaquoit pointed to Osprey.

"When he recovers, I will make him understand that he is to stay here."

Ninigret looked toward the interior of the house.

"And the woman?"

"You must go to Mistress Williams and tell her to come here to tend to that one."

Massaquoit sat next to Osprey, who was beginning to stir. He held the knife ready to convince the lieutenant that it would be in his best interest to do as he was told.

"Go on," Massaquoit said to Ninigret. "The woman might rouse and decide to run."

Ninigret trotted off down the road. A few minutes later, Thomasine did get up and stumble toward the door.

"Mistress Williams is coming to tend to your wound," Massaquoit said. He rose so that his body blocked the door. "Go back to your bed and wait."

Thomasine looked down at Osprey, and then at the pistol at Massaquoit's waist.

"He tried to kill me. That Indian boy saved my life."

"He is a good boy," Massaquoit said. "Now go you and lie down."

THIRTEEN

CATHERINE AND PHYLLIS hurried up the road behind Ninigret. Both women were scant of breath as they turned onto the path leading to the Powell house. At the rear of the rise on which Ninigret and Massaquoit had watched the house was a large oak standing by itself. Osprey sat on one side of the tree, Mapleton the other. Their hands were still tied behind their backs with one piece of rope. Another length of rope had been attached to that one, and then wrapped around, and tied to, the tree so that they were effectively tethered. The tree's trunk was of such thickness that neither could reach the knot that fastened the second rope to the first. Massaquoit sat in the doorway to the house. Ninigret trotted ahead. Without getting up, Massaquoit handed the knife to Ninigret.

"Go and watch over those two," he said, motioning to Osprey and Mapleton. He got up as Catherine approached. Phyllis lumbered up behind.

"She is inside," he said. "Sometimes she sleeps. Sometimes she thinks she will leave. That is why I sit here."

Catherine started to walk into the house, but Massaquoit stayed her with a touch of his hand on her arm.

"There is s trunk of clothes in the storage closet behind the room. You might want to look at it."

"First I must tend to her," Catherine said.

Massaquoit looked at Phyllis.

"Maybe Phyllis can examine it while you look at the woman. Then you both can look at her. I have already done so."

Catherine nodded and led the way into the house.

"What is he being so mysterious about?" Phyllis asked.

"I think I know, but you go before and look in the closet."

Inside, they found two lit candles on the table, which had been pushed close to the bed. Phyllis picked up one and walked to the door to the closet. Catherine moved the other candle closer to the edge of the table and then she sat down on one side of the bed. A rug served as a blanket, and it was pulled up over Thomasine's head. Catherine drew it down until she could see the face. She felt the cheek and forehead. They were no warmer than what would be natural to sleep. Thomasine stirred and opened her eyes. She seemed not to recognize Catherine. She sat up quickly, and then her face contorted in pain. She looked toward her leg.

"I remember now," she said.

"Let me see it."

Thomasine shook her head.

"It is nothing," she said.

"Mistress Williams," Phyllis called. "Come here and have a look in the trunk."

Thomasine shrugged and then smiled. She threw the rug off, and with a grimace, extended her leg toward Catherine.

"I do not think it matters any longer," she said.

Phyllis stepped to the bed, holding her candle over her

head so that its pale yellow light illuminated the bemused expression on her face.

"There's clothes belonging to some man there," Phyllis said.

"They are my brother's clothes," Thomasine said.

Catherine meanwhile had unwrapped the wound. The ball from the pistol had ripped through the calf, which was swollen and discolored at that point. Catherine ran her fingers over the skin adjoining the wound. She pressed hard enough to feel the bone. It did not seem to be broken. The wound was deep, but it appeared clean. Catherine applied a comfrey poultice. She expected Thomasine to pull away, but she did not. It was as though she had resigned herself to some fate that she had long tried to elude. Catherine lifted the shift a little higher so she could wrap the wound in a new bandage. She saw the edge of a fresh scar just above the knee. She took the candle off the table and held it above the scar. Then she replaced the candle on the table.

"So you see how it is," Thomasine said, with a bright and sassy edge to her voice.

"I see a wound like I treated on your brother."

Thomasine lifted her hand to her head and pulled off her blond wig. Beneath it was the shorter blond hair of Thomas. His face was now sullen, with a touch of suggestive sensuality, just as it was the night Catherine had come to the Powell farm to treat the old man's wounded hand. The voice altered too, dropping to a lower register.

"It is my leg you treated," he said.

"I had some idea," Catherine began, "but not . . ."

"But not this?" He put the wig back on. "It is a fine wig, made of my very brother's hair." His voice rose to its female pitch. "But what about this?" Thomasine asked.

She pulled up her shift. Catherine started.

"Bring your candle closer," Thomasine said in a seductive whisper, "and have a good look."

Catherine motioned Phyllis to bring her candle. Phyllis held it a few inches over Thomasine's groin, and then she let out a gasp. Catherine ran her eyes over the hairless pubic area, pausing first on the penis, as thin as a twig and hardly an inch long, but with an unmistakable, miniature glans and foreskin. She continued down to the lips of the vulva.

"I feel nothing down there," Thomas said. He lifted his tiny member. "It does not work as a man's," he said. His fingers went lower. "And this gives me no pleasure." He then put the wig back on and lifted the shift to reveal two small, but well-formed breasts. A thin tuft of blond hair grew between them. "The men like these," she said.

"But Nathaniel?" Catherine asked.

"He loved me," she purred. "But he was afraid, as well."

"What did he fear?" Catherine asked.

The voice was Thomas's. "Why his father, you, the good people of Newbury. He knew how my sister was. He met her in a tavern, you know. I tried to take her away, for I knew what trouble she could cause. But she would not listen. And Nathaniel would not be put off."

"But you came with him from Barbados. You left your sister behind."

Phyllis let out her breath as though she had been holding it in as she witnessed this scene. Catherine glanced up at her with an expression that ordered her silence. Phyllis nodded.

"After my sister married him, we talked. We decided that she could come after. That I would be his companion for a while. You see, he must have one or the other of us, and after a while he did not care which." He settled back onto the bed. "I am so tired," he said.

"I know," Catherine said, "but tell me about the farmer."

"He wanted only to use me. He did not know about my sister until he forced her to show herself, and then he would not keep his filthy old hands off of me until I sank my teeth into them. But you know about that."

"And then?"

"And then, Master Worthington set his lieutenant to chase me away, but old man Powell would not let him near me. He was stronger than you would think. They fought. I started to run. The lieutenant tried to hold me, but I got away in the snow. I watched him go back into the house. The old man was lying on the floor."

"What happened later, when Nathaniel was killed?"

Thomas dropped the wig to the floor, shut his mouth hard, and closed his eyes. He would talk no more.

"Why, I never thought—" Phyllis began.

"I don't imagine you did. Nor did I. Not the full measure of it."

Massaquoit had been standing wordlessly in the doorway. He came in now.

"The sun will be down soon," he said.

"Did you hear and see?" Catherine asked.

"Yes."

"I would like to bring Thomas to my house, to keep an eye on him."

"Are you going to call him a man, then?" Phyllis asked.

Catherine looked at the wig on the floor.

"He is now."

"I have two poles outside," Massaquoit said.

"Take his blanket," Catherine replied.

Phyllis carried one end of the litter Massaquoit fashioned, and Ninigret the other as they walked toward Catherine's house. Catherine walked next to the litter, stroking Thomas's hand. Massaquoit held the rope that bound Osprey and Mapleton. The two walked side by side, their heads almost touching as they talked. Then Mapleton cursed his companion, and Osprey responded in kind. They banged into each other but could do little damage with their hands still bound behind their backs. Massaquoit waited until they tired, and they resumed walking, this time stretching the rope to its limit between them.

Once at Catherine's house, Massaquoit secured them to the tree near his wigwam while Ninigret and Phyllis carried the litter inside. Catherine walked to where Massaquoit stood near the tree. She looked at Osprey and Mapleton, who now sat staring in opposite directions. From time to time, one of them would turn to mutter a curse over his shoulder at the other.

"Are they secure enough?" Catherine asked.

"They are."

"For the night?"

"Yes."

"Good. I can tend to Thomas. I will give him a tea that will make him sleep." She walked back into the house. A few moments later Ninigret emerged.

"I will watch first," he said.

Massaquoit nodded and stooped to enter his wigwam. He suddenly felt very tired.

He started awake with the sun. He crawled out of his wigwam. Ninigret was sitting, eyes fully open staring from Osprey to Mapleton, both of whom lay asleep on the ground. Osprey was snoring loudly.

"Why did you not wake me?" Massaquoit said. He felt a flush of shame warm his face.

"I am young," Ninigret said, "and I was not tired. You have them so well bound," he continued, "there was no danger."

Catherine came out of her house holding a half loaf of bread. She handed it to Massaquoit.

"I thought you might be hungry. Phyllis is baking a fresh loaf. I am to see Master Woolsey."

Massaquoit looked toward Osprey and Mapleton, who were now awake and sitting with sullen expressions at opposite ends of their tether.

"Yes," Catherine replied, "and the one inside, also. Those two might be hungry as well."

Massaquoit broke the bread into thirds, and handed two pieces to Ninigret.

"Eat one. When you are finished, you can stuff a crust into the mouths of those two dogs." He turned to Catherine for confirmation. "They deserve no better, do you think, after twice trying to take our lives?"

"A crust is too much," Ninigret said.

"A crust does fine," Catherine said, and she walked off toward the road.

Massaquoit and Ninigret sat a few feet from Osprey and Mapleton, who were chewing the remains of their crust when two men came up to Catherine's front door and knocked. Massaquoit saw Phyllis open it and talk to one of the men. She pointed toward Massaquoit's wigwam, and then the two strode toward it, followed by Phyllis, wiping her hands on her apron as she hurried to catch up with them. She did so just as they planted themselves, legs akimbo in front of Massaquoit, who rose slowly to greet them. Both constables wore swords at their sides.

"We are here under the orders of the governor to take custody of your prisoners, and to request your presence at the meetinghouse this morning so as to explain your actions."

Ninigret, who had remained sitting, leapt up.

"Perhaps you can ask those two dogs how it is they offered us such violence."

The constables' faces darkened. One pulled his sword out of its scabbard.

"There is no need," Massaquoit said. He walked to the

tree, cut the rope, and led Osprey and Mapleton to the constable. The one who had drawn his sword used it to cut through Osprey's remaining bonds. Osprey rubbed his wrists, and then held out his hand.

"My pistol, if you please. And my knife."

Massaquoit slapped its butt end hard into the lieutenant's outstretched hand. Ninigret placed the knife on top of the pistol. Osprey smiled, and bowed.

"And what of me?" Mapleton asked.

A constable took the end of the rope attached to the boy's hands.

"Come along," he said. "Master Worthington wants to be sure he has a chance to talk with you."

Massaquoit and Ninigret watched the constables leave with Osprey and Mapleton.

"We had no powder or ball," Ninigret said.

"Nor need," Massaquoit replied. He turned to Phyllis. "How is your patient?"

"Stronger," Phyllis replied.

"Good. For I have an idea."

"Should we not wait for Mistress Williams to return?"

"We can join her at the meetinghouse."

"He is doing much better," Dorothy said as she led Catherine into the front room, where Woolsey now sat at his desk poring over a page in his ledger book. He looked up and beamed at Catherine.

"We have done remarkably well with this voyage of the *Good Hope*. When it reaches England and sells our cargo of tobacco and sugar, we will make out handsomely." He paused. "I have heard some say that this tobacco is a savage vice. What think you, Catherine?"

"I think I am glad of our profit, Joseph." She placed her hand on the ledger page. "But it is a very different business I have come to discuss with you. Thomasine was, but for the intervention of Massaquoit, and his new friend Ninigret, dead at the hands of Osprey and Mapleton."

Woolsey removed Catherine's hand and shut the ledger book with an audible thud. His smile turned to a distasteful frown.

"This is Samuel's doing," he said.

"There is more, much more," Catherine said.

"Then you must tell me," Woolsey urged.

Catherine pulled up the cane-backed chair.

"Take a breath," she said.

Woolsey obeyed.

"Now, then," Catherine went on, "you recall meeting Thomasine, Nathaniel's intended."

"Yes."

"And you recall her brother, Thomas, Nathaniel's friend."

"Indeed."

"They are the same."

"Brother and sister?"

"They are one person, who is now recovering in my house from a wound from the lieutenant's pistol."

"One person, you say."

"Yes."

"How?"

"God can explain the reason, but I have seen with my own eyes. He, she, is both man and woman, or perhaps neither."

Woolsey sank back into his chair.

"Wondrous," he said.

"Indeed. And the cause, no doubt, that both Nathaniel and Isaac are dead."

FOURTEEN

S AMUEL WORTHINGTON DID not offer a greeting, not even
 a polite lift of his head to acknowledge their presence,
as Catherine and Woolsey walked into the meetinghouse.
He turned instead to whisper something to Lieutenant Osprey, who sat next to him on the foremost bench. Wequashcook stood at the end of the bench, holding the rope
that still bound Frank Mapleton. Behind Mapleton were the
two constables. Catherine noted with dismay that Osprey
again had his pistol tucked into his cloth belt. Governor
Peters sat behind the table, which had been taken from the
closet behind the pulpit as it customarily was when the
house of God was transformed to serve the laws of man.
At his side was Minister Davis, whose facial expression
indicated he would have been much happier in his accustomed place in his pulpit. Peters motioned for Woolsey to
take a seat next to him.

"Mistress Williams," Governor Peters said, "Master Worthington has brought to me a grievous account of your
Matthew's interference in his attempts to resolve a matter
touching his family and, in particular, the estate of
Nathaniel."

Catherine took the brass button out of her pocket and tossed it on the table.

"Ask him to explain that, if you please," she said.

The governor picked up the button and passed it to Woolsey, who laid it on the table in front of him.

"A button," Peters said.

"From his man's coat, found not far from Isaac Powell's body. He has said as much to me," Catherine said.

Peters looked toward Osprey.

"I did so," the lieutenant replied. "I explained how I found the man dead and started to follow his attackers, only to be discouraged by the cold and the snow."

Catherine faced Osprey.

"And how happened it that you were there?"

"On my business," Worthington interjected. "My family business."

Massaquoit entered, walked over to Catherine, and whispered in her ear. She nodded, and he returned to the door, where he remained standing.

"And what was that business?" Catherine pressed.

Worthington glowered.

"I do resent your intrusion, Mistress," he said.

"No more of an intrusion than a pistol ball," Woolsey said.

Worthington looked at Massaquoit.

"Her savage, Matthew, there, can best answer that."

"I think not," Catherine said. "Massaquoit, would you, please?"

Massaquoit walked out the door. He returned a moment later with Thomas, who had one arm wrapped around his neck, and the other supported at the elbow by Phyllis. Thomas was wearing a man's leather doublet and breeches, but also a woman's apron and white cap over his wig. In a collective gasp, Governor Peters and Minister Davis drew in their breath, and each sought to gather the escaping air into words. But before either could, the three walked to the front of the meetinghouse, where Thomas proceeded unaided to stand in front of Osprey.

"He shot me." The voice had the high, seductive tone of Thomasine. It dropped now. "He had attacked me before, when I lived with Isaac Powell."

Governor Peters recovered first.

"Mistress Williams, what means this creature in this costume?"

"Why, only that the outer can accurately manifest the inner."

"That creature beguiled and seduced my son," Worthington said in an explosion of anger. "I did not know its full nature until just now."

Thomas's face blanched.

"I must sit," he said in a soft woman's voice. Massaquoit aided him to the bench across from Worthington, who continued to glare at him. He looked at Worthington. "I did marry your son," he said.

Governor Peters stood.

"Constables, we must retire for a few minutes. Guard the door."

The constables took positions on either side of the door while Peters, Magistrate Woolsey, and Minister Davis walked to the far corner of the meetinghouse. There, with heads bowed toward each other they conferred. After a few moments, Governor Peters reached out his long arm and beckoned Catherine to join them.

"You have seen this person's private parts?"

"I have."

"Man or woman?"

"Both and neither. A male organ that does not function and female ones that will never have a babe or suckle one."

"Wondrous strange," the governor said.

"Not so," Minister Davis responded, his eyes full of the

truth of the idea he had just discovered. "This creature, for creature it is, made from God, comes to remind us of God's shaping hand, for as all learned men agree, a woman is no more than a partially formed man, and lest we forget, this creature's bizarre nature, standing as it does between both, reminds us of our creator's intentions."

"All learned *men,* indeed," Catherine said, "do believe that. Say you, then, that a woman is almost a man, or is it rather a woman is rather more than a man?"

"Enough," the governor said. "We need to resolve these issues." He walked back to his place at the table, followed by Woolsey and Davis. Catherine returned to a place next to Thomas. She noted that Worthington had been in close conference with Osprey.

"If it please you," the merchant said, "the lieutenant would like to offer a statement."

Osprey rose.

"After many untoward and uncivil scenes in his house, Master Worthington, to protect the honor of his son, sent that creature, who was then dressed as a man called Thomas, away. Nathaniel protested, so Master Worthington permitted Thomas to stay at Isaac Powell's farm just until he could leave on the next outward bound ship. Which he did not do, and when he did not, I was sent to have a talk with him. Old man Powell, perhaps misunderstanding my mission, strove to block my conversation, saying the lad was his own to do with as he wanted. He came at me with a knife. I defended myself. Then I tried to grab hold of the lad, who escaped my grasp and ran. That is how Isaac Powell came to be dead and my button at the scene."

"And the rest?" Woolsey demanded.

Osprey smiled.

"It would not do anybody any good to know exactly what happened there, I thought, so I made it out to be an Indian attack, which it like enough could have been, seeing as what happened at Westwood. I had seen what savages do to their dead victims when I was in Virginia."

Peters looked toward Thomas, who was leaning against Catherine.

"What he says is true," Thomas said.

"How came my son to be dead?" Worthington demanded. "I care not for the miserable old sodomite of a farmer. We are well rid of him, however his death occurred."

"For that you will have to ask him," Osprey said, pointing to Mapleton. Then he looked toward Massaquoit. "That savage over there knows well enough I was with him when the boy was killed, and that one"—he indicated Thomas—"was in the tent with 'em. Those two know, if anybody."

Thomas got unsteadily to his feet.

"Nathaniel wanted me to go away when my sister came. He said he could no longer countenance my company. When I told him that I could not leave, that I must stay with my sister, he became angry. We quarreled." Thomas switched to his woman's voice and stretched his arm toward Mapleton. "And then, hearing us so, that one came into the tent with his knife drawn. Thomas tried to protect Nathaniel, but could not. I am certain it was that one. Thomas was stabbed. So was poor Nathaniel. That is all I know."

"Lies," screamed Mapleton, rising to his feet. The constable pulled the end of the rope, and jerked him back. "When I came into that tent, they was both lying on the ground bleeding, they was. I had no weapon, I stabbed nobody. I only ran for help."

"William," Worthington said, and Wequashcook stepped forward.

"I was outside the tent so as to be near Nathaniel as his father had asked me to do. I heard loud voices and saw a knife blade slit the tent. I looked in, and I saw that boy"—he gestured toward Mapleton—"with a knife in his hand. It had blood on it. Nathaniel and Thomas, both of them, were on the ground. Then, as he said, he ran out, leaving them to die."

Again Mapleton surged to his feet. This time he had the rope wrapped around his hand, and he managed to jerk himself free. He bolted toward the front door. Osprey raised his pistol with a casual gesture and sighted the running boy. Just as Mapleton came abreast of the lieutenant, he turned his startled eyes. The last thing he saw was the flash from the muzzle. The retort echoed through the meeting-house and Frank Mapleton collapsed.

Catherine hurried to his side. It took her only a second to see that the bullet had entered his chest above his heart, which no longer beat. There was not much blood, but he was most certainly dead. She rose to her feet, looked to the magistrates and minister behind the table, and shook her head.

Worthington strode to the body and looked down at it.

"I will see to this one's burial." He pointed at Osprey. "Do you have further use for him?" he asked the governor.

Peters, his face ashen, rose to his feet.

"This is most regrettable," the governor said. "Keep your man close by you until we reach a determination. We will hold you to his presence, should we desire it."

Worthington nodded.

"Pick up that trash," he said to the lieutenant.

Osprey lifted the pouch from Mapleton's waist, shook it to hear the coins jangle, and then motioned to the constable who had been holding the rope. The lieutenant took the feet, the constable the arms, and they walked out. Worthington watched them leave and then turned to Thomas.

"What intend you to do with that one?" he asked the governor. "I am of the opinion it had a hand in my son's murder."

Governor Peters shook his head.

"William seems to place the blame on the dead boy. I am content to leave it that way." He glanced at Woolsey.

"That is well," Woolsey said. "For I fear that dead lad took the truth to the grave with him. Your lieutenant is a dangerous man. We cannot prove he willfully killed Isaac, but the farmer is dead. And now we have seen him act with a rash hand."

"The boy you are willing to call my son's murderer was making his escape."

"Rash, nonetheless," Peters said.

"I will have him on the next ship to Barbados. My plantation there requires a strong hand to control the Africans that I am now importing."

"Good riddance to him, then, say I," Woolsey declared.

Minister Davis cleared his throat. He looked at Thomas.

"As for that one, I would have it live among us, dressed as it is, half man, half woman, to show the Lord's purpose in the Creation, a woman on her way to being a man."

"Perhaps she can be put into service as a woman," Peters said, "and so dressed."

"I think not," Catherine said. "Is it not for Thomas or Thomasine to decide?"

Massaquoit strode forward.

"If you English cannot decide, I can help. He or she will be welcome among my people with my mother, Minneseewa, on Munnawtawkit."

Relief spread over the governor's face and a smile widened Woolsey's mouth while the minister's face dropped into a frown.

"Then it is settled," Governor Peters said.

Thomas got up. "Do I not have an opinion?" he asked.

"No," Peters said, "the matter is decided."

"I am content, nonetheless," he replied.

FIFTEEN

T HOMAS SAT AT the table and spooned the stew Phyllis
had ladled onto his trencher. Phyllis still stood, pot in
one hand, ladle in the other, but her eyes on Thomas.

"I am sorry to stare," she said, and moved to her place
at the table. She filled her own trencher and sat down.

"I am well used to it," Thomas said, in a soprano voice,
now edged with a deep sadness. "I have spent much of my
life as a woman, some of it as a man. I did love Nathaniel,
in my way, but I could not please him. Either as woman
or man. And Master Worthington did not want me to live
even after his Nathaniel was dead."

"Are you certain you want to leave us?" Catherine asked.

"Oh, yes," Thomas said. "I am willing to try to live
among the savages."

"If you so choose," Catherine said, permitting a stern
tone to tinge her voice, "you must begin to learn not to
use that word."

Thomas reddened, the first blush of shame Catherine
had seen on his face.

"I, more than most, should understand that," he said.

Edward's eyes remained fixed on his food.

"You can look up, you know," Phyllis said.

"I can, but I choose not to," he replied.

"This morning," Thomas said, "Massaquoit will take me to his mother on that island. Then, Edward, you do not need to fear looking upon me."

"That will please me," Edward said.

In his wigwam, Massaquoit sat across the fire from Wequashcook. He stirred the pot of samp with a wooden spoon. Ninigret squatted a respectful distance from the two older men.

"Why?" Massaquoit asked.

"I said what I knew. Maybe a little more than I knew. Let the English kill each other. I am content with the result. One English boy dead, one English soldier on his way to Barbados. One English merchant who trusts me and will do business with me."

"Ah," Massaquoit said, "I see, but do you know who you are?"

Wequashcook sucked the samp from his spoon.

"Very well."

Massaquoit stood with the shallop's steering oar in his hand while Ninigret hoisted its sail. Thomas, again wearing a scarlet bodice, green hat, and green gown, sat in the stern. He had a small pile of men's clothing at his feet, leather doublet and breeches, and the cloak he had wrapped himself in the night he walked from Isaac Powell's house to the tavern in Newbury Center. The breeze filled the sail, and the shallop crested gentle swells as it headed out of the harbor. Thomas sat in silence until the vessel was far enough off shore that the retreating figures of Catherine and Phyllis, who had seen them off, had all but disappeared. He stood up, and with great deliberation tossed first the doublet, and then the breeches, into the water.

"Thomas is not coming back."

"It is well," Massaquoit replied.

"Then you know?" Thomasine asked.

Massaquoit nodded.

"I listened very hard to what Wequashcook did not tell me."

Thomasine sighed.

"Thomas did not mean to kill my Nathaniel, but . . ."

Thomasine sat back down and forced a bright smile.

"I will miss my brother, but maybe it is better that he is gone."